In the bedroom [illegible] drawer of his dresser, searching for the engagement ring. It wasn't there. *I know I put it in here somewhere.* He opened the second drawer. Tossed T-shirts around. No ring. Starting to panic, he jerked open the third drawer. The tiny blue box, snuggled in the corner of the drawer beneath his rolled socks, winked up at him. His shoulders sagged in relief. He reached in, grabbed the box, and opened it.

Empty. No ring.

Oh, crap. Where is it? His eyes darted around the room. He dashed to the laundry basket, flinging dirty clothes left and right as he dug for the last pair of pants he wore. Images of the diamond ring devoured by the washing machine flooded his mind. His pulse pounded. He collapsed to the floor as his fingers brushed the hard, circular object in the front pocket. *Thank God, I didn't wash it.*

When he returned to the living room, the engagement ring nestled safely in the bottom of his front jeans' pocket.

Broken Toys

by

Glenda Thompson

This is a work of fiction. Names, characters, places, and incidents are either the product of the author's imagination or are used fictitiously, and any resemblance to actual persons living or dead, business establishments, events, or locales, is entirely coincidental.

Broken Toys

Contact Information: info@thewildrosepress.com

Cover Art by *Kim Mendoza*

The Wild Rose Press, Inc.
PO Box 708
Adams Basin, NY 14410-0708
Visit us at www.thewildrosepress.com

Publishing History
First Crimson Rose Edition, 2020
Trade Paperback ISBN 978-1-5092-3379-3
Digital ISBN 978-1-5092-3380-9

Published in the United States of America

Dedication

To Darlin'—thank you for believing in me,
for pushing me, and for teaching me the difference
between a clip and a magazine.
You will always be my heart.

~

To Jenn—thanks for the swift kicks to my backside
when I started lagging or threatening to give up.
And for the chocolate…always the chocolate.

~

To my wonderful support system
at 10-Minute Novelists—you know who you are.
I never would have finished this story without you.
Thanks for the encouragement.

Chapter One

As Alyssa Sanders ran through the thick South Texas brush, blood trickled from a gash on her forehead. Mixing with sweat, it dripped into her eyes, burning and blurring her vision.

Bare feet rasping over rock and sand, she floundered to a stop, doubling over and gasping. The hot night wind lifted her hair from her face. Mesquite and cactus thorns punctured her aching soles. Bloody scrapes stung her knees from the many falls she'd taken while racing through the darkness. Sucking in a ragged breath, she choked on the smell of rotten eggs.

"Sour gas," the stranger said, bending over beside her. "From the oil wells."

Concern smoldered in his eyes, stirring mixed emotions within her. *Was it caring—or excitement?*

"Here, put this on." He straightened and placed his navy baseball cap over her hair, tucking the platinum lengths from sight. "It will make you harder to see."

He crept forward, inching his way around the prickly pear. She hesitated. Who was this young man? Why was he helping her? True, she was a whisper younger than the other girls, but that only put him closer to their age than hers. Why wasn't he helping one of them escape? Trusting a different young man—one she had believed with all her fourteen-year-old heart was her prince charming—caused her capture in the first place. How long ago had it been? She had lost all track of time while being confined in the cage.

The stranger grabbed her. The cap tumbled from her head. His calloused fingers, rough on her tender young skin, spun her to face back the way they had come. "Do you want them to catch us?" He yanked on her arm, tugging her forward. "I can always take you back, you know. Less hassle on my part."

In the distance, the metal storage container where she had been imprisoned loomed, a darker shadow among the shadows cast by the meager light of the crescent moon. Heat lightning crackled overhead, dancing from cloud to cloud. The flashes made the container appear to move, as if it chased her. Despite the unseasonably oppressive heat of Texas in late April, a shiver raced down her spine. *Oh my God! He wouldn't actually take me back, would he?*

A surge of panic paralyzed her. She forgot to inhale. Dark spots danced on the edges of her vision. Tremors cascaded over her limbs.

"Hey, breathe, okay? I didn't mean it. Not really."

She drew in a whooping gasp of air. Only this young man, this dark-haired, blue-eyed stranger, offered her hope of freedom. *I just want to go home.* Tears tracked through the dirt on her face.

Trust him.

She scooped the ball cap from the ground and shoved her hair back beneath it. She held her hand out to him. His massive hand engulfed her tiny, trembling one. His fingers entwined with hers as he drew her through the gloom. She drew comfort from the strength of his hand.

Dawn lurked just over the horizon, a sullen vow to

steal the protective shadows from the field and illuminate their flight.

"Hurry," he said, pushing her onward. "Stay down. We can't let anyone see us."

Bent low at the waist, they plunged haphazardly through the dry, hip-deep grass. Its sharp edges ripped at her arms and face. The tall grass rustled as they struggled through it. She stumbled and fell, collapsing from hunger and exhaustion. A whimper of pain escaped. "I am so tired."

"Shh!" he whispered harshly, whipping his head back the way they came.

What did he hear? She strained her ears for any sound of pursuit. The rushing of her pulse pounding in her ears drowned out everything else. The mournful howl of a coyote split the pre-dawn air, followed by the yipping replies of the rest of the pack. *Dogs? Are they using dogs to track me?*

She spun wildly, peering in all directions. Tall clumps of blooming prickly pear obscured her vision. Tension churned in her belly. Squeezing her eyes closed, she wrapped her arms around her stomach and rocked back and forth on her knees.

Dear God, I promise I will never sneak out again. Please. I want my mommy.

****

As Seamus Gorman slammed open the door to his son's makeshift taxidermy shop, hot humid air followed him inside. "Patrick?" he bellowed. "You in here?"

He paused in the doorway, adapting to the dim interior light. The windows, covered with black paint, contributed to the gloom of the ramshackle barn. Seamus dragged a hand across the back of his neck. All the sightless, glass eyes staring down at him from the animal heads lining the walls gave him goose bumps. He shuddered, shaking off the premonition of unease. Movement at the back of the shop caught his attention.

"I figured I would find you hiding in here, boyo. Quit your arsing around. We've got driveways to pave. Get your ass up and out to work. We're already behind schedule."

His voice echoed off the walls, a rough scratchy sound that assaulted the eardrums. Hints of his Irish heritage clung to his speech. His entire persona screamed used car salesman: loud, brash, and pushy. The only things missing being gaudy gold chains gleaming against a hairy chest and a heavy, gold nugget pinky ring.

"Shut the door, Da. You're letting flies in." Patrick stood from where he kneeled behind an antique display case, rolling his neck on his shoulders and wiping his hands on stained blue jeans.

Seamus stepped into the barn and drew the door closed behind him. Shutting out the harsh Texas sun plunged the shop back into its former cave-like murkiness. The dim light of one bare bulb dangling from the ceiling did little to dispel the shadows.

"Stop acting the maggot. We need to start the jobs before the *gits* change their minds. Or their nosy kids talk 'em out of it."

The single window air-conditioning unit wheezed as it struggled to cool the space. He skirted around enormous glass aquariums sitting on a rusty, industrial workbench. Heat lamps above the glass cases kept the creepy crawlies inside underneath shredded paper and wood shavings. A tiny tremor crawled down his spine.

He raises flesh-eating beetles, and he's worried about flies?

Seamus crinkled his nose as he walked deeper into the shop. A noxious, more immediate odor overcame the sickly-sweet odor of rotting meat. The shop reeked with it. "What is that *manky* smell?" He plucked a freshly laundered handkerchief from his pocket and covered his mouth and nose. "What have you been doing now?"

The closer he got to his son, the stronger the stench became. A few feet from the counter, the mixed odors of burning flesh and feces hit him full in the face. He hurried around the display case and looked down.

"No!" He slammed a gargantuan fist against the glass top so hard it splintered. Slivers of glass embedded themselves in his hand. As he gagged, the handkerchief fluttered to the floor. "No, no, no, no."

An emaciated teenage girl lay crumpled on the dirty wooden floorboards at his son's feet. Her head rested in a slowly widening pool of blood that turned her platinum hair a rusty shade of copper and seeped in ever-expanding circles beneath the counter and beyond.

Her bloodshot, green eyes widened at Seamus's arrival. Bruises, both fresh and faded, covered her face. Cigarette burns marred the skin of her inner arms. A filthy cloth, shoved in her mouth and tied around her head, muffled her cries. Cuts, human bite marks, and dried blood decorated her naked body. A teardrop of blood cut a path through the dirt caked on her porcelain cheek. Her eyes fluttered closed.

Prickly heat raced through Seamus as he shoved his son out of the way and dropped to his knees beside the girl. Ignoring the fresh blood dripping from the cut on his hand, he placed two fingers against the girl's neck to search for a pulse. Skin cool and clammy. Pulse weak and thready but there, barely there. He glanced up to stare at his son—and saw him clearly for perhaps the first time. Blood spatter covered Patrick from head to toe as he idly twirled a blade between his fingers.

He jammed his finger into the boy's chest. "How many times have I told you not to play with the livestock? We're running an old-fashioned cattle drive. You and your pretty-boy Romeos round up the livestock. I'm the trail boss driving them to auction. The cartels are the railroad shipping north, or overseas, or wherever they end up. Not my concern. Our job is to get them safely to the railhead." He shoved his son away so hard the boy stumbled. "You, *idjit,* how thick can you be?"

Patrick lowered his eyes. He ducked his head, raising his shoulders like a puppy cringing away from a blow. The perfect image of submissive obedience.

Unfooled, Seamus caught the flash of malevolent hate glittering in his son's eyes before a blank expression claimed the boy's features. "You listen when I'm speaking to you, ya useless *poxy little shite.* Do you realize how much money you just cost me?"

"I'm sorry, Da. Really sorry. I only wanted a bit of fun." The boy swallowed hard. He muttered a few more indistinct words.

"What did you say?"

Patrick spoke up without lifting his gaze from the floor. He raised his hands, palms up. "I guess I got a wee bit carried away."

"You *guess?* Really?" Seamus's voice rose with each syllable. He pointed at the brutalized girl. "You call that *a wee bit*?" Disgust laced each word. "I truly have no words."

The boy raised his chin just a fraction, his eyes meeting his father's in a tiny show of smug defiance. "You didn't want this one anyway, Da. The boys grabbed a bad one. She was damaged goods. Once the makeup and clothes came off, she was a brutal mess." The son laughed, a cold, dark laugh. "And that was before I started on her. Scars everywhere. She wasn't very bright either. She actually believed I was helping her escape."

Seamus clenched his hands at his sides to keep from wrapping them around his son's throat. As his pulse hammered in his ears, spots formed on the corners of his vision. He focused on the face of his one and only child.

All color faded from Patrick's face as he took a quick step backward. He held his hands up to block his father's approach. "Seriously, Da, no one would have paid much for her. I did you a favor when you think about it, keeping you from offering subpar merchandise."

A growl slipped from Seamus's lips. He advanced another step. Patrick moved back, hands still extended. "Da, if ye…"

"Shut the *fook* up." Seamus raised his clenched fist. A muffled moan drew his attention back to the girl. "Hand me that tarp behind you. Now."

Eyes closed; Seamus squeezed the bridge of his nose. With a deep sigh, he kneeled beside the child lying on the floor. He draped the tarp over her naked body and drew the gag from her mouth. Gently, he brushed the hair from her pallid face, examining the damage inflicted by his son. With a tender hand, he wiped the tears from her face, slid the back of his hand down her cheek in a soft caress. "I'm so sorry, sweetling. It shouldn't happen this way."

A bowie-style knife whispered out of the leather sheath in his boot. Muscles in his forearm rippled as he grabbed the knife and slit the girl's throat from ear to ear, slashing open her windpipe while severing both the carotid artery and jugular vein. The smell of hot iron flooded the space. Warm blood splattered, creating a brilliant red abstract painting over the floor and walls. Arterial spray splattered as high as the cedar beams of the roof.

For several long seconds, the only sound heard was the whistle of air bubbling through the gaping, bloody wound. Gradually her pulse stilled and her heart stopped. Pale, green eyes glazed over with the opaque covering of death.

Seamus rose slowly to his feet, the weight of what he had just done crashing against his shoulders. Scooping his handkerchief from the floor, he methodically wiped the blood from his face. He glanced down at himself and then glared at his son. "You made the mess. You clean it up. I have to change. Get cracking. We still have paving to do."

Patrick's eyes lit up as they darted from the fleshing machine to the terrarium housing the beetles. A tremor raced down Seamus's spine. Gruesome images of what he imagined his son doing to the body turned his stomach.

"Don't worry, Da. I've got this."

That's exactly what I am worried about. Seamus started to the door, stopped, and turned back to face his son. "And you, or one of those boyos of yours, need to find me a replacement—soon. I've already paid for twelve spots on the auction website, and I will deliver twelve." He paused, his hardened glare crawling up and down his son's solid frame. "One way or another."

****

Patrick wiped a drop of blood from his cheek with the back of his hand as he watched his father stalk from the shop. Absentmindedly, he touched the tip of his tongue to the smear of blood. *Copper pennies.*

He scanned the body lying on the floor and then his taxidermy shop. His eyes locked on the pale, white bone of a European-mounted deer skull. He smiled. The stew-like smell of muscle boiling from the bone when he'd peeled the skin off tickled his memory. Trophy mounts, all of them. Even the girl. An idea crept in. He flexed his hands; the smirk plastered on his face widening. "Don't worry, Da. I've got this. No one will ever find her."

He walked to the bench of tools mounted on the side wall. He picked up and discarded the bone saw. Lovingly, he fondled a variety of knives before deciding on a small skinning knife with a gut-hook on the end. The weight of it felt good in his hands, balanced. He rarely used this particular knife, so he drew the edge of the blade slowly across the tip of his finger to test the sharpness. A thin, red line of blood welled up. As he sucked the blood and glared at the old, wooden door his father had just stormed through, Patrick smiled again.

This time, his smile reached his eyes.

One day, Da—maybe one day real soon—no one will be able to find you either.

Chapter Two

Texas Ranger Noah Morgan sat in the parking lot of the Bennett County Law Enforcement Center. Engine running and air conditioner blasting in his unmarked four-wheel-drive truck, he dragged sweaty palms down his freshly pressed and starched black jeans before picking up the tiny, blue-velvet, square box sitting on the truck console beside him. A tingle of fear crept over his broad shoulders, tightening his muscles.

What if she doesn't like it?

He opened the lid to stare again at the golden rays of sunshine sparkling off the engagement ring he'd just purchased during his lunch hour. The one-carat, pear-shaped diamond solitaire nestled in a delicate lace of quarter-carat emeralds and—according to the salesperson—would melt any woman's heart.

He sure as hell hoped so.

Doubt taunted as it always did when a voice from the past began to echo inside his head. *The ring? Sure, she'll love it. But you? No one wants you. You're a broken toy.*

Panic bubbled in his chest, creeped its way into his throat, choking him. He squeezed his eyes closed. Images—memories—of a different ring, a different time, danced across the inside of his eyelids. He heard the muffled laughter of his older cousin's taunts. *Broken toy, thrown away, broken toy, go away. Nobody wants you; nobody loves you. Broken toy, broken toy, broken toy.*

Cursing, he inhaled as deep as possible and held the breath for a slow count of five before exhaling completely. *Cat is not Maeve, and you are not...*

A sudden thump on the hood of his truck pulled his attention from the past. His eyes popped open. He tossed a casual salute to the uniformed patrol deputy crossing in front of his truck.

Noah closed his eyes again. *You were a different person back then.* He repeated the deep-breathing exercise, mentally counting down from ten. When he reached the number one, he inhaled again and held the breath. He pictured himself on one knee. Smelled the rose petals scattered around him. Heard the words "Catalina Maria Ramos, will you marry me?" Envisioned her throwing her arms around his neck and saying, "Yes, yes, yes."

Slowly he blew out the held breath, emptying his lungs, and felt better immediately. *Who knew this self-hypnosis crap actually worked?*

He felt a grin tug at the corners of his lips. A glowing warmth spread through his chest. *Why wouldn't she want to marry me? She already puts up with me on a daily basis.*

Snapping the box closed, he gently lobbed it into the glove compartment. He tugged his shirt cuffs down to cover his wristwatch and straightened his tie. Today's silk tie boasted a vintage map of the Goodnight-Loving cattle trail. The ranger dress code called for a long-sleeved button-down shirt and a tie. It didn't specify what kind of tie, so Noah searched for old-time vintage flash. Anything to irritate the big boss.

After grabbing his summer straw cowboy hat off the passenger seat, he secured the glove box with his key before stepping out and locking the truck. Placing the hat firmly on his head, he strode across the steaming asphalt of the parking lot. He approached the double glass doors set in the limestone façade of the building that housed the Bennett County Sheriff's Department, the county jail, dispatch center, and the Department of Public Safety offices. Years ago, someone above Noah's pay grade convinced the county legislators to go in on the joint effort to save the taxpayers a bit of money. The way the oilfields worked these days, the county never knew if incoming taxes would provide a feast—or dry up like a year-long famine.

Two young boys darted out from the automatic doors, ducking around him before racing toward the grassy stretch of land on the other side of the Life Flight helipad. Noah couldn't help but grin at their youthful exuberance before turning back to enter the building.

Pure chaos greeted him—and wiped the grin right off his face.

The acrid smell of scared sweat and dirty diapers competed with overpowering orchid- and rose-based perfumes, a restless rustling mixed with whispering and whimpering. An older, silver-haired lady sat far away from everyone else—at least, as far away as she could get in the overcrowded room. She clutched a lace-trimmed handkerchief and a beaded crystal rosary between gnarled fingers. Tears shimmered on her cheeks. Her prayers, in Spanish, added to the pandemonium spilling through the public waiting room.

Regret propelled him forward as he wove his way

through yelling toddlers, children begging moms for coins to put in the vending machines, and crying young women holding squalling infants. He stopped beside the praying woman and rested his hand gently on her shoulder. *How many times had Nana sat in a room like this? Waiting on me or my cousin?*

Squatting beside her, he whispered words of comfort in her ear. She patted his hand and crossed herself, smiling through her tears.

Rising to his feet, Noah nodded to her and walked toward the locked door separating the secured, employees-only area of the law enforcement center from the public areas. A group of gangsta wannabes, covered in ink and dressed in baggy pants, gathered in front of the bulletproof reception window. The group broadcast hostility, muttering fiercely and flashing gang signs at the weary receptionist.

The apparent leader of the pack stepped in front of Noah, crowding his personal space and blocking access to the door. The thug folded his arms across his chest, the sleeves of his blue plaid flannel shirt covering the worst of the sweat stains on the wife beater beneath it. Chin raised defiantly, he bobbed his head and eyeballed Noah as if daring him to pass.

Noah rested his right hand loosely on the butt of his .45 caliber 1911. He raised his left eyebrow. "Do we have a problem here?"

Short and stout, the thug resembled a fireplug. An inked dragon curled down his neck. The dragon's tongue tickled his jaw while the tail disappeared beneath his dingy white tank top. The thug took another step into his personal space, throwing his arms down and chest out in a challenge. "What if we do?"

Towering over the man, Noah flashed an arctic smile and stepped closer to the thug, causing the wannabe to stumble back. The muscles in his arms and hands tightened. A spike of adrenaline enhanced his senses. Every whisper, every movement around him was amplified. He leaned forward, deepened his scary smile, and drawled, "I imagine I could help you fix it."

A tense moment of silence passed. The thug swallowed hard and stepped back. His chest deflated. He raised his hands in a gesture of surrender. "No, boss, no problem here."

He slunk back to his buddies who laughed and rattled off something in rapid-fire Spanish too quickly for the ranger to translate it. Shrugging off his buddies, he raked Noah with a glare of pure hatred.

With a shake of his head, Noah tapped lightly on the bulletproof glass in front of the reception desk. A buzzer sounded, and the door next to the desk unlocked with a subtle click. He shoved through and waited near the door until it closed and locked behind him.

Sylvia Castillo, the law enforcement receptionist, grinned at him. "Hey, Easy Money, whatcha' up to?"

"Living the dream." A bouquet of brightly colored posies perched next to the nameplate on her desk. He snagged one from the vase and presented it to her with a flourish and a grin. "Just living the dream."

Swatting his arm, she giggled. "Get on with yourself, rotten boy, before I tell that pretty girl of yours, you're misbehaving again."

"What the heck happened out there?" He gestured toward the crowd in the waiting room. "This place was a ghost town when I stepped out for lunch."

"You know about last night's gang fight out on the

east end of the county?"

"Yeah, the commotion came across the radio, but it sounded like your patrol deputies had everything under control. What does the fight have to do with this afternoon's crowd? I could have sworn visiting day was Tuesday, not Thursday."

"And you would be right. Judge Karnes came in today to magistrate last night's detainees. One of the wise-ass bangers mouthed off at the beginning of the court session and seriously pissed her off. She set everyone's bail at the maximum—like three times higher than normal."

"Oh, crap. That's going to stir up the locals."

"Yep. She decided to treat them all like felonies." Sylvia shrugged. "It's well within her rights, but hell, they didn't even hospitalize anyone last night. Anyway, they"—she gestured toward the people overflowing the waiting area—"are all here to talk to the sheriff, not that he can do anything about it."

"Lucky man." Noah grabbed the mail from his box. "Let me guess. No one's sons, husbands, baby-daddies, boyfriends, brothers, buddies or whatever did anything wrong. They weren't even there, right?"

Sylvia's laugh was a silver peal of delight. "You got it in one. Guess we now know why they pay you the big bucks. Even the ones arrested on scene claimed they weren't there."

"Good luck sticking to that story." As he headed down the hallway toward his office, the click of his boot heels echoed against the tile floor. He called back over his shoulder, "Holler if you need any help."

****

Holding an ice-cold can of soda in each hand,

Noah leaned against the wall across from the office door of his fellow ranger and best friend. He watched Rhyden Trammell tuck a cell phone between his ear and shoulder while struggling to dig a set of keys from the front pocket of his starched jeans.

Rhyden's eyes widened at something said on the other end of the telephone conversation. He fumbled the keys as he tried to unlock his door. "Really?" Sarcasm dripped from the single word. "And whose brilliant idea was it to take a group of high school seniors to a bluff overhanging their favorite swimming hole to take class pictures?"

Cell phone still clamped to his ear, he bent to scoop the keys from the floor, straightened and managed to unlock his office door in one long, smooth move. "Did you really believe no one would jump? It's a hundred and two in the shade. When I was in high school, I would have jumped. Hell, I'd probably do it today."

Noah leaned against the doorjamb as Rhyden flipped on the stark fluorescent lights and tossed his bundle of keys onto the messy desk. They landed with a solid thud between two empty coffee-stained Styrofoam cups and a stack of unfinished reports.

After hanging his silver belly beaver cowboy hat on the antler of the trophy twelve-point whitetail buck mounted on the wall, he waved Noah into the office. "No, I understand," he continued into the phone. "Yes, ma'am. No, ma'am. Okay. Got it."

He stepped around the desk and plopped down into his office chair. Scrubbing a hand through his coal black hair, he sighed. "YouTube, huh?" He wiggled his mouse to wake up his computer. Quickly he entered his username and password. Still on the phone, he said,

"No, no, you are right. Disrespectful and insubordinate. Yes, ma'am. You do what you need to do, and I will handle it on my end when I get home from work. Thank you for calling." He disconnected the call. The cell phone dropped to the top of the desk, landing next to the keys.

"What did she do now?" Noah asked as he sauntered through the open doorway and handed his buddy the can of soda. "Steal a bus? Burn down the school?"

Rhyden cracked the tab on the can. "Thanks." He gestured toward the computer monitor. "Give this a minute to warm up. Apparently, my darlin' daughter is a star. She's already gone viral." He sighed. "Twelve years of school—and nothing but straight As. Never been to the principal's office. Never been in trouble once. And now? Three weeks left until graduation—three measly weeks—and she's in trouble. I really don't know what to do."

Noah perched on a corner of the desk for a better view of the computer monitor and took a sip of the frosty cherry-amaretto-flavored cola so popular in this part of Texas. Now and then he found himself craving the spicy ginger ale he grew up with in South Carolina. Within seconds, a shaky cell phone video filled the screen. High-pitched shrieks and giggles, lower octave whoops and hollering echoed from the speakers. On the screen a petite redhead in a lacy green tank top and jeans took a running leap off the bluff.

The video followed her over the edge and recorded her landing with a giant splash in the murky green river water below. When she surfaced, she shook her wet hair out of her face before thrusting her arms in the air, her fingers hooked in the familiar Texas Longhorn victory sign. The kids on the bluff erupted in cheers.

Soda squirted from Noah's nose. "Wait a minute." Flabbergasted, he glanced at his best bud. "*Senior* insanity? You mean our precious Little Miss Goody Two Shoes Bree is in trouble? I just assumed we were talking about another Wild-Child Samantha stunt." He wiped soda from his chin and laughed. "Way to go, Aubree. It's about time she acted her age instead of like a middle-aged matron."

"Go ahead and laugh, 'Uncle' Noah. I ought to make you go to the principal's office where I'm expected to drop off a written apology from her to Principal Harkness and the teacher who chaperoned the photo shoot. And don't let Bree hear you call her goody two shoes. She'll have your butt for breakfast."

"Hard Ass Harkness is principal now? Who let that happen?" Noah shuddered. "That woman hates me. You'll be much better off without me in tow, partner."

"Why would Harkness hate you? You don't even have kids."

"Thank God. Can you see me as a father?" Noah held up a hand to ward off the response. "Never mind. It's a long story. Way before Cat. Let's just say Harkness and highballs don't mix. Don't ask."

He sank into one of the cushy, brown leather visitor chairs in front of Rhyden's desk, leaned back in the chair, and propped his boots on the corner of the messy, mahogany desk. "I'm still having a tough time wrapping my mind around the idea of Bree thwarting authority. I'm more used to seeing rebellious behavior from Sam, not her responsible big sister."

"Wanna see the video again?" Rhyden knocked

Noah's boots off his desk. "Get your feet down. Nice boots, by the way. Fancy-schmancy. You auditioning to be a sheriff's office investigator?"

Noah straightened up in the chair and grinned. "Aren't they, though? Cat had them custom made for me at that place in Weslaco." He raised his foot, tugged up his pants leg, and turned it from side to side to show off the boots. "She even had them put my badge on them."

"You must have done something right."

"Yeah, that's what she said." Noah waggled his eyebrows, and his grin lit up the room before he sobered. "So what's going on with Bree?"

"It's this new boy she's seeing."

"Do we need to go have a talk with him?"

"Hell, I don't know. She is extremely secretive about this one, very un-Bree like." Dropping his head into his hands, Rhyden massaged his temples before dragging his hands down his face. "At times like these, I almost wish her mother was still around."

Noah crossed himself. "Heaven forbid."

"I said *almost.* But seriously, I don't know what to do. Bree won't even tell me the boy's real name. She just calls him Prince Charming. She doesn't want me to scare this one off. She's afraid I will go all Ranger Dad, run a criminal background check on him, and interrogate him." Rhyden made eye contact with Noah and smirked. "You know. Like we did the last one."

They shared a look before bursting out in laughter. "Anyway," Rhyden continued when the laughter subsided, "all she will tell me is he's new to town, works for his dad, and apparently has to-die-for biceps gagging noise. "Actually, she didn't tell me the last part. I overheard her talking to her friend, Jenn."

"And you're letting her get away with not telling you who he is? Seriously?"

"Just wait. Your day's coming, and I hope you have twin girls—better yet—triplets. Yeah triplets, blonde like you but gorgeous like Cat. And I hope they act just like you." Rhyden paused, took a swallow of his soda. "You know, when you have a boy, you only have to worry about one prick. When you have a girl, you have to worry about all the pricks."

Noah choked; more soda spewed. After putting down the can, he wiped his face on the back of his hand. "I cannot believe you just said that."

"Why not? It's true." Rhyden let both shoulders sag. He leaned back in his office chair. "What am I supposed to do? As Bree continually points out, she will be eighteen in a few weeks. She's always been a straight arrow. Responsible as all get out and has never given me one reason not to trust her."

"Keep telling yourself that. You want me to ask Cat to talk to her? See what she can find out?"

"No offense to your girlfriend, but what's she going to do? Hell, I don't even know what I'm supposed to do."

A sharp knock on the door interrupted Noah before he could respond.

"Ranger Trammell?" Brook from dispatch, with a voice like cool silk and legs that went on forever, stood in the doorway.

At the sound of her voice, Noah saw his partner straighten in his chair, tug at his collar, and smooth down his tie before waving her into the office. "What's up, Brooke?"

The curvaceous blonde nodded a greeting to Noah before turning her attention back to Rhyden. "I really hate to bother you, sir, but would you mind taking a nuisance call for me?" She bit her lower lip. "I know you don't normally respond to calls like these, and I wouldn't ask, but this poor man has called at least a half dozen times now. Most of my patrol guys are tied up on the north end of the county, working an eighteen-wheeler rollover. The rest are on the east end with a motorcycle versus school bus accident. And the peacocks, um—I, uh—I mean the investigators—" A blush spread across her face.

Rhyden waved it away. "We know what you mean. Where are the illustrious investigators?"

Face still flushed, she said, "At the courthouse, discussing what color shirts to wear to the press conference this afternoon." Appearing to have overcome embarrassment, Brooke popped both hands onto her shapely hips. "I swear they're worse than a bunch of high school girls planning for prom."

Noah smothered a laugh that ended up sounding like a hog's snort.

Rhyden only raised one eyebrow. "Press conference? Hadn't heard about that."

"Channels Five and Twelve called about the gang fight last night. Someone told the press the fight was a turf battle between rival cartels." Brooke rolled her eyes. "As if. Anyway, the investigators caught wind of it and plan on taking credit for breaking up the 'vicious and highly dangerous' fight."

Noah rubbed his jaw. "Funny. I don't remember hearing any of their unit numbers communicating on the radio last night during the altercation."

Brooke smirked. "No, you didn't, did you?"

"Ah, business as usual, I see," Rhyden said. "Sure. I can help you out. Whatcha' got?"

"Some old guy complaining about Travelers who booby-trapped his driveway. I think he's German. He's kind of hard to understand."

Noah slid both palms up and down the side seam of his jeans to ease the sudden itch in his hands. His chest tightened and his stomach churned. "Uh—Travelers, you said?"

Brooke, already walking out the door, glanced back over her shoulder at Noah. "Traveler, Gypsy, Paver, whatever name they're using these days. We've had a sharp increase in complaints against them over the past few weeks for scamming the elderly, although this is the first call accusing them of out-and-out sabotage. I guess it's that time of year again." She turned back to the hallway, her blonde ponytail flipping flirtatiously as she headed back to the Communications Office.

Rhyden stood and grabbed his hat from the deer's antlers. "You got anything going on right now? I know it's not in your region, but I wouldn't mind the company. A little testosterone to combat all the estrogen I'm dealing with at home. Wanna ride along?"

Dread threatened to overwhelm Noah. He ground his teeth but said nothing.

Hat in hand, Rhyden tapped him on the shoulder. "Hey, are you coming?"

Noah started. "What?"

"Do. You. Want. To. Come. Along?"

Needing to know what was going on, while at the same time wanting to be a million miles from here, he aimed for nonchalant. "Sure. Why not?"

Chapter Three

While heading to the nuisance call in Rhyden's unmarked truck, Noah's thoughts whirled like a red sand dust devil. He tried inhaling and exhaling to ease the churning in his gut, took slow deep breaths like the hypnotherapy app on his phone taught him. No results.

Panic built in fast increments inside his chest at the same rate acid burned a fiery trail up his esophagus. He adjusted the air conditioning vent to direct a stronger airflow at his face and wished he had a peppermint candy to settle his stomach. Reaching into his pocket, he fingered his lucky talisman, a fouled spark plug.

"Hey, you okay over there? You're awfully quiet."

"Me? I'm fine." Noah shot Rhyden a wicked expression. "Just wondering when you'll ask her out."

"Ask who out?"

"Don't play dumb. You know who. Brooke."

"Brooke?" Rhyden flipped on his left turn signal. "From dispatch?"

Noah cocked his head to the right and grinned. "No, Sister Sally Brooke from the convent."

"Aren't there rules against dating in-house?"

"I'm sure there probably are. Even if the sheriff's office has rules against fraternization, they don't apply to you. We don't work for the sheriff." Noah tapped the silver badge on his chest. "Rangers, remember?"

"Funny, ha-ha…not." Pulling up on the street in

front of the two-story white limestone house on Sage Drive, Rhyden placed the vehicle in park and stepped out. "Why would she want to go out with me?"

Noah unfolded himself from the passenger side of the pickup. He stretched and studied Rhyden from across the hood. "Dude, you have got to get over the number Cara did on you."

"For your information, I happen to have a date with the reports clerk this weekend, the brunette."

Noah raised both hands in mock surrender. "Just saying. And good for you."

Together, the two men advanced up the gravel pathway toward the house. Before they reached it, the front door, fashioned out of rustic cedar, slowly swung inward. An elderly man dressed in faded denim overalls stepped out. Short and stout, the guy resembled a cranky St. Bernard with bushy whiskers framing deep jowls and a professional drinker's red bulbous nose.

Directing his comments over one shoulder and back into the house, he barked, "*Ja, ja. Sie sind hier.* I said I would handle it." He slammed the door and limped out to meet the men as they approached.

"Good afternoon, sir. I'm Ranger Trammell. This is Ranger Morgan."

"Rangers, huh?" The old guy leaned heavily on his mesquite cane and inspected them before shaking their hands. "They sent the big guns this time. 'Bout time. Didn't think that girl would ever get me help. Had to call a dozen times."

"What can we do for you, Mr.…?" Rhyden asked.

"Schmidt, Gunter Schmidt. I'll tell you what you can do for me. You can arrest those damn Gypsies is what you can do for me. Or better yet just shoot 'em."

Swallowing a chuckle, Noah asked, "Could you give us a little more information, Mr. Schmidt?"

The man gestured for them to follow him. "I told my wife not to hire those men. I knew they were no good. Shifty-eyed sons of bitches. Smooth talking used car salesmen if you ask me. But no, the wife, she knows better. She *always* knows better. Married sixty years and the damn woman knows everything. Just ask her."

Schmidt yanked a blue and white bandana from the front pocket of his overalls and mopped the sweat from his face. "I should have known better. I never should have married the old battle ax. We were dating—she was cute as a button and tiny, too—curves in all the right places. I asked her for a glass of iced tea. She went to the kitchen, came back, and handed me a glass. I took a long sip and damn near choked. Told her 'there's no sugar in this tea.' She looked me square in the eye and said, 'No, there's not.' No sugar, can you believe it? Damned if I ain't been drinking unsweetened iced tea ever since. Do you have any idea what it's like to go sixty-plus years without a single drop of sweet tea except for the ones I can sneak in when she goes to Fredericksburg to visit her sister?"

Rhyden and Noah exchanged glances, faces reddening from suppressed laughter. Rhyden cut into Mr. Schmidt's monologue. "Sir, as much as I can sympathize with you for the loss of sweet tea, it's downright criminal, but I don't think you want us to arrest your wife. Can you tell us why we're here?"

The old man shoved the bandanna back in his pocket. "Sure, go ahead, laugh. Hardy-har-har."

"Mr. Schmidt?"

"What? Oh, yeah, sorry. Damned woman just gets

under my skin. See, right here." He pointed to a flat tire on the rear driver's side of an older model Caddy.

"Um, Mr. Schmidt," Rhyden began.

"*Nein, nein*, not the tire." Using the cane, the old man gestured to a spot behind the tire. "Damn Gypsies booby-trapped my driveway. Just because I'm German doesn't mean I had anything to do with Hitler. Hell, my *grossvater* immigrated to the United States in 1888, the year of the three fat ladies. I ain't no damned Nazi. Never sent no one to one of those horrible camps, neither. Those *mistück* men charged me a small fortune to refinish my driveway, which was perfectly fine to begin with and didn't need refinishing in the first place, but my wife…anyway, they charged me a fortune and did a half-assed job. See? They left a piece of metal sticking up. Ruined my tire."

Both rangers moved to the sedan and squatted on their boot heels. Noah slid a black pocketknife from his front jeans pocket and used it to pry at the sharp piece of metal embedded in the hot asphalt.

Rhyden came to a standing position and stepped to the edge of the driveway where Mr. Schmidt waited, watching. "Sir, I'm sorry, but there's not much we can do for you. Shoddy work isn't a crime. Should be, granted, but it's not. You need to go down to the office of the local Justice of the Peace and file a civil suit in small claims court."

Out came the blue and white bandanna again. Mr. Schmidt mopped his forehead. He gestured angrily with his cane. "What about my frickin' tire?"

"Mr. Schmidt, do you have a spare?"

"Of course, I do. What fool kind of question is that? First, you tell me you can't help me, then you ask me stupid questions. I thought rangers were the top dogs. What kind of idiot question is that?"

Over by the back of the Schmidts' vehicle, Noah tucked his head to hide a chuckle. Rhyden took a deep breath before responding. "I'm sorry, sir. Let me reword the question. Where is your spare tire? Ranger Morgan and I will be happy to change it for you."

"Bah! I pay Triple A enough every year. About damned time they earned some of it. They can damn well come out and change the tire. What I want to know is who will pay for the damn thing? It's ruined. Can't be fixed."

Rhyden reached for his wallet. "I have Judge Nelson's card…"

Noah interrupted him. "Hold up, Rhy. There's something over here you need to see."

Puzzled, his partner said, "Excuse me, Mr. Schmidt." He stepped back over to where Noah still squatted behind the flat tire.

With the tar-covered tip of his knife, Noah pointed to the oddly shaped piece of metal he had pried from the driveway. With a rounded, mushroom-shaped head on one end, the object angled outward and down to form a sharp point on the other end. This point had punctured the vehicle's tire. "Do you recognize this? Or those?" he asked, pointing at small, weird shaped rocks also covered in tar.

"No. Can't say I do. Do you?"

Noah winced as he rubbed a hand over one hip. "Unfortunately, I do." He tugged his cell phone from his shirt pocket and typed a few words into the browser. When the website he was searching for finished loading, he turned the screen to face his partner.

Rhyden studied the piece of metal on the ground, comparing it to the image on the phone. His gaze wandered to Mr. Schmidt and back to the metal again. "You sure?"

"Pretty sure."

"Well, hell."

"Exactly." A heavy sigh slipped from Noah's lips. "Do you want me to tell him, or do you want to do it?"

"I'll do it."

"I'll call Martin over at the jail and ask him to haul the halogen lights and generators out here before the sun goes down. Maybe have him grab water and pizzas, too. It's gonna be a long night. Better get the crime scene crew headed over from Austin as well."

Rhyden pulled on his earlobe. "Do you think we should call over to Southwest Texas University for their forensic anthropology team?"

Noah shrugged. "And show them what? A piece of metal and a handful of potential bone fragments? I think it would be a waste of time. Don't they need a skeleton or at least a partial skeleton to work with? I think our best bet will be tracing down the serial number on the hip replacement, but we'll wait and see what the crime scene crew thinks. They can decide if they need more help or not."

"All right. Crap, I promised Bree I would be home in time for her to go to Jenn's house tonight. I need to call the girls and let them know I won't be home for dinner. Again."

"Go ahead," Noah said. "Call the girls. Whoever finishes first deals with Mr. Schmidt."

After ending his calls, Noah returned to where the elderly man still fumed, carrying a consent-to-search form. He held up a placating hand before the man could start in on him. In a grim tone, he informed Mr. Schmidt things were more complicated than a shoddy driveway repair and a flat tire.

"You found a *what* in my driveway?" he bellowed, staggering against his cane.

"Mr. Schmidt, would you like to sit down?" Concern tinged Noah's voice. *Please do not pass out.* "Can I help you inside where it's cooler?"

With the temps running in the low triple digits and the humidity hovering around ninety percent, Noah could count the rivulets of sweat trickling down his back causing his shirt to stick to his skin. The smell of melting tar in the driveway burned his nose. He could just imagine how the combination of the acrid odor of asphalt, the stifling heat, and the shocking news must affect the elderly man. He grasped Mr. Schmidt by the elbow to lead him into the house.

The grumpy old geezer jerked his arm from Noah's grasp. "*Mein Gott* in Heaven. I don't need your mollycoddling. I'm old, not stupid. I need you to tell me one more time exactly what you found and what it means. What happens next?"

Noah removed his hat and ran his sleeve across his forehead and down his face before returning the hat to his head. *Why do I work for a department that demands a cowboy hat be worn as part of our uniform any time we are outdoors, regardless of the weather?*

He brushed his dress code thought aside. "Sir, are you sure you don't want to go inside? Maybe sit down? Cool off?"

Schmidt waved the suggestion aside, irritation clear in the motion. "Just spit it out."

"All right. The piece of metal we pried from your driveway appears to be a surgical implant device, the kind used in hip replacement surgery. We suspect some of the rocks we found may be pieces of bone, teeth even. We've called in the necessary people to take care of identifying these things.

"While we wait for the mobile crime scene lab from the Texas Department of Public Safety to arrive from Austin, I need you to sign this consent-to-search form. Next, Ranger Trammell and I will photograph the scene to preserve it *in situ*—as it currently is."

"Now you wait one cotton-picking minute," the old man growled. "How long will all that take? What if I don't want to sign your *verdammt* form? I need my car. The old lady has several doctors' appointments in San Antonio this afternoon."

Noah lifted his hat again and brushed sweat off his forehead before it rolled into his eyes. "Tell you what. Sign this piece of paper giving us permission to search your driveway, and as soon as we finish the photography, Ranger Trammell and I will change your tire. Then you can pull your car out of the driveway. If you don't sign it, we will have to find a judge and get a warrant. Going the warrant route will delay things considerably."

Noah shrugged. "The choice is yours. Either way it goes, you won't be able to pull back in for some time. We're going to have to tape off your driveway and process it as a crime scene. Is there maybe somewhere you could stay for a few days?"

"Crime scene?" Mr. Schmidt crumpled as if he'd been kicked in the solar plexus. Bewilderment flooded his features. For the first time since the rangers arrived, the man looked *old.* "My driveway is a crime scene?"

"I'm afraid so, sir," Noah said, using the tone he reserved for scared kids, grieving family members and sagging old men who hadn't tasted sweet tea in more than sixty years. "Hip implants, bits of bone and teeth are not normally used for road base. It looks like someone may have disposed of a body in your driveway."

Chapter Four

Bree shimmied out of her wet blue jeans while balancing a cell phone between her chin and shoulder. "If I'd known swats with a board over wet jeans stung so much, I might not have jumped off the cliff. Archaic custom—corporal punishment. Why do I have to go to the only school in the state of Texas that still beats students for showing a bit of spirit, a bit of independence?"

"Who are you talking to?"

Bree jumped. Samantha, stood in the doorway. "Not you." She stalked to the door and slammed it in her sister's face.

Sam slammed her fist against the closed door and yelled, "How rude!"

Bree's cell phone chirped, showing she had a new text message. The alert had sounded nonstop since she left school. Her phone was blowing up as her friends told her how many hits her video had gotten on Facebook and YouTube.

Going viral! Her chest puffed up with pride after reading the number of videos confirming the popularity of the stunt at the bluff. *Told him I could be spontaneous. Can't wait till he sees the video.*

She imagined the expression of pride her new boyfriend would bestow on her. Her thoughts darkened as they drifted to her father. He definitely would not be proud. *I hope the school doesn't call him. Can't believe I actually jumped.*

After a soothing, hot soak in her claw-foot bathtub filled with lavender-scented bubbles and surrounded with vanilla candles, she dried off with a fluffy, purple towel, then sprinkled baby powder on her legs. The powder helped as she wriggled into her favorite pair of super-soft, faded, skin-tight jeans.

Flopping down on her back on top of her turquoise and empire blue duvet, she lay back to fasten her jeans. She sucked in her stomach as tight as possible and fastened the button at the waistband. Fighting with the zipper came next. She grabbed a wire coat hanger and fed the hook into the hole at the end of the zipper tab. Using the hangar for leverage, she wrestled the zipper all the way up. *There. At last.*

She struggled to her feet and dropped into a couple of grand *pliés* to stretch the jeans enough to allow her to breathe. She slipped into her favorite blingy tank top. Before she forgot, she threw a loose, button-up denim shirt over it. Carefully buttoning up the shirt, she left it untucked just in case her dad came home before she left. “Yeah, right. Like that's ever going to happen.”

She was supposed to be spending the evening at Jenn's house. “Dad may not be the brightest crayon in the box when it came to his daughters, but even he would question why I'm so dressed up to hang out and watch movies at my bestie's house.” Excitement sizzled through her insides. *I can't wait to see Prince Charming!*

A flash of apprehension dampened the excitement. She had never lied to her father before. She hated lying now, but she didn't know what else to do. Dad would never let her date PC. He'd say her boyfriend was too old. He'd also say she couldn't go out with anyone who wasn't in high school. She was afraid to even think her sweetie's real name. Sometimes she believed her dad was psychic and could read her mind.

Her old man would interrogate him faster than a duck on a June bug. Just like the last one he scared off. And the one before that one. "Not my fault PC was homeschooled and graduated two years early. Besides, I'll be eighteen soon. Age is all in your head, anyway. You are only as old as you feel."

Bree yanked her closet door open and dropped to her knees as she rummaged through the piles of stuff on the closet floor. *It's not fair. I make straight As. I go to school. I come home from school. I cook. I clean. I take care of my sisters.*

She grabbed her left cowboy boot from the bottom of one stack and tossed it onto the floor near her bed. She kept rummaging for the right boot. Just thinking about all the things she did raised her temper. "I don't skip school. I don't sleep around. I don't do drugs." She snagged the right boot and scooted over toward her bed. It was too hard to stand up yet in the tight jeans.

"Hell, I don't even drink—which is more than I can say for Sam. If Dad doesn't loosen up a little, I may have to start."

Leaning her back against the bed, she tugged on her boots. Crawling up the footboard to a standing position, Bree bent forward from the waist and dragged a brush through her hair. She flipped it back, smoothing the flyaway hairs from her face. Grabbing her lipstick off the dresser, she touched up her lips. She stepped back and checked out the finished product in the mirror from several angles. She grabbed her lipstick and pink, custom-made pocketknife off her dresser but discovered her jeans were too tight for them to fit in her pockets. Instead she stuck the tube of lipstick down into the top of her left boot and her knife into the right. She spun in circles, then smiled at herself in the mirror. *Prince Charming will love this outfit on me. I hope.*

Guilt skittered through the back of her mind. *Why doesn't Dad trust me? I'm not Mom.* Anger mixed with the guilt. *I've never done one thing—not one teensy, tiny, itty-bitty thing—to give him any reason not to believe in me.* As if on cue, barking split the air as her phone rang with her father's personalized ringtone.

"Hey, Dad."

"Hey, sweetie. Everything okay on the home front?"

With a fast glance around the war zone of her room, she lied her ass off. "Sure."

"Anything happen at school today you want to tell me about?"

"Really, Dad?" *I'm not falling for that.* "Save it for Maddie. I'm not five anymore."

"Uh-huh. Well, okay, we'll talk about school later. Can you make sure the girls get fed? I'm tied up on a case but should be home by bedtime. Let Maddie know I'll be there to read her a story and tuck her in."

Sure you will. Fat chance on that promise. I'll be dealing with Maddie's tears…as usual. Thoughts of PC rushed through her. *Shit.* "But, Dad, I was going to Jenn's house tonight. Can't Sam do it?"

"Sweetie, I need your help. I want to have a house to come home to when we're done. Remember the last time Sam tried to cook? The kitchen curtains still smell like smoke. Why don't you invite Jenn to our house? And remind Sam she's still grounded."

"But Dad..." Bree stopped mid-whine. *What a great idea. Dad won't be home. I can invite Prince Charming over for dinner.* "Fine, Dad," she muttered in one of her best I-hope-you-realize-the-sacrifice-I'm-making-for-you voice.

It wouldn't do for her father to figure out she now wanted to stay home and cook. He'd get suspicious if she gave in too easily. Pouring on the sarcasm, she continued, "I'll give up another night of freedom to take care of *your children* for you. It's not like I have a life or anything."

"Okay, sweetie." Her sarcasm never registered. "I appreciate it. Maybe I can make it up to you this weekend. Listen, Uncle Noah needs me. I've got to run. Love you." The phone disconnected before she could respond.

Aaaarrggghhh!

Bree squeezed her cell phone into the back pocket of her jeans, shrugged out of the oversized work shirt, tugged off her boots, and danced down the hallway to the kitchen. "Maybe after I put Maddie to bed, Prince Charming and I can snuggle up and watch a movie. Just the two of us, all alone, in the dark. I wonder if I can get Sam to sneak out and spend time with her friends?"

She sent him a text.

—Trapped at home. Want to come to dinner?—

—Sure—

Excitement tingled as she sent a quick text to Jenn.

—Don't need u to cover for me. Deets later. Love ya—

She bounced on her toes as she waltzed around the

kitchen gathering ingredients for jambalaya.

Five-year-old Maddie wandered into the kitchen dragging Fred, her bedraggled, well-loved teddy bear. She hopped up on a rustic brown, high-backed, swivel bar stool at the moss-green granite countertop and perched Fred on the stool beside her. Fred had been a gift from Uncle Noah. “Whatcha’ doing?”

“Cooking dinner. What are you doing?” Bree added the chopped green onions to the fresh crushed garlic, yellow onions, and red cayenne peppers sautéing in the melted butter.

“Can I help?”

“Not right now, baby, but you can add the rice when I’m ready, okay?”

“Okay.” Maddie twisted a length of hair the color of corn silk around her finger. “I’m bored. Where’s Daddy?”

“He’s at work with Uncle Noah.”

A pout clouded the pixie face. She grabbed Fred from the seat beside her and hugged him to her chest. “Daddy’s always at work.” Tears filled her eyes. “Why does he like work better than us?”

“Oh, baby.” Bree tossed the chicken chunks into a pot of boiling water already containing slices of link sausage and cubed ham steak, washed her hands, and scooted around the counter to gather Maddie into her arms. *Thanks a lot, Dad.*

“He doesn’t like work more than us. He promised he’d be home in time to read you a bedtime story.”

“Yeah, right.” Maddie pouted.

Bree glanced at the ground sausage and venison waiting to be browned with the sautéed onions, peppers, and garlic. She closed her eyes. *Lord, give me strength.*

Opening her eyes, she asked, "Where's Sam? Why don't you and Fred get her to read a book to you? Or better yet why don't you read one of your new library books to Sam?"

"She's too busy putting gunk on her face." Maddie's lower lip stuck out. "Nobody wants to play with me."

"Gunk?"

"You know, like Unca Noah says, paint for what you ain't."

Bree gave Maddie a little squeeze and walked back to the stove. "Why is she putting makeup on? She's not going anywhere. Dad said she's grounded."

Maddie lifted one shoulder up in a shrug. "She said if you didn't get grounded for the stunt you pulled at school today, then she wasn't grounded either. Are you grounded? What did you do? You don't get in trouble. Sam and her friends call you Miss Goody Two Shoes."

A hot flush crept up Bree's chest. She slammed the glass lid down on the stock pot. "Goody Two Shoes? I'll show her Goody Two Shoes." Deftly, she drained the grease from the ground meat before liberally adding Slap Ya' Mama Cajun seasoning. She stirred the mixture, viciously scraping the wooden spoon hard against the sides of the pan.

"Bree?" Maddie's voice trembled.

She took a moment to paste a smile on her face before turning to face her sister. "What, baby?"

Maddie peeked over the top of Fred's shabby, semi-bald brown head. In a tiny, squeaky voice, she asked, "Are you mad at me?"

"No, I'm not mad at you." She lifted the pan of seasoned meat and dumped it into the stock pot where the chicken, link sausage, and ham boiled. Setting the now empty pan down gently in the charcoal granite sink, she wiped her hands on the ivy-printed kitchen towel hanging on the oven door. "You can add the rice, shrimp, and the crawfish, but be careful. Don't let the water splash you. It's boiling and will burn you."

Maddie dropped Fred on the bar stool, grabbed a kitchen chair from the breakfast table, and dragged it across the hardwood floor. Bree hurried over and picked up the chair before it could scratch the wood.

After they finished stirring in the final ingredients, including Bree's super-secret one, Maddie proudly put the lid back on the stock pot. Bree turned the heat down to medium-low. She took her youngest sister by the hand. "Come on. Let's go see what Sam's up to."

Sam stood in front of the mirror in the bathroom attempting to straighten her naturally curly hair. Anyone looking at the three girls side by side would never guess they were sisters. Bree resembled her mother—at least as best as the teen remembered her mother. Petite, barely topping four foot eleven inches and curvy. Board-straight, waist-length copper hair cascaded down her back. Wispy bangs framed high porcelain cheekbones dusted with freckles.

Sam, on the other hand, took after their father. At fifteen, she stood five foot eight inches—only an inch shorter than her dad—with no curves whatsoever. Not to say she was a stick. Sam's frame leaned more toward athletic. Graced with curly, blue-black hair, olive skin, and dimples, Samantha would make a great runway model if she put any effort into it. Unfortunately for the modeling world, she would rather work on muscle cars and play football with the boys. The only trait shared by the two older girls were their eyes. Upturned, almond-shaped hazel eyes laced with flecks of gold and green sparkled in both their faces.

Maddie resembled neither of the sisters nor her dad. Waves of thick, platinum-blonde hair surrounded golden tan skin, chubby pink cheeks, and chocolate brown eyes. When Sam was being mean, which was often, she would tell Maddie they'd found her under a rock and hauled her home for a pet. This invariably caused a storm of tears from the sensitive five-year-old.

A hint of sage with undertones of burning hair lingered in the bathroom despite the fan sitting on top of the toilet tank, blowing air out an open window.

"What do you think you are doing?" Bree asked.

Sam stuck her chin up and out defiantly. "Great-Grandad said smudging the house chased away negative spirits."

Bree waved her hand in front of her face, fanning away the smoke residue. "Do you really think sage will hide the smell of skunk weed?"

Samantha drew herself up to her full height, puffed up like a bullfrog. "It's not—" Avoiding eye contact with Bree, Sam turned back to the mirror, adding another coat of midnight black mascara to lashes that didn't need it. "I am quite sure I have no clue what you are talking about."

"Right." Bree drew the word out. "Where do you think you are going?"

"What's it to you?"

Bree tapped the toes of her right foot on the ceramic tile floor, her arms folded across her chest, as she stood in the doorway. She waited without saying another word.

"Fine." Sam fluffed her hair. "I'm going to meet my boyfriend at the park. And I'm late already." She shoved her way past Bree. "He can't stay long because he has to have dinner with his family at his grandmother's house."

Maddie piped up. "Bree said you're not going anywhere because you're grounded. And you can't have a boyfriend. You're too young. Dad said so. I'm telling."

"Shut up, pipsqueak," Sam growled.

Maddie darted behind Bree and snuck a peek out around her waist. The five-year-old stuck her tongue out at Sam. "I am not a pipsqueak."

Sam made a fast movement toward Maddie who squealed and ducked back behind Bree.

Bree said, "I didn't ground you. Dad did."

"I don't care what he said. You publicly disrespect a teacher and the principal, and you don't get grounded. I commit one teeny-tiny prank, and I'm grounded for the rest of my life. It's not fair."

Maddie piped up like a parrot. "Dad said life and fair are both four-letter words, but that's all they have in common."

Sam stomped toward Maddie. "If you don't shut up, I will rip your little head off."

"Sam, stop it. Maddie, shut up." Bree shifted away from the bathroom door. "And Sam, shutting the school down for three days by putting a chemical concoction in the air-conditioning ducts is not a 'tiny prank.' It's borderline terrorism. You're lucky they didn't press charges. You cost the school district a ton of money, and now we have to go to school on our bad-weather days to make up for it."

"What do you care? You like school." Sam shrugged. "I don't see what the big deal was. It was funny. No one got hurt." She stopped and examined Bree as if seeing her for the first time. "What are you all dressed up for? And where is Dad anyway?"

"Dad caught a case. He's working late."

"Nothing new there." Sam grimaced. "He's always at work. Not sure why he even had kids in the first place. You still didn't tell me why you're all dolled up."

Bree glanced over her shoulder, checking for eavesdroppers, not that anyone else was in the house. She stared at Sam, measuring. "Promise not to tell?"

"Of course. We're sisters, aren't we?"

She would love to share her delicious secret with someone who would understand and keep it a secret. She cast another quick glance around, her gaze landing on Maddie. "Mads, why don't you take Fred and go to the living room? You can watch any movie you want."

Maddie eyed her sisters, looking from one to the other and then back again. The little girl shook her head side to side. Waves of silky, baby-fine blonde hair whipped around her face as if in a windstorm. "Nope. No way. No how. I'm not going anywhere." She folded her arms over her chest and dug her heels into the hallway flooring. "I'm your sister, too, and you can't make me."

Sam cracked her knuckles. "Wanna bet, pipsqueak?"

"Enough already. Fine, but you can't tell anyone either, okay?" Bree turned to Sam. "I mean it. Neither one of you can share a word of this with anyone."

"What about Daddy?" Maddie asked.

"Especially not Dad, understand? Pinky promise?"

Sam held up her hand, little finger extended. “Pinky promise.”

“I still don’t know why I can’t tell Daddy.”

“Maddie!” Bree glared at her baby sister. “Either promise or leave.”

Mimicking the older girls, Maddie held up her hand. The three girls interlocked pinkies and shook.

Bree leaned toward her sisters and whispered, “Since Dad won’t be home until late, I invited my boyfriend to supper.”

“Boyfriend?” Sam fell back. “Shut up. You mean Mr. Hottie also known as Prince Charming in your journal is real? I thought you made him up.”

“Wait, what?” Heat crept up Bree’s neck. “You read my journal? How could—”

Before she could finish her sentence, her guilty sister squealed in delight. “He’s here. His Mustang just pulled up. Love those pipes and glass packs.” She paused for a moment as if confused by something. “How did he find out where I lived?” She shook her head and beamed a smile that lit the room. “Who cares? Just shows how smart he is, right? I bet he got tired of waiting at the park because I am way late. He has to go to his grandmother’s. He doesn’t want to, but his parents demanded he show up for dinner.”

Bree and Maddie trailed Sam as she dashed to the front door. Bree watched Sam fling open the door, squeal in a most un-Sam-like way, and raced into her boyfriend’s arms.

To be more exact—she raced directly into the arms of Bree’s Prince Charming.

Chapter Five

As the sun disappeared beneath the curve of the horizon, the roar of generators powering the halogen lights filled the air, and the mobile crime scene unit rolled up. Noah and Rhyden climbed out of the pickup truck where they'd waited, soaking up as much air conditioning as possible following the Schmidts' departure for their afternoon round of doctors' appointments.

After handshakes and introductions all around, the senior crime scene technician asked, "So what do we have here?"

Black and yellow caution tape fluttered in the breeze, blocking off the crime scene. As Noah spoke, he pointed to the yellow, plastic evidence markers dotting the driveway. "We're hoping you can tell us. We've located what we believe is a hip implant and possibly some tar-covered bone fragments."

"What makes you think it was a hip implant?" the tech asked.

With a wince, Noah instinctively rubbed his left hip. "Unfortunately, I have one of my very own. Souvenir from a wreck I had back in my teens."

"Ouch," she replied, face grim. "Well, alrighty then, a sifting we will go."

The tech walked to the rear of her van and helped her partners finish unloading equipment as two unmarked Bennett County vehicles arrived on scene. Damon Tesler and Brian Coer, investigators from the sheriff's office, climbed out of the trucks and strutted up to the scene.

Noah chuckled. "Brooke wasn't kidding. They really do coordinate their outfits." He gave them a quick once-over. "Matchy-match right down to their gun rigs."

Tesler and Coer both wore black jeans, lime green shirts, and fluorescent yellow ties. Their leather gun belts matched their boots. They headed straight to the temporary command station where boxes of pizza sat.

Rhyden shook his head. "They may dress prissy, but honestly, they do an excellent job. Did you see how quickly they cleared the Vasquez murder? Most ricky-tick. They impressed me."

He and Noah followed the crime scene tech to the back of the van and offered to help carry equipment. After she turned down the offer, Noah handed the tech a business card. "Keep me informed on whatever you find, please. We have several patrol deputies on standby if you need them, and I see Bennett County's finest have just arrived on scene as well." Gesturing toward the card, he said, "My cell number's on the back. Call if you need anything or if you find anything important."

****

As the moon rose above the horizon, in response to a call from the crime scene unit, Noah and Rhyden returned to the Schmidts' residence. Upon their arrival, the lead crime scene technician led them past the screen shakers to a long, white plastic table set up under a blue canvas tent. The yellow numbered evidence markers now sat in shallow bins on the table. With a somber expression, the tech gave both men a tour of the evidence collected from the driveway.

Turning back to the truck, Noah squeezed the bridge of his nose between his thumb and middle finger before dragging his knuckles across his forehead in an attempt to relieve the pressure building behind his eyes. *I don't have time for a migraine. Not now.*

"Been a hell of an evening, hasn't it?" Rhyden took a deep swallow from the semi-cool bottle of water he had just rolled across the back of his neck. He held a second bottle out to Noah.

"Thanks." He twisted the cap off. "That's one way to put it. A hip implant, thirty-seven possible bone fragments, and a handful of teeth. Hell of a nuisance call, huh?" He took a long swig off the bottle as he examined the remains of Mr. Schmidt's driveway.

Rhyden shook his head. "Who the hell crushes up a body and uses it for road base?"

The beginnings of anxiety skittered down Noah's spine. *I sure hope I don't know the answer to that question.* Fine muscle tremors started in his fingertips and began a slow trip up both arms. "I guess that's what we have to figure out. Along with whose body it is. Did you know hip implants have serial numbers on them?"

"To be honest," Rhyden said, "I never really thought about it one way or another, but I have to say I'm glad this one does."

Noah slid his fingers in a reverse pinching motion over the surface of the phone, enlarging the image of the hip implant because the numbers and letters etched into the object were barely legible. He then emailed the picture to the office so an admin could research the manufacturer, where the implant had been installed, who did the actual installation and when.

"Come on," Rhyden said, "I need to head back to the house. I've already missed several texts from the girls." He checked for messages and grunted. "Huh. That's weird."

"What?"

"No text messages. The girls rarely call me anymore. They usually text. Apparently, it's uncool to actually speak to your parental unit." He dialed the house number. It rang and rang. No answer.

Noah chuckled as he climbed back into the passenger seat and fastened his seatbelt. "And there you have reason number six hundred and seventy-eight why I don't have children. You give them life. Feed them. Nurture them. And they cast you off like a dirty sock when they don't need you anymore."

He studied the driveway where the crime scene technicians still labored at scooping up and sifting the contents of what used to be Mr. Schmidt's driveway through three screens of increasingly finer mesh. "I don't envy them when Mr. Schmidt gets home. He's gonna pop a gasket when he sees his driveway."

"I can hear him now." Rhyden started the engine while punching in numbers on his phone. "No answer from either Sam or Bree. Bree, I understand. She's always misplacing her phone, but Sam's has practically grown to her hand. I'll try the landline again."

"Do you want to skip the office and go straight to the house? Check on the girls? You can take me back…"

The radio squawked. "Bennett County to 1541."

"1541, Bennett County," a deputy responded. "Go ahead."

"Bennett County, 1541, we have a domestic disturbance at 225 Redbud in Magellan. Neighbors report fighting in the front yard. Repeat physical disturbance at 225 Redbud."

Rhyden reached up and turned down the volume on the radio. Shooting out a hand, Noah stopped him. "Wait a minute. The address sounded familiar."

"I wasn't listening." Rhyden grabbed the microphone mounted on the dashboard, picked it up and keyed the mic. "819, Bennett County, repeat traffic please."

"10-4, 819. Domestic disturbance, 225 Redbud in Magellan. Report of minors fighting in the yard. No weapons."

"Son of a..." Rhyden whipped his truck out into traffic, squealing the tires and flipping on his lights and sirens. "That's *my house*."

Noah braced himself against the dash as Rhyden slid around the corner of Elm onto Redbud. A minute later, they pulled into his driveway. Rhyden threw the transmission into Park so hard and fast it gave Noah whiplash.

Bree and Sam rolled through the front yard, yanking hair, scratching, kicking, and biting. A crowd of neighbors gathered around the edge of the yard enjoying the show. Some held up their cell phones to record the action.

Rhyden leaped out of the truck, leaving the engine running and the door open. Moths flew in, swarming the cab light. He ran straight to the girls. "Stop it. Stop it right now."

Noah stretched across the console and shut off the engine. Blaring sirens drowned out the ticking of the cooling engine as a marked county unit, red-and-blue lights flashing, rolled up behind the truck. A second unit quickly followed.

He climbed out and walked around the front of the truck. Closing the driver's door, he leaned against it. Showing his badge to the deputies, he waved them to a stop. "He's a ranger, too. Those are his daughters. Let him handle it. Please."

The girls fought across the yard, rolling in and out of the splashes of pale-yellow light provided by the security light and the red-and-blue puddles from the Bennett County units' overheads. They screamed, punched, and tried to subdue one another with jiu-jitsu choke holds.

Rhyden dove into the fray. "Break it up. Now."

The girls ignored him. Noah gasped in shock as Bree drew back and punched Sam square in the face. Blood spurted from her nose.

Bet Rhy wishes he hadn't taught the girls how to fight so well now. Noah laughed. *Damn, I love those girls.* He searched for Madison, the baby. He spotted her on the porch, wringing her hands and hopping from foot to foot.

A shriek drew his attention back to the older girls. Sam grabbed Bree's hair and yanked. A handful came away in her fist.

Noah grinned as he remembered scuffling with his older cousin. With Mom dead and Dad in prison, Grandda and Nana had raised him. He couldn't remember why his cousin lived with them, too, but he did. Grandda always let them duke it out when they were younger. Not so much as they got older. Noah's expression darkened with memories. Unconsciously, his hand slipped into his pocket to roll the spark plug between his fingers.

Cursing pulled him back to the present just as Rhyden caught an uppercut to the chin meant for Bree. Noah winced. *That will leave a mark.*

The sheriff's deputies started forward again to help break up the fight. Noah held up a hand to stop them. Placing two fingers in his mouth, he let loose with a loud, shrill, ear-splitting whistle.

The girls jerked to a stop. They saw Noah and the neighbors gathered on the outskirts of the lawn. Sheepishly, they broke apart, panting. They glared at one another, then slammed into the house through separate doors.

Rhyden rubbed the bruise forming on his chin as he approached Noah and the deputies. Crimson embarrassment stained his cheeks. He held out a hand for the deputies to shake. "Gentlemen, I am so sorry."

Maddie flew through the grass and latched onto Noah's leg. "Unca Noah." She tugged on his shirttail. "Unca Noah, Unca Noah, Bree and Sam were fighting. Sam kissed a boy. Ewww! He put his tongue in her mouth. I saw him. Why would you put your tongue in someone's mouth?" She wiped her hand across her mouth as if she were scrubbing away a kiss. "Everybody in my school knows boys have cooties. Bree cried and yelled, and then she hit Sam, and Sam hit her back, and the stupid boy ran away."

As she paused to draw in a breath, Noah smiled down at the pint-sized bundle of energy wrapped around his legs, uncertain how to respond. Before Rhy's ex-wife, Cara, walked out on Rhyden and the girls a few years back, Noah had never been around young girls—ever. With his own situation, he had been so lonely and in such pain. He recognized a similar pain in his fellow ranger. Gradually, through work, they became close friends, and eventually Noah had been adopted into the family as an honorary uncle.

"Unca Noah, are you listening to me?" She tugged on his shirt again before thrusting her arms up in the air. "Pick me up."

Rhyden walked up and scooped Maddie into his arms, rescuing Noah. "You okay, pumpkin?"

The little girl wrapped her arm around her father's neck, turning her attention to him. "I called you, Daddy, but you didn't answer. Why? I called you. A bunch of times. Like a bazillion times. Boys are gross. I'm never gonna like boys." She shook her head emphatically. "Nope, never ever."

Noah ruffled her hair. "If only, Miss Priss. If only." He made eye contact with his partner and nodded to the house. "Why don't you go ice your chin and check on the girls? I'll deal with this out here and catch a ride back to the station with one of the deputies."

A deep sigh cscaped Rhyden. "Thank you," he said, with an expression of extreme gratitude. Repositioning his youngest daughter on his hip, he said, "What do you say, Maddie girl? Want to go see if your sisters have killed one another yet?"

Noah chucked Maddie under the chin. "See you soon, li'l raccoon."

"After while, crocodile." The youngster offered him a fist bump before snuggling down on her daddy's shoulder. "Come on, Daddy, let's go inside."

Noah turned to the crowd of bystanders who were busily reviewing and sharing the videos they had taken on their cell phones. *Great, the Trammell girls are going viral twice in one day. They're gonna be stars.* He cleared his throat. "Okay, folks, show's over. You can all go home now. And by the way"—sarcasm dripped from his next words—"thanks for all your help."

He stepped over to the deputies who were still standing by their vehicles. "Sorry about this, gentlemen." He shrugged. "Teenagers. What can I say?"

****

Darkness shrouded the covered porch lining the front of the house. He approached on foot, drifting through the shadows, staying out of sight. The absolute last thing he wanted to do was disturb the elderly neighbor's yappy dog. He tugged off his boots and carried them up the steps. He avoided the third step, which he knew from observation creaked. Once he reached the porch, he paused, casting a furtive glance around the neighboring houses. *So far, so good.* No one noticed him. He dropped his boots on the porch, cringing at the slight thud.

Creeping forward, he drew near the front door. Ever so slowly, careful not to make a single sound, he tested the front door. Unlocked. He twisted the knob until the latch released with an almost inaudible click. He stopped and listened. No reaction. *Really, people? Will you never learn to keep your doors locked? As much crime as there was in the area and still doors were left unlocked.*

He nudged the door open. Again, he waited. No reaction. He stuck his head in the door and scanned both directions. No one in sight. Silently, he slipped through the door, drawing it closed and locking it behind him. He stood in the entryway, clothed in shadows, gathering his thoughts.

The scents of garlic and onion tickled his nose. His stomach growled, reminding him it had been hours since he had last eaten. Following his twitching nose, he drifted down the hallway toward the kitchen on silent feet. He lurked in the hallway, watching and listening.

Music floated from a radio sitting in the window over the farmhouse sink. He watched the slender Hispanic woman dance around the kitchen in her sock-clad feet. *Her socks don't even match.* A flash of pure heat seared his brain, shooting straight to his groin, as she bent over to check the contents of the oven. He snuck up behind her. Swiftly, he grabbed her around the waist and tugged her back to his chest.

"Ooof!" The air left his lungs as her elbow connected sharply with his solar plexus. He released her and stepped back.

She spun, a butcher knife flashing in her hands. She pulled up short. "Damn it, Noah, I could have hurt you. You know better than to sneak up on me."

He raised his hands in surrender. "I know. It's late. I thought you'd be asleep, but then I saw you in the kitchen, all bent over like that…" He shrugged. "What can I say? I couldn't help myself. And why the hell wasn't the front door locked?"

Catalina Ramos glanced up at the clock on the microwave. "Damn. It's later than I thought. Why don't you ever come home at a decent hour? Where have you been?"

Laughter bubbled past his lips. "Breaking up a

brawl at Rhy's house."

"A brawl? Rhyden had two dates show up at the same time?"

Noah snorted. "That'll be the day. Boy can hardly handle one female at a time. His ex really screwed him up." He shook his head and related the events of the evening to Cat, finishing with "Poor Rhy. I don't know who to feel sorrier for—him or the girls."

Cat removed a pan of bubbling lasagna from the oven and placed it, steaming hot, on the trivets sitting on the dining room table next to a green salad. "Would you grab the dressing out of the fridge? And where's my kiss?" She reached back into the oven and pulled out the garlic bread. Still holding the foil-wrapped bread in her oven-mittened hands, she asked, "Should I volunteer to talk to the girls?"

Noah snagged a kiss as he headed to the refrigerator. "I offered your services already. Rhy declined. But stay ready, just in case. I bet he may change his mind and be calling for help before too terribly much longer. I wish you could have seen the look on his face when Sam popped him square on the jaw. Priceless."

He tiptoed up behind her, leaned over, and kissed the neck exposed by her spicy cinnamon espresso ponytail. He whispered in her ear, "Have I told you yet today how much I love you?"

She leaned back against him and raised her lips for a kiss. "I love you, too, babe, but next time you sneak up on me like that, you may end up on the floor bleeding. Fair warning."

"Lock the door, and I won't be able to sneak up on you." Noah took the bread from her hands and placed it and the salad dressing on the table. He spun Cat around for a proper kiss. After releasing her, he laughed again and said, “And have I told you lately how grateful I am we don’t have children?”

Noah wasn’t sure what to make of the emotion flashing through Cat’s eyes as he sat down and filled his plate. Before he could ask her about it, she spoke up. “How was your day? You seem a little off. Everything okay?” She picked up her own plate, grimaced, and placed it back down.

Flashes of childhood memories of being part of an outlaw Traveler group brought a frown to his face. Fear that his secrets could be exposed turned the lasagna to sand in his mouth.

Chapter Six

Plastic skateboard wheels scraped against concrete. Exhilarated whoops split the air. Shouts from the skaters were easily heard over the tinny rattle of the pickup's exhaust shield. Patrick Gorman sat in his Great-Uncle Paddy's lime green F-100. It wasn't like his great-uncle needed the truck, considering he currently sat on death row for first degree murder.

Engine running, a/c blasting semi-cold air through dusty vents, Patrick watched teenagers in the skate park grind ledges and rock to fakies on the ramps, waiting for the perfect target.

There.

On the far side of the park, a lone figure hovered on the outskirts of the action. Longing almost vibrated off the teenager dressed in a shapeless, long-sleeved, button-down man's shirt and baggy blue jeans despite the heat. The young woman sulked, leaning against the trunk of an ancient oak tree, left thumb tapping against the fingertips of her left hand, moving rapidly from fingertip to fingertip.

He jerked the keys from the truck's ignition, climbed out, and wandered over to where the teen stood. As he approached, she jerked her sleeves down—but not soon enough to cover the thin, pink scars parallel-parked on the inside of one arm from elbow to wrist.

Patrick smiled inwardly. *Jackpot.*

Tapping a cigarette from a soft pack of smokes, he raised his chin in greeting. “Got a light?”

The girl narrowed a pair of cocoa brown eyes. Her shoulders hunched forward. She tugged on her shirt sleeves, tugging them farther down over her hands. Sweat glimmered along her hairline, darkening her greasy brunette hair a shade or two. “What do you want?” The finger tapping picked up pace.

Patrick held up the cigarette. “Just a light.”

“Don’t smoke.”

With a shrug, he slipped the cigarette back into the package. “Don’t skate either, do you?”

She cocked her head. “How do you know I don’t skate?”

“No board. Why are you here?”

“What difference does it make to you?”

“None, I guess. Aren’t you hot?”

“Again, what’s it to you?” She stepped away from him, crossing her arms across her chest and turning her back to him. “Just leave me alone.”

“Hey.” He raised both hands, palms out. “Just trying to be friendly. I’m new in town. Wanted to make a friend.” He gestured toward the skaters doing heel-flips, ollies, and grinds. “These losers suck. You seemed interesting. You don’t wanna be seen with me, no skin off my nose. It’s all good.” He turned to walk away.

Voice hesitant, she called out. “Hey, wait.”

Patrick smiled inwardly. *Hook, line, and sinker.*

Fumbling in her pocket, the teen withdrew a silver Zippo lighter engraved with a skull and crossbones over the background of an American flag.

"Here." She tossed the lighter to him.

Patrick snagged the lighter from the air. He slid a cigarette from the crumpled red-and-white cellophane package, tucked the filter between his lips, and clicked open the lighter. The scent of lighter fluid seeped into the air. He struck the flint wheel with his left thumb. The wheel scratched, and the spark flickered to life. Bending forward, he held the lighter to the end of the cigarette. The blue flame danced as he took a deep drag. Blowing out gray-white smoke, he clicked the lighter closed. He bounced the Zippo in his hand, enjoying the weight of it, before he tossed it back. "Thought you didn't smoke."

"I don't smoke—cigarettes."

"What do you smoke?"

The girl stared at him, lost in thought.

He waved his hand in front of her face. "Hello? Anyone home?"

She blushed, a soft tinge of red creeping up her chest and neck. "Sorry."

"Penny for your thoughts?"

Her blush turned to a crimson red and flashed from her chest across high cheekbones to the roots of her hair. "Has anyone ever told you your eyes look like someone pushed sapphires into your face with a sooty finger? Or that your voice sounded like melted, dark chocolate?" She slapped her hand across her mouth and mumbled, "Did I really say that aloud?"

Patrick chuckled, a deep, warm sound. "What's your name?"

"Rochelle."

"So, Rochelle, you don't skate. You don't smoke…" He paused. "Cigarettes. Whatcha' doing hanging out at a skate park wearing long pants and longer sleeves in triple digit heat?"

****

Patrick climbed the three metal steps leading to the door of his Great-Grandda's recreational vehicle. Grandda said he was too old to be living under his parents' roof and let him crash in the RV. Laughter echoed through the open windows. He paused on the top step and listened to the chatter of his crew waiting for him inside. The voices were too muffled for him to make out what they were saying.

Tugging the door open, he stepped in and kicked off his shoes before stepping on the carpet. Grandda was cool with him staying there, but Nana would scalp him alive if he messed up her beige carpets. "Got another beer?" he asked.

One of the guys reached into the mini-fridge and pulled out a can. He tossed it to Patrick, who caught it with one hand. He dropped onto the sofa by the door. Scanning the living area of the RV, he cracked open the frigid can of beer and took a long pull. Three deeply tanned, blond men ranging from seventeen to twenty-two sat at the tiny, built-in dining table. A fourth leaned against the miniscule counter next to the gas stove.

"Where's Trevor?"

"Working on a new conquest. Cute, young thing he spotted outside the zoo yesterday afternoon."

"Good thing," Patrick grunted. "Da's not happy. We're coming up short on the livestock count. You think Trevor can wrap this one up and get her in a cage in the next day or two?"

Two of the guys exchanged a loaded glance before one said, "I'm sure T plans to get *him* in the kennel tonight or tomorrow."

"I don't care if the kid is a he, a she, or an it. The auction's coming up soon."

The seventeen-year-old tapped his fingers on the Formica tabletop. "How much longer are we going to play Romeo and grab kids? How many do we need? When do we get paid for the ones we already brought you?"

Patrick mimicked the boy. "When do we get paid?" He stood and threw the now-empty beer can at the teen before stalking toward him. Slamming his hands on the table in front of the boy, he leaned in close and dropped his voice to a low whisper. "When do you think we get paid? Hmmm?"

Beads of sweat pooled on the teenager's upper lip as the color faded from his face. He stammered, "Um…af-after the auction?"

"There you go. Figured it out all by yourself, did ya'?" He stalked back to the sofa. "Get me another beer. I need progress reports from all of you. Now."

Before anyone could respond, the door swung open, and a chubby, pink-faced boy of seventeen entered the RV.

"Hey, Trevor. Did you get the boy tucked away in the storage unit?"

The one known as Trevor cleared his throat. His Adam's apple bobbed as he swallowed hard. "Fuck no. Damn pigs stopped me for rolling through a stop sign. Took the kid home instead. Figured it wasn't worth the risk of being seen with a missing kid."

Patrick pressed his lips into a white slash. "We need a replacement like yesterday." He scanned the room, making eye contact with each of his Romeos.

An older redhead seated at the kitchen table ran his hands down the front of his jeans. He tapped the table and said, “Shouldn’t be a problem. I’ve never seen so many kids starved for attention. It’s like shooting fish in a barrel.”

“Well you better straighten your aim. Da’s getting antsy. It’s almost time to move these kids to pre-production holding. Time for their fifteen minutes of fame—dark web style.”

Grabbing a beer from the mini-fridge, Trevor asked, “What are we going to do about the five-o? What if they stop us when we’re moving the kids? They’re everywhere.”

Patrick cracked open a fresh beer and smirked. “Don’t worry about the *peelers*. I’m taking care of it.”

****

Bree watched her dad carry a sleeping Maddie to her bedroom. After tucking the youngster in, he quietly stepped out of the room and shut the door. She cringed as he headed to the kitchen calling for Sam and herself to follow him.

Here we go.

Rhyden wrinkled his nose as he sat at the dining room table. “What did you burn?” He waved a hand in front of his face, stood, and walked to the kitchen sink where he opened the window. He reached over and turned on the exhaust fan above the stove.

He resumed his seat at the head of the table. The girls, both sulking, sat to either side of him. “Never mind.” He looked from daughter to daughter, taking in the scratches and bruises forming on each of them. “Who wants to tell me what the carnival sideshow out front was all about?”

Both girls began speaking at once.

He held up a hand. "One at a time, please."

Bree cut her eyes over at her sister, Sam. "It's all her fault. She threw herself at my boyfriend."

"Your boyfriend?" Sam shrieked. "He's *my* boyfriend."

"Why you little—"

Rhyden slammed his hand down on the table. "Enough. I don't even want to hear it. I'm done. Sam, you just earned another two weeks on your grounding."

"But Dad…"

"Want to make it a month? Go to your room."

"That's not fair." Sam shoved the chair away from the table. "You let Miss Precious Goody Two Shoes get away with everything. Why am I grounded?"

"Samantha Elaine Trammell, to your room—now."

Sam glared at her father and her sister before stomping from the kitchen and down the hallway. Thunder reverberated through the house as she let the bedroom door slam.

Rhyden dropped his head into his hands. He squeezed his eyes shut. Taking a deep breath and letting it go, he raised his head and locked his gaze on Bree. "Want to tell me what's going on with you?"

Bree looked away, examined her hands resting in her lap with great attention. Keeping her voice neutral, she replied. "I don't know what you mean. There's nothing going on with me."

"Aubree Nicole, look at me."

"Why?"

"Damn it. I'm too tired to play games. Who is that boy? What the hell is your problem?"

Bree jerked her head up and met her father's eyes.

"My problem? What the hell is my problem?" She threw her hands up in the air. "I don't have a problem. I don't even have a life."

"Bree..."

"Dad, I'm seventeen years old. These are supposed to be the best days of my life. A carefree time to have fun and make memories to look back on when I get older. Instead, I'm a seventeen-year-old slave. All I do is clean your house, cook your meals, and take care of your children. You have no clue what goes on around here, do you? How could you? You're never home."

"Now, Bree..."

The angry teenager pushed away from the table and stalked to the stove. She dumped the jambalaya into the garbage can beneath the sink. She scraped away the scorched rice clinging to the sides of the stock pot. Deliberately, with great care, she placed the pot in the sink, filled it with scalding water and dish soap. Turning off the water, she turned to face him.

Voice quavering, she asked, "Do you know how many nights a week Maddie crawls into my bed because she has nightmares? Or what she named the monster that lives under her bed? Do you know how many times Sam has skipped school this semester? Do you know she smokes weed in the bathroom and tries to hide it by burning sage? Do you even know when my graduation is? Or where I plan to go to college? Do you even care?" She sniffed, holding back tears.

"I depend on you. You've never minded before. You know how important my work is."

"Obviously, it's more important than your family. Now I understand why Mom left...and I don't blame her. I can't wait to get out of here."

"That's not fair—"

Her pulse pounded in her ears. Clenching and unclenching her fists, she narrowed her eyes and walked toward the hallway. As she drew even with her father, she said, "Aren't you the one that always said life and fair are both four-letter words, but that's all they have in common?" Spinning on her heel, she dashed to her bedroom. She barely closed the door and collapsed on her bed before dissolving in great, gulping sobs.

****

Noah tapped on the open door of Rhyden's office with the knuckles of his left hand. A leather binder embossed with an image of the Texas Ranger badge dangled from his right. "So how did it go last night after I left? How are the girls?"

"Grounded for the rest of their natural lives." Rhyden raised his eyes to the ceiling. "God save us from teenage girls and their hormones." He gingerly rubbed his chin, right on the spot darkened with the shadow of a bruise. Changing the subject, he nodded at the folder Noah carried. "Results from the Schmidt crime scene?"

"Partially. Definitely bone fragments and teeth. They're still trying to run down the serial number on the implant. No idea why it's taking so long." Noah dropped into the visitor chair and studied the whiteboard lining one wall of the office. Lists of names, dates, and ages covered it. Maps, smothered with colored push pins, papered the adjoining wall. "You've been busy."

Rhyden sighed again. "Unfortunately, yes. I started out searching for missing elderly people over the past year in our county and all surrounding counties. Only three of those reported missing have yet to be found. I contacted the persons who filed each report. None of the missing have had a hip replacement."

"Okay." Noah waved at the massive list of names and dates covering the board. "Then what's all this?"

Before Rhyden could answer, Sarah, the long-legged brunette reports clerk from the sheriff's department, stormed into the office, no smile, no word of greeting, and slammed a file down onto Rhyden's desk hard enough to make coffee cups and soda cans rattle. Turning on one stiletto heel, she stalked out, leaving a cloud of some high-falutin' perfume in her wake. Both men heard the furious rhythm of heels against ceramic tile as she moved down the hallway at a brisk pace.

Noah let out a long, low whistle. "I'm guessing the date didn't go very well last weekend?"

"Date? What date?"

Noah lowered his chin, tilted his head to the side, and raised his eyebrows. "Really?"

Dawning realization showed in his partner's eyes. "Oh shit. I was supposed to meet her at the Silver Spur Saturday, wasn't I? Fuck! Maddie's hamster died, and she was inconsolable. We had to do the whole beloved pet funeral. I totally forgot about meeting Sarah, and I forgot to call. Damn, damn, double damn. No wonder she's pissed. She thinks I stood her up. Man, I don't have time for this shit."

"Uh—technically, you did stand her up. I'd say you dorked the pooch. I told you not to dip your pen into company ink."

"*You* told me? You're the one pressuring me to

date Brooke. Don't make fun of me. Being a single parent is challenging work."

"Maybe if you worked harder on some of those hot dates, you wouldn't be a single father anymore." Noah waved his hand at the whiteboard again. "Let's get back to something you are good at. If you eliminated all your missing elderly, what's all this?"

"I expanded my parameters to all missing persons over the past three years in the state of Texas, regardless of age. The number of missing people, especially children, shocked me. So I tightened the parameters back down to our county, Atascosa, Frio, LaSalle, Medina, Live Oak, Bee, and Karnes counties. The results are still high but not nearly as astronomical as the entire state. Just removing Houston, Dallas, San Antonio, and Austin made a dramatic difference." Rhyden leaned back in his chair and studied the board. "Do you see what I see?"

Noah scanned the notes on the board. The dates people, especially the younger ones, went missing seemed to jump out at him. The majority of the incidents occurred between June and November. "Hurricane season?"

"Seems like we have a major uptick in disappearances each year between the first of June and mid-October. Most of the missing are between the ages of eleven and sixteen. Three times as many females as males."

"Why hasn't anyone noticed this pattern before?"

"Could be because although they were all reported missing here in Bennett County, not all of them reside here. Some were in the area on vacation when they disappeared." Rhyden spun around in his chair, tapping his fingers on the armrests. "What is so special between June and October? Besides it being hurricane season? I don't think storms are responsible for all these missing children."

"June to October," Noah mused, thinking. "Migrant workers? Don't we also see an increase in the number of stolen vehicles and coyotes running illegals at the same times?"

Rhyden twirled his chair back to face the desk and tapped a few keys on his computer. "Guess what else increases between June and October? Reports of Traveler scams against the elderly. Which reminds me, we need to go talk to Mr. Schmidt again."

Travelers. Again.

"You know, we never did actually see Mrs. Schmidt, and Mr. Schmidt didn't seem very pleased with her. Maybe we'll get lucky, and we've already met our driveway cut-up."

"Ha-ha, not. The way he kept glancing back at that closed door like he was afraid of her, I think she would be more likely to do him in than the other way around. We need to collect more information about the paving company his wife hired."

Heat suffused the nape of Noah's neck. A lone drop of sweat took its time rolling down his spine. He fought the urge to squirm in his chair; instead, he stood. "Do you really think Travelers could be running a human trafficking ring out of Bennett County?"

"Travelers and human trafficking? Huh. It could fit the pattern, couldn't it? The dates on the complaints filed regarding their scams do seem to coincide with the majority of the dates on the missing persons reports. I hadn't thought about that."

Fuck me and my big mouth. Bile flooded the back of Noah's mouth. *I know they live on the other side of the law, but they couldn't be, no way, not stealing children. That's too wrong, even for them.* The walls started to close in on him. He fingered the spark plug in his pocket.

"I'm gonna check on a few things. Find out what's taking so long on tracking down the information on the serial number of the implant. I'll let you know if I find anything."

****

Less than an hour later, weight crushing his shoulders, Noah walked back into Rhyden's office. He half-heartedly waved a leather binder in the air. "Results finally came in." He collapsed into his usual chair and handed the binder over. "Not good news, either."

Rhyden opened the binder. On top of the stack of lab reports sat an eight by ten glossy color photograph—a school portrait of a fourteen-year-old girl. The photograph showed platinum hair dropping behind narrow shoulders, sky blue eyes surrounded by a bit too much eye makeup, freckles, and a wide, quirky smile above a crooked, faded scar on her chin. A touch of mischief danced in her eyes.

"Meet Alyssa Sanders," Noah said. "Five years before that photograph was taken, she was involved in a nasty car wreck. The truck she was riding in flipped end over end before landing against a tree and killing everyone inside except her. Toxicology reports showed the driver, her stepmother, had a blood alcohol content three times the legal limit. Alyssa had to be cut out of the wreckage. Doctors gave her less than a twenty percent chance of survival, and they said if by some miracle she lived, she'd never walk again. She surprised them all. Multiple surgeries, several years of physical—and mental—therapy, but she did it. Alyssa was one tough cookie."

"Okay." Rhyden shook his head. "What does Alyssa Sanders have to do with our crime scene?"

"Guess what one of those many surgeries included?"

Rhyden lowered his head into his hands and groaned. "Hip replacement?"

"Bingo."

"This just keeps getting better and better. Bad enough we have a murder on our hands, but I thought, with a hip replacement in action, we were dealing with an elderly victim. No less a crime but at least the victim would have had the chance to live a full, rewarding life."

He stared across the desk at Noah, a bleakness in his expression. His voice sounded like ground glass. "Now you're telling me our victim is a fourteen-year-old child who hadn't even really lived yet? One who had already survived so much. Damn, she's almost the same age as Sam."

Noah made a quick scan of the whiteboard again. "Huh."

"Huh, what?"

"Why isn't her name on the board?"

"What?" Rhyden spun back to his computer and typed a search into the missing person's database. He picked up the report Noah carried into the office and double checked his spelling. "That's weird. No one reported her missing."

"Are you sure?"

"I just double checked. No Alyssa Sanders reported as missing any time in the past three years. Has the next of kin been notified of her death yet?"

"I was heading there next. What kind of parent doesn't report their fourteen-year-old daughter as missing? I can't imagine not reporting my child as missing, and I don't even have children. Do you think the family could be involved?"

Rhyden stood up, grabbed the keys off his desk and his hat from the deer horns. He tossed the keys to Noah and scooped up his laptop. "Let's go find out. You drive. I want to check a couple more things on the way."

Chapter Seven

Noah turned onto a long, winding driveway. Cheerful sunlight, a clear blue sky, and billowing white clouds mocked the darkness of his mission. He drove past a well-landscaped lawn, coming to an easy stop in front of a rambling, ranch-style home surrounded by an old-fashioned veranda complete with Craftsman-style porch columns. A pair of white, wooden rocking chairs framed a bay window. The pastel yellow paint on the exterior of the house appeared slightly faded in contrast to the deep red and hot pink geraniums sitting in round clay pots balanced on the cracked alabaster porch railings. The high-pitched whine of a push lawn mower's motor echoed behind the wooden privacy fence surrounding the backyard.

In his mind, he saw a different house, in a different town, different state over a thousand miles away. Brilliant, neon colors—turquoise blue trimmed with butter yellow and highlighted with splashes of Aztec gold—adorned a bungalow style home with a deep, covered porch. The scent of heirloom roses wrapped with sugar cookies and the tinkling sound of wind chime upon wind chime flashed through his memory.

Were the police officers gentle with Nana when they broke the news? Or were they brusque because of who the family was? Did she mourn, or was she glad I was finally out of her hair once and for all?

His chest tightened as he envisioned the scene: her gray head shaking in denial; a hand to her bright pink lips to hold back a cry of anguish; Grandda wrapping her in his arms, supporting her. *I wonder what they placed in the casket to accompany me to the afterlife. Did they even bother with a casket since there was no body?* Hot tears stung his eyes. *I'm so sorry, Nana. I didn't know what else to do.*

Rhyden tilted his head and raised an eyebrow. "You okay over there, buddy?"

Noah took a deep, cleansing breath and straightened his shoulders. He blinked back the tears. Patting his shirt pocket, he verified his badge was present and recognizable. He removed the keys from the ignition. He exhaled slowly before turning to face Rhyden. "Yeah, man. I just hate these things."

"You're not alone."

Noah opened the pickup door and sat for another moment before stepping out. Straightening his hat and taking another deep breath, he said, "Come on. Let's get this done."

Together, they approached the front door. Noah pressed the doorbell. Peals of classical chimes rang out. Footsteps echoed in response to the call of the bell before a slightly rounded blonde in her mid-forties opened the door. Noah whipped the cowboy hat from his head and held it between his hands where he turned it nervously.

The blonde looked from their faces to their badges to the hats in their hands before returning her gaze to their faces. She looked past them to the unmarked truck sitting in her driveway. Confusion and fear clouded her eyes. "May I help you?"

Noah asked, “Are you Mrs. Charlotte Sanders? I mean Whittier. Mother of Alyssa Sanders?”

She nodded, a hand going to the strand of pearls at her neck. “Yes, I am. Is she at the hospital? Damn it. I knew I shouldn’t have let her go stay with him. Why didn’t that blasted man call me?”

Noah turned to his partner with a raised eyebrow. Rhyden shrugged. “Ma’am? Who is Alyssa supposed to be staying with?”

Mrs. Whittier rolled her eyes. “Only the biggest mistake of my life—her father. Not that I’m not grateful for the children but that man. Sometimes I wish I had never met him. Just let me grab my bag, and I’ll be ready to go.”

“Ma’am,” Noah asked, “may we come in, please?”

She gestured toward his truck. “Shouldn’t we be going? My baby girl needs me.”

“Please?”

“Oh, of course. I’m so sorry. Where are my manners?” Flustered, she stepped back from the doorway, motioning for them to enter. “Please. Please come in.”

Mrs. Whittier led the way into a comfortable living room filled with an eclectic mix of simple and ornate furnishings. A wall of windows flooded the room with warm light. She rolled the pearls between the fingers of her left hand and gestured to an upholstered sofa with her right. “Please, have a seat. Would you like something to drink?”

“No, ma’am. Thank you.” Both rangers remained standing. “Is your husband home?”

As if summoned by Noah’s question, a gangly young man in his late teens, wearing a sweaty university T-shirt and matching forest green gym shorts, walked in from the back of the house. He wiped perspiration from his face with a paper towel. He glanced around the room, taking in Noah and Rhyden before turning to Mrs. Whittier. “Mom? Everything okay?”

“Yes, sweetie, everything’s fine. Your sister got hurt at *his* house and these men are here to take me to her. I told Peter it was a bad idea to let her go stay with your father. The man hasn’t been a part of your lives in years and suddenly pops up out of the blue and wants her to come stay with him. She’s not strong enough, and God knows he’s not responsible enough to care for a young girl. Now she’s been hurt—in his supposed care—again. One thing’s for sure, it will never happen again. My poor baby. I was just coming to find you.”

Noah watched the color fade from the young man’s face.

“Are you Justin Sanders?” Rhyden asked, holding out a hand. “Alyssa’s brother?”

“Yes, sir.” The young man wiped his palm on the leg of his shorts before taking Rhyden's hand in a firm grip. His voice wavered just the tiniest bit. “What’s this about?”

“Sweetie,” Mrs. Whittier placed her hand on her son’s shoulder. “I told you what it’s about. Alyssa’s hurt. We need to go to the hospital.” She turned to the rangers. “Which hospital is she at?”

“Would you please be seated? Both of you?” Noah nodded toward the floral sofa opposite two matching wingback chairs. “Is Mr. Whittier home?”

She perched nervously on the edge of the sofa cushion while her son balanced on the arm beside her.

She shook her head. “No, he’s at work but should be home soon.” She stood. “Justin, call Peter, please. Have him meet us at the hospital. Shouldn’t we be going?”

“Please, Mrs. Whittier, be seated.” Noah gestured to the chairs. “May we?”

She checked her watch. Tapped her toe impatiently. “Of course, of course. Please.” She settled back onto the edge of the sofa.

Noah and Rhyden each took a seat on one of the wingback chairs.

Justin wrapped his arm protectively around his mother’s shoulders. “What’s going on? This is about my sister, right? Is she hurt?”

An edge of anger showed in Mrs. Whittier's voice. “If my baby girl is hurt, I need to get to her. We’re wasting time here.”

Rhyden began to speak, but Noah gave a subtle shake of his head, indicating he would handle this. Scooting closer to where the pair sat, he began, “Mrs. Whittier, Justin, I regret to inform—”

“No. No, no, no.” Mrs. Whittier stuck her fingers in her ears and shook her head like a kindergarten child. “I’m not listening, and you can’t make me. The bastard paid you to do this, didn’t he? I am not listening. I bet you aren’t even real rangers.” Her voice ramped another couple notches. “It isn’t true, and it won’t get him out of paying child support, either. Oh, no. He’s got four more years to go. Sorry bastard.” She pulled her hands from her head and glared at Noah. Jumping to her feet, she pointed at the door. “Out. Get out, get out, get out.”

Rhyden stood and stepped toward Mrs. Whittier, but before he could reach her, Noah embraced her and gently edged her back to the sofa. He kneeled beside her and turned to Justin who stared blankly in shock. "Is there anyone we can call for you? Your father? Your stepfather? Another family member or friend?"

Justin stared back with no expression on his face.

Noah gently shook the grief-stricken young man. "Justin?"

As Mrs. Whittier wailed, Rhyden withdrew the file from his binder and found Mr. Whittier's cell phone number. As he was dialing, a voice from the entryway called out. "Charlotte? Honey? Who's here?"

A man stepped into the living room, taking in the scene. Immediately, he rushed to his wife's side. "Here now, what's going on?" His chest puffed up. "Who are you people, and what have you done to my wife?"

Noah stood and stepped back a few paces, giving him and Justin room to comfort Mrs. Whittier. He introduced himself and Rhyden to the man.

"Sir," Rhyden said, "I was just trying to call you. I'm glad you are here. We have news of your stepdaughter."

"Alyssa? What has that man done now?" he demanded. "She's staying with her biological father for a month. Is she hurt? In trouble?"

"Mr. Whittier." Noah glanced over at the man's wife who glared at him from the protection of her husband's arms. He stopped and took a deep breath before beginning again. "I regret to inform you your daughter is dead."

Mr. Whittier staggered, caught himself, then straightened his spine and squared his shoulders. "Impossible. She's at her father's. If anything had happened to her, he would have called us." An expression of uncertainty crossed his face. "Unless…was there an accident? Was he drinking and driving again?"

Mrs. Whittier shook her head. "No, Alyssa is fine. I would know. A mother always knows." She rounded on the rangers, hands fisted at her sides, eyes shooting sparks. "Why are you doing this to us? I don't understand."

Noah tugged a miniature spiral notebook from his shirt pocket. "What is the name of her father? Where does he live? When did she go, and when was she expected home?"

Justin squirmed beside his parents. He tugged at the collar of his T-shirt before shoving his hands into the pockets of his shorts. "Um…"

Noah waited.

"Oh, crap." The boy turned to his parents; tears rolling down his cheeks. "She didn't go to Dad's."

"What do you mean she didn't go?" Mr. Whittier yelled.

Justin tucked his head and mumbled.

"Speak up, son," his stepfather demanded.

Justin raised his head and blurted, "She skipped as soon as you dropped her off last weekend. She said she was tired of being treated like a china doll and wanted to have some fun. She and her friends were going to the beach. One of the girls' cousins had a beach house on Port Aransas. They were gonna crash there."

"But her father," Mrs. Whittier said. "If she didn't show, he would have called us. Even he isn't *that* irresponsible. Right?" She turned from her husband to her son and back again. "Right?"

Justin's face reddened. His voice dropped an

octave lower, shame coating every syllable. "He didn't know she was coming. He never called in the first place. Alyssa made it all up." He faced his mother and stepfather, begging forgiveness in his voice. "We didn't think it would hurt anything. I'm so sorry. She just wanted to live a little bit."

Eyes rounded in what Noah assumed was shock and anger, Mrs. Whittier reached out a palm and slapped her son's face. The resounding crack reverberated through the now silent room. Grabbing her phone, she dialed Alyssa's number. The tinny sound of a voicemail greeting echoed through the speakers. She dialed again with the same results. "Alyssa Lynn Sanders, you call home immediately. This is not funny."

She threw the phone down on the sofa cushion and turned back to her son as if to strike him again. Her husband grabbed her hands and whisked her away from Justin as more tears rolled past the reddened handprint on the teenager's face.

She jerked away and spun on the rangers. She jabbed a finger into Noah's chest. "And you. How much are they paying you to play this horrible joke on me? Hmm? How much?"

"Mom, it's not a joke," Justin pleaded. "Nobody's paying anybody. Alyssa just wanted a little freedom. We didn't think…"

She rounded on him once again. "No, you didn't think. You never think."

"Mom." He ran a hand through his sweaty, blond hair, leaving a row of porcupine quills in its wake. "Ever since the accident, you treat her like she needs to be kept in bubble wrap and placed on a shelf. She's a teenage girl, not a doll. She just wanted to live a little."

Mr. Whittier turned from his stepson to the rangers. "Where is our little girl?"

Noah and Rhyden exchanged another uneasy look. Rhyden went first. "Mr. Whittier, the coroner's office will be in touch when they can release Alyssa's—" He paused, his voice faltering. "—remains."

"Remains?" Mr. Whittier collapsed onto the sofa next to his wife. "You mean her body, right?"

An awkward silence filled the room as Noah and Rhyden exchanged another weighted glance. Noah motioned Rhyden to stay close to Mrs. Whitter who dissolved into tears. "Mr. Whittier, may I speak to you in the other room for a moment?"

"What? Why?"

With another uneasy glance at Mrs. Whittier, Noah said, "Please, sir, if we could step into the other room for just a moment."

"Fine." Mr. Whittier squeezed his wife's shoulder before standing. "Justin, take care of your mother. I'll be right back." He led the way into the kitchen, a bright, breezy room with a beachy feel just off the living room. "Now, what is it you so obviously don't want my wife to hear?"

Noah pulled a wicker chair out from the kitchen table. "Would you please have a seat?"

With a heavy sigh, Peter Whittier dropped into the chair. He leaned forward, resting his arms on his knees. "Spit it out already. Please."

Still, Noah hesitated, gathering the words in his head, trying to make what he needed to say easier for the man sitting in front of him to hear. Finally, realizing there was no easy way to put it, he sat in the chair next to the man and looked him straight in the eyes. "Sir, there is no body for the coroner to release to you. I can't go into too much detail, and believe me, you don't want me to, but what we found of your daughter—stepdaughter—included her hip implant, some bone chips, and a handful of teeth."

A bemused smile lit Mr. Whittier's face. "No body? So you don't know if it is my Alyssa, do you? It could be anyone else who has had a hip replacement. Maybe some old guy. How do you even know those are human remains? Maybe they are animal bones? And the hip replacement was defective and never used? Huh? What about that? It's not my Lyssa." He stood. "I know it's not. You can leave. Now."

"Sir, please. The serial number engraved on the implant matched that of the appliance the surgeon installed in Alyssa after her car accident a few years ago. That's how we were able to track you down in the first place. I would like to ask your wife and stepson for a DNA swab so we can do a reverse comparison with one of the teeth. Then we will have one hundred percent confirmation on identity."

Mr. Whittier shook his head. "My wife needs me. You can show yourself out." He turned to face Noah, anger painted across his features, and said, "I can't believe you came in here and scared her. I know it's not our Lyssa. It can't be our baby girl." He walked back into the living room where his wife, still weeping, clung to her son.

Placing one hand on her shoulder, Mr. Whittier placed the other beneath her chin and lifted it so she could meet his eyes. "Honey, it will be okay." He stroked her hair. "They don't know for sure it's Lyssa.

They don't even have a body."

Anger flashed in her eyes. "Then why the hell did they do this?" She glared at Noah and Rhyden. "How could you?" She pulled away from her son's arms to advance on them. "Do you get some kind of perverted kick out of causing pain?"

Noah cut him off with a shake of his head. In a voice as smooth as glass, he said, "Mrs. Whittier, I apologize for upsetting you. We have compelling evidence pointing to this being Alyssa. To confirm it or disprove it completely, we need a DNA cheek swab from you and your son. Can we do that now, please?"

"Fine. Do your swab, then get the hell out of my home and don't come back."

Rhyden collected DNA samples from the lady and her son with quick efficiency. While taking Justin's sample, he asked, "Can you provide me with names and numbers of your sister's friends?"

He glanced at his parents. Turning back to face Rhyden, he shook his head.

"Please. It could be important."

"I—" He clamped his mouth shut and left the room.

Meanwhile, Noah again kneeled next to Mrs. Whittier. "I'm terribly sorry to have upset you. Is there anyone I can call for you? A friend or family member? Maybe a neighbor?"

She shook her head, looking oddly composed and in control. "We don't need anyone. It's not our Lyssa. You'll see. It can't be."

With a nod, Noah laid a business card on the arm of the sofa. "If you think of anything or have any questions, please feel free to call me, day or night. My cell number is on the card as well as my office number." Rising to his feet, he asked, "Mr. Whittier? Could you please walk us to the door?"

Mr. Whittier held his wife tight for a moment before releasing her and stalking to the door, stiff spine and choppy steps betraying his fury.

At the door, Noah stopped and turned to face the man. "I know it's hard, but for a moment, please set emotion aside and think about this logically. How else could the implant from your stepdaughter's hip have ended up in our crime scene? You know I'm telling you the truth. What reason would I have to lie to you?"

As denial faded from his face, despair hit the man hard. Noah saw the exact moment hope disintegrated and crumbled to dust. Grief stole his voice. Moisture gathered in his eyes as he nodded.

Noah placed a comforting hand on the man's shoulder. "Please. Prepare your wife. We will need to come back a little later to ask more questions about Alyssa, her friends, and her disappearance. We hate to intrude during this painful time, but we really need those answers if we are going to bring the person or persons who did this to justice. Please don't be too hard on your stepson." Noah paused and stepped back. "Again, I am truly sorry for your loss."

Back at the truck, both men silent and lost in thought, Noah placed the key in the ignition but didn't turn it. "Well, that sucked." A million questions raced through his mind, one on top of the next. "How could they not know she was missing? I don't get it."

Before Rhyden could answer, a knock on the driver's side window startled them. Justin stood beside the truck, a hot-pink, faux-leather journal in his hands.

Noah rolled down the truck window.

Justin thrust the journal into Noah's face. "Here. It's Lyssa's diary. Maybe something in here will help. I didn't want to tell Mom and Dad, but it wasn't her friends she was going to the beach with. It was a new boyfriend she's been hiding. He's older, and she knew our parents would pitch a bitch fit if they found out she was seeing him. She's not supposed to date until she's sixteen according to Mom. I don't know his name. She called him by some silly initials. Maybe you can find his name." He wiggled the journal. "I haven't read it." Guilt blanketed his features. Tears filled his eyes. "If only I…" His voice broke.

Noah took the journal and handed it across the seat to Rhyden. Opening the truck door, he stepped out and opened his arms to the young man. As Justin clutched onto him like a drowning man hanging onto a life preserver, Noah said, "Son, this is not your fault. Should you have tried to stop your sister? Probably, but it was her decision. Should you have told your parents? Most likely, but I don't think it would have changed anything. If she didn't want to be found, they would not have found her whether you ratted her out or not. Let go of the guilt. You can't change anything."

Rhyden held up the journal so Justin could see it. "Thank you for this. I'm sure it will help. Now, go back inside and help your parents as much as you can. If you think of anything else, anything at all, please call us."

Chapter Eight

The clatter of the school bell woke Patrick from a power nap in the front seat of his great-uncle's truck. The double doors of the school flew open, and students swarmed down the front steps. He grabbed a black trench coat off the seat beside him. He curled his lip in disgust as he slipped it on and scrambled out of the pickup truck.

Fuck, this thing's hot. Why do all the weirdos wear these damn things, anyway? What's the deal?

Hiding his greater interest in getting off school property and out of the stifling jacket, he strolled around the front of the truck and leaned against the hood. The black of the jacket looked like an oil stain against the lime green paint of the truck and came close to matching the illegally dark tint on the windows.

Shoulders hunched, head tucked, a dark-colored backpack draped across her shoulders, Rochelle moved slowly, reminding him of a turtle plodding her way to the bus line. She kept her gaze on the ground, hiding her face from the other students behind a curtain of shaggy, unkempt brown hair.

"Hey, beautiful," he called out.

No reaction, just a slow, steady pace forward, lost in her own world. Other students swirled around her in clumps of threes and fours as if she didn't even exist. Here and there girls tossed lustrous, shiny hair over their shoulders as they scanned the crowd to see who was calling them "beautiful."

"Roc."

No response.

"Rochelle." He placed two fingers in his mouth and whistled, a high piercing sound. "Hey, Rochelle, over here."

She stumbled to a stop, shoved the hair out of her eyes, and peered in his direction.

He pushed off the truck and sauntered over to where she stood. He dropped his voice into that smooth, sexy, melted dark chocolate sound he knew girls loved. "Hey, beautiful."

She scanned the area around, beside, and behind herself, seeing no one near. She pointed at herself and mouthed, "Me?"

He smiled. "Yes, you."

Several groups of girls stared at them, turning their heads from him to her and back again before giggling and whispering furiously. Patrick narrowed his eyes and glared at the giggling girls. "Fucking bitches. Don't let them bother you." He paused, his voice dropping to an ominous tone. "They'll get what's coming to them."

Rochelle raised her head high. Eyes narrowed, she flipped off the girls with both middle fingers, and drew closer to him.

He took both her hands in one of his. With the other, he brushed a lock of hair off her cheek, tenderly tucking it behind her ear. "Of course, I mean you, beautiful." He kissed her blushing cheek. "Want a ride?"

She peered at his truck and then back at the school buses. "Uh…I…uh…"

He let go of her hands and shrugged. “Never mind. Forget it.” *Dangle the bait, then take it away.* He turned his back on her and walked back toward his truck, keeping an eye on Roc in the reflection of his truck windows.

She hesitated a moment longer, turning her gaze from him to the buses, back to him.

He kept moving.

“Wait! Wait a minute. Wait for me. Can I ask you a question?”

Keeping his back turned to her, he smirked. *Gotcha.* Slowly, he drew to a stop and waited for her to catch up to him before he turned to face her. “For you, beautiful, anything. What do you want to know?”

Arms wrapped around her chest, she gazed up at him from under the fringe of her bangs. “Well, um,” she stammered, “what’s your name?”

Laughter rolled off his tongue. Ireland deepened his voice. “Patrick Cillian Gorman, my lady.” He bowed with a flourish and held his hand out to her. “I usually go by PC because my uncle’s name is Patrick, too.” He winked at her. “But for you, my gorgeous princess, you can call me PC because I plan to be your prince charming.”

High color flashed up her chest to her cheeks. She bounced on her toes. A smile shot from her entire face. Her eyes sparkled, and the air surrounding her seemed to dance with elation.

He opened the driver side door of his truck. Sweeping wadded-up hamburger wrappers and empty French fry containers from the seat to the floor, he motioned for her to climb in.

Rochelle slid across the cracked, black vinyl seat

that had to be blistering the back of her legs. She didn't seem to notice or mind the heat or the scratches.

Patrick smiled. "So, beautiful, where would you like to go?"

****

Noah laid Alyssa's journal open, facedown, in his lap. "Have you read any of this?" he asked.

"No, not yet," Rhyden said. "Why?"

"You might want to. This secret boyfriend thing reminds me an awful lot of your situation with Bree."

"I don't have a situation with Aubree. She's just not communicating with me right now. Besides, after the massive scene with Samantha, she's dumped the stupid idiot. One thing about my eldest, you don't cross her and walk away unscathed. Let me tell you *that* girl can carry a grudge. She's over this whole secret boyfriend thing."

"Listen to this." He picked up the journal and began to read. "I'm in love. There. I said it. All other boys pale in comparison to him. Just the sound of his name makes my heart sing. He wants me to call him PC. I'm his fairy-tale princess, and he's my prince charming. My heart is soaring like an eagle above the clouds. He makes me feel alive."

Noah tossed the journal on Rhyden's desk. "Whatever. I really think you should at least skim through it. The guy even uses the same initials—PC. Prince charming? Really? Where do these girls come up with this shit?"

Rhyden raised one eyebrow, picked up the journal, and flipped through a few pages. He shrugged. "Beats me. I'll never understand teenage girls. Not even my own. Same initials, huh? I guess with all the fairy-tale movies being re-released, it's not surprising. Every little girl seems to dream of finding her prince charming. Hell, even the grown-up girls seem to be searching for a fairy-tale ending. Did you find anything helpful in here?"

"Not really. Just a lot of rambling about how mean her parents are, how they don't trust her for no reason known to her, how her mother is overprotective, how they don't understand her, etc., etc., etc. The last few pages talk about how gorgeous this PC guy is, how different he is from all the 'little boys' her age, how she could drown in his deep, blue eyes. Truly stomach-turning."

Rhyden set the journal on the corner of his desk. "I'll look through it, but Bree's over the guy she was seeing. And if you can't find anything useful in it, I doubt I will either. I do think I need to have another chat with my daughter and find out everything I can about this character she was seeing. I don't think there's a connection, but you never know."

"On another note," he continued, "I've been researching some of the paving companies. I think we need to go visit Mr. Schmidt again."

Images of what the driveway looked like the last time he had seen it raced through Noah's mind. "Do we have to? He's going to be one pissed-off old geezer."

Rhyden chuckled. "I bet he will, but, yeah, I don't see any way around it. Grab your stuff. Let's go."

****

They pulled up in front of Mr. Schmidt's house, parking on the street next to the old man's boat-size vehicle. What used to be the driveway now held giant potholes where asphalt had been dug up and sifted by the crime scene techs. Snippets of yellow-and-black crime scene tape flapped in the breeze.

As they stepped out of their unmarked unit, Mr. Schmidt raced out of his house, waving his arms. "*Nein, nein.* Go away." He made shooing motions with the mesquite cane. "*Mein Gott!* You are more trouble than you are worth. I call you about Gypsies doing a shoddy job on my driveway and next thing I know; I don't have a driveway anymore. You and your Tyvek-suited gorillas destroyed it—chopped it up and carted it off. Go away. At least when *der Zigeuners* left, I still had a driveway."

"Mr. Schmidt," Noah began. A yellow jacket wasp buzzed his ear. Noah waved it away and tried again. "Mr. Schmidt…"

The wasp landed on his cheek. Noah swatted it away, but not before it stung him. *Damn it.* His cheek felt like a cigarette cherry landed on it. Almost immediately, the bite began to swell, then itch, and his tongue started to feel furry.

Mr. Schmidt sniggered. "No more than you deserve, tearing up my driveway the way you did."

Before Noah could retort, Rhyden stepped up. "Mr. Schmidt, we are sorry for the inconvenience. As soon as the crime scene teams tells us they are finished, we will have someone from the county's maintenance department come fix your driveway."

"And what's that going to cost me?"

"Not a penny. Not one red cent. May we come in, please? We need to ask you a few more questions regarding the pavers."

The old man eyeballed his front door. He appeared to shrink a size or two. "If you don't mind, I'd prefer we stay out here. The missus is napping, and I don't want to wake her. Besides, she won't let you have sugar in your tea, either."

Noah chuckled.

"What's so funny?" Schmidt demanded. "You think I'm joking?"

Noah swallowed his mirth. "No, sir. I'm sure you are quite serious, and we definitely have no desire to disturb her. How is your wife today?"

"Bah! You didn't come to ask about her. What do you want to know?"

"We need to ask you about the paving company. We tried investigating the name you gave us, but we can't find a listing for them or any other information. Did they happen to give you a receipt or a card with a telephone number or address on it?"

"They damn sure didn't give me no receipt, but I think the wife has a card somewhere. Wait here. I'll see if I can find it."

"Before you go back in," Rhyden asked, "do you think you could also make us a list of any of your other neighbors who had work performed by them as well?"

As the front door closed, Noah and Rhyden returned to the truck. "Told you the old man was afraid of his wife," Noah said.

Rhyden rummaged around in the glove box until he found an anti-sting stick. "Here, try this on your face," he said. "That bite is going to double the size of your head if you don't take care of it. And your head is already big enough, believe me."

"Ha. Ha. Hilarious." Noah tried to swallow. His throat tightened.

Mr. Schmidt returned with a business card and a

short piece of paper bearing a list of his neighbors' names and addresses. *"Heiliger Strohsack."* Mr. Schmidt glanced at Noah. "What's wrong with you?"

Noah glared at Mr. Schmidt and scratched his face. All of a sudden it became more and more difficult to breathe. His vision began to gray.

Rhyden followed the direction of Mr. Schmidt's gaze.

Noah's respirations became labored as his throat continued to swell. His chest tightened. Panic set in. He gasped for oxygen. "Rhy…Rhy…" He tried to speak but couldn't force the words out. Black dots swarmed the air, crowding his vision.

"Why the hell didn't you tell me you were allergic to bee stings?" Rhyden motioned Noah back into the passenger seat of the pickup. He turned to Mr. Schmidt, accepting the card and list. "We'll be back in touch as soon as we can about repairing your driveway. Thanks for the information. I need to transport my partner to the hospital now."

Mr. Schmidt shook hands with Rhyden and nodded to Noah. "*Ja,* his lips are turning a rather interesting shade of blue."

Back in the truck, Rhyden flipped on the sirens and overhead lights as he raced to the emergency room. "Hang in there, buddy. We'll be there most ricky-tick."

Noah just nodded and concentrated on breathing. As his vision tunneled, memories surfaced. *The screech of wounded metal, shattered glass, water roaring around him and over him. Flames dancing on the surface of the water. His lungs tightened, pressure built and tried to escape, but no air could get in. Cold surrounded him. His feet went numb. His hands tingled.*

A spike of pain shot through his skull.

Tires squealed on the pavement as Rhyden slid the truck into the ambulance bay at the emergency entrance to the hospital. “Can I get some help over here?” he yelled toward the paramedics heading back to their ambulance.

A female figure in the ER doorway glanced over one shoulder. “Rhyden? What are you doing here? What’s wrong?” She jogged over to the truck.

As she approached, Noah squinted his eyes, recognizing the figure as Cat. Just her presence calmed him. She took one look at Noah and started barking orders. “Grab a couple of EpiPens from the box. Let’s move him inside. Stat.”

Her partner ran up, EpiPens in hand. She grabbed the first one and jabbed it into the meaty section of Noah’s thigh. With capable hands, she brushed the hair from his clammy forehead. “You'll feel better in a sec.”

Unable to speak, he just shook his head. Raspy, gasping breaths swept a miniscule amount of oxygen into Noah’s lungs. Cat supported him on one side while Rhyden held him up on the other. Together, they quick-stepped it through the ER entrance.

“Hey, you want the gurney?” Cat’s partner hollered from the ambulance.

“Nah, take too long. We’ve almost got him in.” Cat hit the paramedic lock code on the emergency room door to open it, then with Rhyden’s help, half carried, half dragged Noah inside.

After dumping him onto a bed like a sack of potatoes, while waiting for the ER doc to make his presence known, Cat gave Noah a second epinephrine injection. She leaned over and placed a kiss on his forehead. "Babe," she said, "if you wanted to see me that bad, all you had to do was call."

With the struggle for breath easing a bit, he gave her a lopsided grin. "This is nothing. You know I would drive thirty minutes one way any day just to kiss you for ten seconds."

****

Disgusted, Bree tossed her cell phone onto the bed. Sixteen texts in eighteen minutes from the jerk. Ignoring the incessant chirping sound, she flopped onto the mattress, rolled onto her side, and hugged her pillow tight. *Asshole.* She punched the pillow and decided she couldn't cry anymore even if she wanted. Her tears were all used up.

The phone rang again, an actual call this time. She punched the pillow again and glared at the small plastic electronic leash. It fell silent, for only seconds, then began ringing again. Giving up, she tapped accept on her phone. Throat raw, she croaked, "What?"

Silence greeted her. Gritting her teeth, she repeated, "What do you want?"

A subdued whisper responded. "I didn't think you would answer. I've been calling and texting for two days. I planned to leave a message."

"Fine. I'll hang up. I don't want to talk to you, anyway."

"No, please, don't. I'm sorry. I wasn't thinking."

Bree snorted. "Obviously. Did you really think it was okay to cheat on me? *With my sister?* How did you not think you would get caught?"

The boy mumbled, "I didn't realize Sam was your sister."

"And that makes it okay?"

"Please. Please don't hang up. I really am sorry." He dropped his voice in timbre and volume. "I miss you. More than I thought possible. I can't eat. I can't sleep."

"Sounds like a personal problem to me." Bree leaned her head back against the pillows, wrapping a strand of hair round and round her finger. Her face twitched as she bit back the smile hovering on the edges of her lips.

"Can I see you again?" he begged. "Please?"

"I guess it depends."

"On what?"

She rolled onto her stomach, crossing her sock-clad feet in the air. Silky strands of hair slipped between her fingers. "What time you plan on seeing my sister again."

"Bree, baby, please. That won't ever happened again. I made a huge mistake. Forgive me? Please?"

"Don't baby me. You two-timing, chicken-shit ass wipe. What was your *huge* mistake? Seeing someone else? Not realizing she was my sister? Or getting caught?"

"Come on, Bree, please? I'm begging you."

"Well, bless your pea-picking little heart. Give me one good reason I shouldn't just hang up this phone."

An hour later, when she finally hung up the phone, Bree grinned from ear to ear. Warmth rippled from the tips of her toes to the top of her head. Picking up her body pillow, she squeezed it tight, slipped off the bed, and danced around the room.

Chapter Nine

Noah slipped into the dining room. As he watched Cat fiddle with the place settings on the table, the weight of the day lifted from his shoulders. He was home.

"Hey, babe," she said. "You're running late, later than usual. I should have known you wouldn't take it easy despite what the doctor advised. How are you feeling?"

She stepped around the dining room table where she carefully placed china plates, cloth napkins, and utensils. The pretty, white plates glowed in the flickering light from long tapers resting in fancy candlesticks. The candlelight sparkled off her dangly earrings and reflected from her long, shimmery silver blouse. Soft black leggings and bare feet completed the image that filled his heart with warmth.

She pressed the back of her hand against Noah's forehead briefly before dropping her hand to rest against his chest. With the other hand, she casually picked up his wrist, placing her fingers on the inside below the base of his thumb. She glanced at the wall clock and began counting under her breath.

Left hand still tucked behind his back, Noah leaned forward and whispered, "You know I know what you are doing, right? My pulse is fine."

An enticing blush blossomed on her cheeks. She

dropped his wrist and stepped back. “Fine. So sue me for caring. I just wanted to make sure you were doing better. You were in pretty rough shape when they brought you into the ER. I can’t believe you disobeyed the doctor’s orders and went back to work.” She rolled her eyes. “Never mind. Yes, I can.” She poked a sharp-tipped fingernail against his shirt, one poke for each word. “But I still think it was stupid.”

With a flourish, he pulled two roses from behind his back. The entwined flowers, one red and one white, were meant to be a symbol of unity, his very own unspoken proposal. At least, that’s what the florist said.

He thought of the small blue box tucked securely in his pocket. *Now?* He slid the delicate petals of the blooms down Cat’s nose and across her lips—lips that parted ever so slightly—in a soft caress. “Much better now, *anamchara,* much better.” A tender smile lit his eyes from within. He whispered, “What would I do without you?”

“*Anamchara?* What does that mean?”

“I’m almost positive it means ‘soul mate.’ It’s what my dad used to call my mom, you know, before—well, when they still liked each other.”

“You never talk about your parents. Why not?”

Damn it, why did I use that *word?*

Mood broken, he handed her the roses and stepped away. He stared down at his empty hands. Melancholy seeped into his bones. Shaking it off, he forced a bright note into his voice. “And how was your day at work? Other than saving the life of your favorite man?”

“How did you know about that?” Cat teased. She stretched up on her tiptoes and pressed a kiss against Noah’s still-swollen cheek. “Poor baby.”

With a graceful turn, she headed back to the dining table and added the roses to the brightly colored springtime arrangement already sitting between the candlesticks.

"That's right." Noah followed her. "Poor baby, indeed, and don't you forget it," he said as he nuzzled the back of her neck.

With a giggle, she thrust him aside.

He swept Cat off her feet and into his arms. "Push me away, will you? What happened to 'poor baby'?"

She whooped and wriggled, trying to get down.

He adjusted his grip, tossing her over his shoulder like a sack of rice, and headed for the French doors on the back of the house. With her tucked in his arms, he slipped out of the house.

"Put me down, you big oaf. Where do you think you're taking me?"

"Shh," he said, tightening his grip. He carried her through the gate into the neighbor's yard. Sticking to the shadows, he made his way over to the older couple's trampoline.

"What are we doing here?"

Noah gave her butt a light swat. "Hush." Inside the house, the neighbor's yappy kick-dog barked up a storm. He watched the heavily curtained windows. No light shone through. No one, other than the dog, moved. "The Burtons must not be wearing their hearing aids tonight," he said. With a slight oomph, he tossed Cat onto the trampoline before climbing on himself. He tugged her onto her back beside him, staring up at the Milky Way.

"We really need to get one of these," he said. He rolled onto his side and rested on one elbow, gazing down at Cat. He rocked forward and placed a kiss smack dab in the middle of her forehead. "I…" He kissed her on the chin. "…love…" He dropped a kiss on the tip of her upturned nose. "…you." He wrapped his arms around her and tugged her close. *Mine,* he thought as he kissed her lips passionately. Reluctantly, he drew away.

She placed two fingers on her slightly swollen lips. "What was that for?"

His eyes met hers. He smiled and gently brushed her hair from her eyes. "You just glow."

"What are we doing in the Burtons' backyard in the middle of the night?"

"I think the more pertinent question, young lady, is why do George and Martha have a trampoline, and we don't? Aren't they like ninety or something?"

A laugh burst from Cat's lips. She shot a guilty glance at the back of the neighbors' house. Swatting him on the arm, she said, "You goofball. George is eighty-three, and Martha is only sixty-eight. The trampoline is for when their grandkids come to visit, which they do frequently. You might know that if you ever got home before ten or eleven at night."

"So George has himself a young hottie, huh? Ooof." Noah rubbed his stomach where Cat had just planted her elbow. "What was that for?"

"Smarty-pants. Look," she said, pointing up, "a shooting star."

They watched the stars painting the purple sky. "Aquarids meteor shower is supposed to peak tonight. I thought it might be nice to watch out here with you." He thought about the ring in his pocket. A secret smile slid across his face.

Should I propose? Surrounded by shooting stars? That's romantic, right?

"Okay, what are you up to? You've got that cat-ate-the-canary grin on your face."

"Um…nothing?" He waved the question away. "So tell me, how was your day at work?"

She scooted over and placed her head on his shoulder. "Pretty exciting, actually. I thought we were going to deliver a baby in the back of the ambulance. Mom-to-be's water broke as we were loading her into the box. Jim, the yellow-bellied wuss, took one look at her and decided it was his turn to drive even though it wasn't." She giggled. "I wish you could have seen the expression on his face when she had a contraction, grabbed onto his hand and squeezed before he could escape to the front of the box. No one makes bed sheets that white."

"Why was she grabbing Jim? Where was the dad?"

"On his way. Probably driving over a hundred miles an hour. Baby's premature. Dad's an oilfield guy smack dab in the middle of his two-week hitch. He was still out at the rig in Oklahoma. Thought he had at least another week before the little one made an appearance. At least he wasn't stuck on a rig in Montana or Wyoming."

"Well, did she have a girl or a boy?"

"I don't know. We got her to the hospital in time. They whisked her straight on up to obstetrics." A soft smile lit Cat up from the inside. Her left hand skimmed lightly over her abdomen. She turned her head, meeting Noah's eyes, and shrugged. "I'll pop in tomorrow and check on her if they'll let me. Dang HIPAA takes all the fun out of my job these days. Then, on the way back to the ambulance, I stopped in the emergency room to drag Jim away from his flavor of the month—the new nurse he's always flirting with—and there was the cutest little girl about three years old. Big green eyes, long brown hair, just gorgeous. Jim's nurse friend was trying to pry a plastic bead out of the child's ear."

"Why did she have a plastic bead in her ear?"

"That's what I asked. Get a load of this. She wanted to wear earrings just like her mommy. How adorable is that? The things kids come up with."

Noah swept Cat over the top of him. He sat up with her cuddled in his lap. "At all ages, apparently." He took a moment to tell her about Alyssa Sanders's faking a visit with her deadbeat father to hang out with a boy. He left out the part of the story ending with her unfortunate demise.

Darkness clouded his thoughts as he pictured the bits and pieces recovered from the driveway. The pain Alyssa's family experienced crashed down on him. He increased his grasp on Cat, holding her that much tighter and pressed his lips to her shoulder.

She tilted her head to one side. "Hey, where'd you go just then?"

He wrapped his hands in her cinnamon-coffee hair and deepened the kiss. He lost himself in her embrace.

She broke the kiss with a sigh. She ran her fingers through his hair, brushing the shaggy edges out of his eyes. Sensing his need for comfort, she snuggled deeper into his arms and laid her head on his shoulder. She caressed the back of his neck.

Noah held her even tighter, trying to drive away the gloom. At the same time she began to speak, he spoke over her. "I am so glad we are not having kids."

Cat stilled. She patted his shoulder stiffly and scrambled off the trampoline. Quickly, she turned her face away from him and headed back to her kitchen.

Noah grabbed her hand. He turned her back to face him. Puzzled, he asked, “Did I say something wrong?”

“No.” She forced a smile as she tugged her hand from his grip. “I just don’t want dinner to burn.”

His eyes searched hers. “Sweetie, are you sure nothing’s wrong?”

“Nope,” she replied. “Not a thing.”

He tilted his head and examined her from head to toe. “You’re sure?”

“Everything’s peachy keen. Fine as frog hair. Okay?” She tossed her hair back over her shoulder. “Are you hungry?”

He hesitated. “You’re sure, absolutely positive everything is okay? You know I love you, right?”

Lips pressed closed, she nodded and turned away.

Noah smiled. “Well, in that case, I’m starving. It’s been a really long day.”

****

“Goodnight, Dad,” Bree said as she slipped into her bedroom.

“You sure you don’t want to watch a movie with the rest of us?” Rhyden asked.

Bree faked a yawn. “No, Dad, I’m exhausted. Plus, I’ve got a calculus final in the morning.”

“Finals? On a Saturday?”

Shit. I forgot tomorrow was Saturday. Thinking fast, she said, “Yeah, we have to take them on a Saturday because someone, I won’t mention any names but she lives in this house, is younger than me, and isn’t Maddie, shut the high school down for three days with her stupid little chemistry prank, and now the rest of us have to suffer by going to school on a Saturday."

"I guess those are the breaks, huh? Okay, then. Sleep tight."

Bree shut the door to her room and turned the lock on the knob. *Finally!* Moving quickly, she plumped her pillows and stuffed them into her favorite nightshirt. She tucked them beneath the quilt, leaving just the tail end of the bright red nightshirt visible beneath the edge of the coverings.

One last glance in the mirror and Bree was ready to go. She tugged the safety dowels from the window frame and flipped the locks on the window open. As she raised the glass, a horrible squeak split the air.

Oh shit. She dove to the floor between the wall and the bed. She lay still, holding her breath for what felt like forever, listening. She raised her head above the edge of the bed and squinted through the darkness toward her bedroom door. No one else in the house appeared to have noticed the noise. Sighing, she rose to her feet, brushed off her outfit, and returned to the window.

She slipped through the window and slowly, ever so slowly, eased it closed. She stood still in the shadows behind the house, waiting. *Whew. No one heard me.* Carefully, she tiptoed around the side of the house. Once clear, she darted down the road to the stop sign where Prince Charming waited for her. She opened the door of his muscle car and jumped in. *Home free.*

"Drive," she commanded. "Hurry, before we get caught."

Her boyfriend leaned across the console to steal a kiss. "Hey, gorgeous, great to see you, too."

“Come on, let’s go. Before my dad comes out.”

He put the car in drive and drove to the playground about two miles from Bree’s house. After they parked, he walked around and opened the door for Bree. “My lady.” With a bow, he held out a hand to help her from the car.

Bree giggled as she stepped out of the car and wrapped her arms around his neck. He winced and pulled away.

“Are you okay?” Her boyfriend leaned down and placed a kiss on the tip of Bree’s nose. “I’m perfect now that you’ve forgiven me. Just a little sunburnt.”

“How do you get a sunburn working in an office? Been playing hooky at the river ogling hot girls in bikinis?”

“Um,” he hedged, “I—uh—I don’t exactly work in the office.”

Bree’s face hardened. “More lies?”

“No lies.” His words tripped over one another as he rushed to reassure her. “I was supposed to work in the office with my dad, but he fired me. You know what an ass he can be. This paving crew was short a couple of guys and needed help. So they hired me as a general laborer. It’s a temporary job. They’re only in this area for a few months, but it puts gas in the fuel tank and pays my insurance.”

“Actually, I don’t know. I wonder why? Oh yeah, it might be because I’ve never met your dad. Or your mom either for that matter.”

“Anyway, I’ve been spreading tar on driveways. It’s hard, hot work under the blistering sun. I got sunburned. No river, no bikinis, just work.”

“Uh-huh.” Bree sauntered away, heading toward

the swing sets, exaggerating the sway of her hips.

He followed her. “No other girls for me. You are my one and only.”

She stopped mid-stride at the tone of his voice. She turned to face him, stepping in close and resting her hands against his chest. Tilting her head, she gazed up at him. “You know, when you say it like that, I almost believe you…almost.”

With a laugh, she whirled, and tossing a flirtatious wink over her shoulder, she said, “Race you to the swings.”

****

Declan Gorman, head of the clan and grandfather to Seamus, bellowed from the back office. “Seamus, get in ’ere, laddie. *Noo.*”

While Seamus’ speech sometimes held subtle hints of the old country, Grandda’s words drowned in the heavy brogue he’d grown up speaking, even after fifty-some-odd years in the “new” country.

“Now what?” Seamus muttered under his breath as he rose from his desk and walked to his grandfather’s office.

The old man hunched over stacks of leather-covered ledgers, his thick, white mane mussed from running his hands through it. Big hands—rugged and weather-beaten—clutched a number-two yellow pencil with a well-chewed pink eraser. The pencil all but disappearing in his grasp.

“You needed me, sir?”

“What the bloody hell is going on?” Declan gestured at the books scattered over the top of his desk. “Why are our expenses so high? How can we make a profit like this?”

"Grandda, when are you going to let me introduce this company to the twenty-first century? Those ledger books are antiquated. You know they have these nifty plastic boxes called computers. They even have accounting software on them. You could retrieve all your reports with the touch of a button."

"Bah! And is that magic button going to lower our expenses? Who needs computers? I've been keeping my ledgers for years with no problems, and books don't crash like computers."

"They don't automatically generate balance sheets or profit-and-loss statements, either."

"Profit? What profit? You and that useless son of yours are running my company into the ground. When Ferrell was here, we had more work and got our supplies at better rates. And we damn sure didn't pay temporary laborers thirty dollars an hour. Where is all my money going? Hmmm?"

Careful to keep the old man from seeing them, Seamus held his clenched fists at his sides. *Don't you wish you knew?* He silently counted to ten and thought about the secret bank accounts steadily growing in the Cayman Islands. "Thirty dollars an hour? We don't pay anyone thirty dollars an hour."

He stepped over to the desk and picked up the nearest ledger. He flipped through a few pages before closing the book and examining the cover. "Grandda, these are the 'official' ledgers—for the vultures in the government. See the fleur-de-lis on the lower left-hand corner? We put it on the cover so we would know which set to give the IRS in case they decide to audit us. Remember? It was your idea."

Seamus stepped around behind his grandfather and

unlocked the gunmetal gray filing cabinet in the corner. He tugged open the bottom drawer, emptied the contents, and lifted out the false bottom. Reaching into the far back corner of the file drawer, he came up with an almost identical set of ledger books. He handed these to Declan.

"Harumph. Cursed government. I wish your cousin were here. He knew how to run a business." Heavy emotion laced the old man's speech, dragging the brogue to the forefront. "Damn pity we hud to bury th' laddie at sich an early age. He wis a pure tough laddie."

Seamus ground his teeth. *Here we go again. Perfect cousin Ferrell.* He closed his eyes before his grandfather could register the hate in them. "Ferrell's dead, Grandda. Just like his mother. He's not coming back—ever."

"And whose fault is that?"

"I don't know, Grandda. He wrecked that fancy, overpowered muscle car you bought him. He just had to have it, and you bought it for him. Then he totaled it. Remember?" *I sure do.* A faint smile flickered on Seamus's face.

Tapping the rear of the fancy sports car with the grill guard of my one-ton dually pickup; the smell of burning rubber as I mashed hard on the accelerator. The vibration of the over-revved engine reverberating against my foot as I forced my truck against the rear bumper of that candy-apple red coupe. The banshee shriek of metal grinding against metal, glass shattering, and the guardrail crumpling beneath the force of the fancy muscle car as it careened down the side of the bluff into the river far below. I remember jamming my brakes on hard to keep from following poor, precious

Ferrell over the edge into oblivion. Too bad the river kept Ferrell's car from exploding on impact. I would have enjoyed watching the fireball, maybe even roasting a weenie or two over the flames. It did eventually catch fire, though, didn't it?

"What are you grinning about, lad? Your cousin's dead, and I'm left with you and that daft son of yours to take over my business and the family. We're losing money hand over fist. You think that's something to smile about?"

Seamus schooled his features, hiding the glee he found in his memories. He shook off the past. He needed to transfer more money into the books so his grandfather wouldn't catch on to how much he'd been skimming.

"What are you talking about losing money? We're not losing money, and I'm not grinning."

"Ferrell would never have let the company lose money like this. And he damn sure wouldn't let that whiny little *shite* hide in that dilapidated barn, doing who know what to those poor animals. Hunting's one thing. Torturing animals is something else altogether."

If only animals were all he tortured, Seamus thought.

He slammed a hand on Declan's desk. "Damn it, Grandda. How many times do I have to tell you we are not losing money? Do I not do everything you ask of me? Didn't I give up my wife for you? My son might be better behaved if he had grown up with a mother."

"Wife? You mean the fancy piece of ass you drug down here from the city?"

Seamus stepped away from his grandfather's desk. His hands itched to wrap themselves around the old man's throat. He inhaled deeply and let it out slowly—very slowly. "I can't help it that Ferrell died, but he's been gone a long time, Grandda. I'm still here."

He studied his grandfather's shocked face, noticing for the first time the deep lines, the gray tinge to his skin, the smudged-bruised color of the heavy bags beneath his age-washed eyes the color of faded-denim.

He lowered his voice. "I'm sorry, Grandda, but I am sick and tired of wearing a dead man's boots. They're never going to fit. When are you going to see me for who I am? For all I've done for you? All I've sacrificed for you and the clan? I've never gone away. I've always been here—right here with you—ready to do whatever you asked of me. Why am I not good enough for you?"

"Noo, laddie, ah didnae mean tae offend ye. Things often aren't as clear in this old noggin' of mine as they used to be," Declan said in a voice as thin and leathery as his skin. "Forgive an auld man, wid ye?"

"I know, Grandda, I know. I'm sorry, too. I shouldn't have lost my temper. But, damn it, Ferrell's been gone more than sixteen years, and he's not coming back, no matter how much we wish for it." *I made damn good and sure of that.*

Before Declan could respond, Patrick called from the front office. "Hey, Da, there's a *peeler* on the phone. They want to talk to you."

Seamus drew back his shoulders and nearly cursed out loud. *What the hell do the police want? Did they find the girl? Damn it, I knew I shouldn't have trusted the boy to clean up his own mess.*

Slowing his thoughts, Seamus picked up the telephone receiver on his grandfather's desk. "Good afternoon. How can I be of assistance?" He grabbed one of his grandfather's pencils and a scrap of paper. "Sage Drive, you say? Let me see."

A crash sounded down the hallway. Seamus put the officer on hold and stuck his head out the office door. His son was busy picking up a stack of books containing photographs of jobs completed for supposedly satisfied customers. The boy refused to make eye contact.

As stupid as the boy is, surely he wouldn't bury a body in a driveway.

****

Patrick knocked on the dented metal door of the aging single-wide mobile home. As he waited for an answer, he looked out at the overgrown weed-filled lawn surrounded by a sagging chain-link fence.

"What do you want?" A tall, skinny man wearing an embroidered, pearl-snap shirt and faded blue jeans growled from behind the screen door.

Patrick turned to face the man. "Hello, sir, is Rochelle available?"

"Rochelle, get your ass in here," the man bellowed over one shoulder. "Right this minute."

She slipped into view, clinging to the edges of the room. "Dad? You wanted me?"

Her father jerked a thumb at Patrick. "Door," he grunted as he stomped off.

Rochelle rushed to open the door. "Hey," she said.

"Hey, yourself. Can I come in?"

"Oh." Visible embarrassment washing across her face, she opened the door wider. "Please, come in. What are you doing here?"

The stench of old grease and stale food turned his

stomach as he stepped into the threadbare living room. He leaned over and placed a chaste kiss on her forehead. "I thought we could go grab a pizza or something."

She shuffled her feet, arm down by her side, hand slightly hidden behind her back. Her thumb bounced from finger to finger, faster and faster. "Um…"

"Or not. No big deal."

"Hang on, let me go ask my dad."

As Patrick watched, Rochelle peered around the doorjamb into the kitchen. Before she could speak, her father bellowed, "Who the hell is that punk?"

Patrick stepped up behind Rochelle. "Patrick Gorman, sir. I'd like to take your daughter to dinner if that's okay."

A woman dressed in a ratty terry-cloth robe lounged at a crappy laminate table. A cigarette burned in the ashtray, blue-gray smoke swirling upward to stain the walls and ceiling. A half-empty bottle of vodka sat next to a plastic cup near her elbow. The woman smirked. Rochelle's father stood behind her like the wicked queen's sergeant-at-arms, one hand resting on her shoulder. His other hand slapped angrily against his leg.

Ignoring Patrick, the man barked, "Get over here."

Rochelle stepped closer but kept her distance.

Smart girl, staying out of striking distance, Patrick thought. He moved closer, placing one hand on the small of her back in a gesture of support.

"Little Mama says you aren't speaking to her. Why?"

With a sideways glance at Patrick, Rochelle said, "Dad, please?" Shrugging, she lifted her hands in an I-don't-know-what-you-want-me-to-say gesture.

Her dad crowded into her space. "I asked you a question. I expect an answer. Now."

Beneath his palm Patrick felt Rochelle cringe, but she stood her ground. Her thumb continued tapping against her fingers. "You're the one who taught me if I couldn't say anything nice not to say anything at all. "

"Why you ungrateful little…"

The blow bounced her head off the wall. Blood dripped from her lower lip where her teeth cut it. Patrick surged forward, fists balled.

Rochelle shook her head at him. She stepped between him and her father. Straightening her spine, she squared her shoulders and lifted her chin. Minutes crawled past. Her father shuffled his feet, dropped his gaze. Without a word, head still high, Rochelle swept from the kitchen.

Patrick crowded in on her old man. "If you ever lay a hand on her again, I will rip off your head and shit down your neck. That goes for both of you." Leaving the suitably cowed couple in the kitchen, he followed Rochelle's path. He found her collapsed on her bed.

She turned a silver razor blade over and over in her hand, rubbing her fingers on the shiny, flat surfaces.

"Hey, now, give me that." He plucked the blade from her hands. "Don't do that."

She looked up at him, anguish clouding her eyes. "I just want to feel something. I want to know I'm alive. Know what I mean? I feel hollow, like there's nothing inside me. The blade lets me know different. I lurk behind this mask, trying so hard to be like the rest of them, but I fail at that, too. The herd—no, the flock of sheep, too afraid to think for themselves, realize somehow—or maybe they just sense I'm different, and they band together against me."

He tugged her into a loose embrace. "Who cares what they think?"

She touched her tongue against the still-bleeding spot on her lower lip. Her features hardened. "I know this. I will never be a victim again. Not his, not hers, and definitely not theirs. Her boys will never touch me again. Never!"

Patrick tightened his hold on her. "Her boys touch you?" His stomach fluttered as his thoughts raced. He wasn't sure how he felt about anyone hurting her. Quickly, he tamped down that line of thought. *She's just a mark. Keep it in check.*

She sighed. "They try. Why else would I staple quilts over my windows and keep a dresser next to the door where I can shove it in place to keep the door from opening?"

Releasing the embrace, he leaned away from her. *Time to set the hook.* He took her hands in his and studied them as if too embarrassed to make eye contact with her. "If I tell you something…" He dropped her hands, turned away. "Never mind."

Roc scooted closer, placed her hand on his face and turned his face back to hers. "Please? What were you going to say?"

"I've never told anyone this. You know why I don't go to your high school anymore?"

Mutely, she shook her head. He pulled away from her. She grabbed the pillow on her bed and hugged it tight. "Last year, the biology teacher cornered me in the boys' restroom. He started telling me how cute I was and rubbing on me and then…" Patrick broke off, pretending to be too overcome to speak. He buried his face in his hands.

She dropped the pillow and reached out to him, jerking her hands back at the last moment. “Is it okay if I touch you? If I hold you?”

He nodded, and she wrapped her arms around him, pulling him close. His shoulders shook as if he were sobbing his heart out. The longer she held him, the bigger his smirk became. *Candy from babies.*

Finally, she released him. “Are you okay?”

“Yeah.” He fake sniffled. “I’m fine, but I should go. You didn’t need me to dump this garbage on you.”

“No, don’t ever say that. It’s all good. I’m here for you, but I think maybe you should go now. I’m sorry about the pizza. I’m just not very good company. I need to go for a drive. Clear my head.”

Patrick followed her to the kitchen where she snatched her keys off the counter before heading out the front door.

Chapter Ten

A dark-colored car, foreign make, flashed past Noah, with the bass pounding out of the little car hard enough to rattle the windows on his truck. The engine sounded like a souped-up sewing machine.

Within minutes, static crackled from the radio on the dash of his unmarked unit. "Attention all officers, all units, we have reports of a stolen vehicle. 10-99 out of Hopper's Creek. Be on the lookout for a 2006 Honda Accord, dark blue in color. Believed to be heading west on FM 472."

Noah grabbed the microphone. "832—Bennett County. I may just have seen your suspect vehicle. Did you get a license plate number?"

"10-4, 832. Twenty-eight is Victor-David-Sam Two-Niner-Niner. Repeat Victor-David-Sam Two-Niner-Niner. Registered owner is Bruce Waters of 349 Timberlake Drive in Hopper's Creek."

Noah followed the suspect car. "832—Bennett County. Confirming I have eyes on your stolen vehicle. Lighting them up now." He turned on his lights and sirens. The car decelerated and coasted to a stop on the side of the farm-to-market road.

"10-4, 832. What is your location?"

"We are coming to a stop in front of the abandoned post office off FM 472." Noah pulled in, angling his truck at a forty-five-degree angle behind the little car so he could use the engine block as cover in case the driver began firing at him.

The driver rolled down the window. Music poured out, the bass so heavy Noah felt it reverberating in his chest while still inside his pickup. Stepping out of the truck, he slid his service weapon from his holster and held it at the ready. Remaining behind the truck's door, he yelled at the driver, "Turn off your vehicle and step out. Keep your hands where I can see them."

The engine shut off. Thankfully, so did the punishing bass. The door swung open, and a teenage girl hesitated before clambering out of the car.

Weapon still in hand, Noah continued barking instructions. "Keep your hands where I can see them. Face away from me. Get on your knees. On your knees now. Keep your hands up. Drop to your knees."

The girl complied.

"Slowly, lower yourself, face first, to the ground. Stretch your arms out to the side."

Noah approached the teenager as she stretched out on the ground. After quickly frisking her and finding no weapons or drugs, he tugged both hands behind her back and handcuffed her. He helped her to her feet and escorted her to a safer area beyond the two vehicles. "What's your name?"

Wide-eyed and trembling, the girl stammered, "Ro-Rochelle Waters."

"Miss Waters, I stopped you because someone reported this vehicle as stolen. Do you have anything to say about that?"

The radio unit clipped to his duty belt beside his pepper gun chattered to life. "Bennett County—832, checking your status?"

Noah lifted the radio, keyed the mic, and replied, "832 code four. One detained. Requesting 10-51 to tow vehicle." He replaced the radio on his belt and returned his attention back to the girl. His nostrils flared as he took in her split lower lip and the bruise beginning to form on her cheek. He placed a hand under her chin, turning her face for a better view of the injuries. "Who did this to you?"

Ducking her chin, she winced and shook her head. Stringy hair fell in front of her eyes, hiding her expression. "I—I don't want to talk about it."

"Fine then. Let's talk about the vehicle. Whose car are you driving?"

She met his gaze with her own, though clearly frightened. "Mine. I mean, it's in my dad's name, but I make the payments on it and pay for the insurance."

"I see. Where's your ID?"

"In my purse. On the front seat of the car."

"Have a seat." Noah lowered her to a seated position on the grass and fetched her purse. "Do I have your permission to search your purse and vehicle? Is there anything in here that's going to harm me?"

Tears flooded the teen's eyes. "N-no, y-yes. I mean yes, you can search. No, nothing will hurt you." Mascara streaked down her pale cheeks. A fit of hiccups overtook her, interrupting her muffled sobs.

He fished around inside her bag. *Why do females' purses hold so much crap?* At last, he tugged her wallet from the bag, opened it, and inspected her driver's license. "You're seventeen? Do you realize how much trouble you could be in if you really did steal this vehicle? What's your father's name?"

Sniffling, she said, "Bruce Waters, sir." Rochelle

shrank into herself, raising her shoulders and lowering her head, as if retreating into a shell. Her voice dropped to a barely-there whisper. “But it’s my car. I swear. It’s my car. I didn’t steal it.”

Noah helped her to her feet. “Let’s go to my office and sort this out.”

Twenty minutes later, with the car towed safely to the parking lot of the Bennett County Law Enforcement center, an unhandcuffed Rochelle Waters sat across the desk from him. As she nursed a soda, Noah dialed the number for Bruce Waters. While she picked at her cuticles, he placed the call on speakerphone.

“Hello?” A woman answered the phone, her smoker’s voice raspy and harsh.

“Hello, this is Ranger Noah Morgan with Ranger Company F. May I speak to Bruce Waters, please?”

“Did you catch that ungrateful little bitch?” she growled. “I want my car back. I want it back *now*.”

He raised his eyebrows. “Excuse me. Who am I speaking to?”

“This is Mrs. Waters and you can talk to me.”

“Ma’am, I need to speak to Bruce Waters, please. Is he home?”

“Bruce!” A shrill shriek issued from the speaker. “It’s the fucking pigs, and they won’t talk to me. Get your ass on the phone and send that ungrateful little bitch to jail.”

Muffled voices and scrabbling noises filled the room through the speaker. A male voice dominated. “Give me that.” The sound of flesh hitting flesh followed. “How many times have I told you not to answer my phone?”

From the corner of one eye, Noah saw Rochelle

cringe, then tug her sleeves down both arms, far enough to cover her hands. Her thumb began tapping a rhythm against the tips of her fingers.

A gruff, grating male voice asked, “Who is this?”

“Mr. Waters?” Noah asked.

“This is him. Who is this, and what do you want?”

“Sir, this is Ranger Morgan. Did you report your vehicle as stolen?” Noah glanced at Rochelle who turned her gaze away from his. He tapped his pen against the notepad resting on the desk before him.

A strident, female voice came over the speaker. “Damn right we reported a car stolen. You need to lock up that lying little slut. Nothing but trouble, that one.”

Gritting his teeth, Noah clenched his fists and then shook them loose. With a visible effort, he fought to maintain his calm. “Sir, are you there?”

“Yeah, I’m here. Yeah, my car was stolen. Did you find it yet?”

“I’m sitting here with a Miss Rochelle Waters. Is she your daughter?”

“So her mother says.”

Noah raised sympathetic eyes to Rochelle who blushed bright red and squirmed in her seat. Making no eye contact, she continued to fiddle with her shirtsleeves and sank lower in the chair. He cleared his throat. “Miss Waters claims she makes the payments and pays for the insurance on the vehicle. Regardless, it is registered in your name, and you are within your legal rights to press charges for the unauthorized operation of a motor vehicle. Do you wish to press charges, sir?”

The woman screeched from the background. “Damn right we want to press charges.”

Noah glanced at the teenager slumped in the chair. His focused on the split lip, the bruised cheek. He took the phone off speaker, picked up the receiver, and pressed it to his ear. "Sir, before you respond to my question, I am going to be blunt. If you say yes, we will open an investigation. Allow me to assure you, sir, it will be an extremely thorough investigation. We will need to get the entire story…like where your daughter's facial injuries came from. Given her age, I will be sure to involve Child Protective Services and see that everything which happens in your household—I repeat, *everything*—will be placed under a microscope. So I ask one more time. Are you absolutely one-hundred-percent positive you want to press charges against your daughter?"

Silence greeted his question. In the background, the grating female voice started up again. He blocked it out. "Mr. Waters?"

"Well, uh, we may have been a bit hasty calling the police. No, it's okay. No charges."

After hanging up the phone, Noah rubbed the scar that cut through one eyebrow before turning to the bruised girl. He lowered his voice to the tone he remembered Rhyden used to calm his daughters. "Rochelle, is there anything you want to tell me? Anything I can do to help?"

She grabbed her bag off the table and hugged it to her chest. With one shake of her head, she asked, "May I go, sir?"

Noah stepped around the desk and kneeled beside the girl's chair. "We can help. If you'll let us."

"Please, sir, may I leave?"

With heat behind his eyelids and a lump in his

throat, Noah swallowed defeat and waved wearily at the open door. “Yes, you may go. Sylvia has your keys at the front desk.”

Scrambling for a business card and a pen, he scribbled his cell phone number on the back of the card before handing it to the battered teen. He did not release the card until she raised her eyes to his. “That’s my personal cell number. Please call me if you need anything—anything at all, any time at all.”

With a sharp nod, Rochelle tucked the card in her bag. Ducking her head and raising both shoulders, she darted from the room.

****

“Hey, beautiful.” Patrick waved across the gravel parking lot at Roc. He drew a battered, olive-colored duffle bag from the back of his great-uncle’s pickup. “You ready to go?”

As the dust settled, she stepped out of her car, carrying safety glasses and hearing protectors. With a hesitant shrug, she said, “I think so.”

He almost didn’t recognize her. Her freshly washed hair shone in the sun. A touch of awkwardly applied makeup graced her face, highlighting her eyes. He stepped closer to her and leaned in to press a kiss to her forehead. She raised her head, eyes closed, obviously waiting for a real kiss. He ran a finger lightly across her split and swollen lower lip. “Damn, girl, he really did a number on you.”

Roc shivered. She ducked her head, a curtain of hair falling forward and hiding her injuries. She mumbled, “I don’t want to talk about it.” Tap, tap, tap, tap, her thumb bumped each fingertip.

“O-ka-a-ay.” *This will be even easier than I*

thought. "Are you sure you're okay, princess? You know you can talk to me."

She raised her head. Her cheek was darkened with the purple shadow of a bruise that shone through her makeup. A bitter chuckle escaped her lips. Hands fisted, jaw clenched, she spit out the words. "The son of a bitch tried to have me arrested."

"Which son of a bitch? Your dad?"

"Yeah, the sperm donor." Forcibly, she uncurled her hands. She bared her teeth in a cold smile and said, "But it's okay, isn't it? We're going to change the world, right? Maybe I'll start at home. All change should start at home, shouldn't it?"

A flaming vision of ripping Roc's father's head from his body burned through Patrick's mind. His body tensed before he purposefully relaxed it. *Don't let her emotions infect you. Not your problem. She's just a tool you are using to get the job done.* Still, the thought of inflicting severe pain on her father tantalized him.

Refocusing his attention, he swung the duffle bag over one shoulder and wrapped his other arm around Roc's waist. He dropped a tender kiss on top of her head. "That's right, princess. We'll change the world."

When they reached the shooting bench set up behind the dilapidated barn, he unzipped the bag and began pulling out boxes of ammunition in different calibers. Next, he grabbed two rifles, a shotgun, and an assortment of handguns. Roc's eyes widened. She slid her finger down the glossy, wooden stock of a rifle.

"Here," he said. "Pick it up." Patrick stepped behind her and positioned the long gun in her arms. "Hold it tight, like this, against your shoulder. Press your cheek against the stock like so." He adjusted the gun, helping her hold it tight to her shoulder while bracing her back against his chest. "Now gently, gently squeeze the trigger. Don't pull it."

Roc stopped. "Don't we need the earmuffs?"

"Nah, not necessary. Just focus down range on the target and squeeze the trigger."

"If you're sure?" she asked tentatively. She pressed the butt of the gun back against her shoulder. When Patrick let go, the barrel of the gun dipped.

"Whoa. Here you go." He slid his arms back around her, supporting the weight of the gun. "Focus on the picture I taped to the target."

"Is that your dad?" Roc sounded a bit shocked.

"No way. It's that teacher. The one I told you…well, you know."

"Oh. *Oh! That* teacher. He *needs* to die."

Patrick watched her tighten her grip on the gun. Helping her hold it firmly against her shoulder, he placed his finger over hers and together they applied pressure to the trigger. It slid back until it hit resistance.

"There you go," he said. "A little tighter. Keep squeezing."

Roc pulled the trigger. The kick from the rifle knocked her back into Patrick. She turned to him, a smile lighting up her face. "I did it. I fired the gun."

"Yes, you did. You even hit the paper." Patrick laughed. "A little more practice and you'll be a regular Annie Oakley. You've so got this."

Roc lifted the gun. She pointed it toward the photograph at the other end of the shooting lane. "I want to do it again. I want to blow his face away. Him and all the rest just like him."

Patrick took the rifle from her arms and handed her

a pistol. “Why don’t we try this one next?”

****

In a candlelit, red vinyl booth near the back of the restaurant, Patrick and Roc huddled over a steaming pepperoni pizza. “Are you sure you haven’t shot a gun before?”

She stopped with a slice of pizza halfway to her mouth. A vibrant flash of red rushed up her neck to her face. She dropped the slice back to the plate. “I’ve been shooting with my father since I was six. Today, I pretended I had never held a gun before.” She wrapped her arms across her belly. “I’m so embarrassed. I acted like everything I hate in a female.”

Curiosity swept through him. “Why did you do it?”

She paused before answering, looking anywhere but at him. After a long silence, she met his gaze and blurted, “When you wrapped your arms around me, when I felt your warmth against my back, your strength surrounding me, for the first time in forever I felt safe. More to the point, I felt emotion. The hollow void inside filled me with, I don’t know, joy maybe? Anticipation? Comfort?”

She removed the napkin from her lap and stepped out of the booth. She stood beside the table, digging in her purse. Pulling out her keys, she said, “I’m sorry. I’m an idiot. I’m just going to go.”

Patrick’s skin tingled. His stomach flipped. *What the hell?* No one had ever been so open and honest with him. He wrapped his fingers around her wrist. “No, don’t go. I—”

Before he could finish his sentence, a very pregnant woman carrying an infant and dragging four squalling toddlers knocked Roc into his lap. Without an apology or even a glance back at the couple, the woman and her bevy of brats swept from the restaurant.

"See? That's what I've been talking about." He gestured at the departing family. "Look out the window. Five kids, one on the way. There's no way she can hold down a job with that many kids, yet she's driving a high-priced SUV. Really? People are trapped in a materialistic funk. We need to free them. It's our duty to set them free. We can't build a new world without sacrifice."

Patrick watched Roc closely. *Was she buying it?* He had studied the manifestos of several mass shooters to come up with this line of rhetoric. *Line of bullshit is more like it.*

"Are you sure I'm ready for this? The whole idea scares me."

"Come here." He moved over on the bench and patted it. "Sit beside me."

She scooted in close to him, pressed her thigh tight against his. He noticed the chill bumps that danced on her skin. Wrapping an arm around her, he ran his hands up and down her arms. "Don't you want a free world? One with no pain, no hate, no anger—just love? I know a lot of people won't understand. They will say what we are going to do is wrong, evil. But we are going to be saving these people. Saving them from the government. Saving them from themselves. It will be a day of great deliverance. A day of freedom. All those empty shells pretending to live, we'll fill them with real life. With real love. They'll understand…afterward."

Where the hell do these whackos come up with this shit? Deliverance? Empty shells? Puh-lease!

He fought the urge to roll his eyes, but as he

watched Roc eat up every last syllable, he was glad he had done his homework.

"We're going to do it together, right? Starting on opposite ends of the campus?"

Damn, this is easy. Patrick shoved a piece of pizza into his mouth to hide his smirk. After chewing and swallowing, he said, "Of course. I'll send you a signal. Any day now."

She smiled and tucked her head against his shoulder. "And then we'll be together, forever and ever in paradise until the end of all time. Do you think it will hurt?" She shook her head, touched her split lip. "Never mind. The pain will be worth the reward. Besides, it can't be any worse than daily life in this gray prison."

****

Aubree danced into the kitchen and grabbed a can of soda out of the fridge before skipping over to drop a kiss on Rhyden's brow. "Hi, Dad."

"You sure are in a good mood for someone who has a calculus final today." He placed the case folder he was reviewing down on the granite countertop.

"Calculus final?" *Shit.* She scrambled to cover up last night's lie. "Uh, yeah, um—I got a text from the school this morning saying the teacher called in sick, so they are rescheduling it for next week."

Damn, this lying stuff was harder than I thought it would be. How does Sam do this all the time?

He flipped the folder back open and started turning pages. "That would definitely improve my mood. If you don't have school, why are you up so early?" He flipped the folder back open and started turning pages.

"Dad, don't freak out, but my boyfriend's on his way here to pick me up. We're gonna hang out."

"What boyfriend?" He looked up at Bree. "Never mind. I'm sorry, kiddo, but I need you here. If you don't have school, I don't have to pay a babysitter to keep an eye on your sisters."

"You know what boyfriend. PC."

Pushing his stool away from the counter, Rhyden faced his daughter. "When are you going to stop with all this PC stuff and just tell me the boy's real name? I thought you had dumped him after the stunt with Sam."

"That was a mistake. Everyone is entitled to make one now and again. Isn't that what you always tell us? Besides, he didn't really like Sam. He likes me, just me."

"Uh-huh. Fine. I still need you here." He closed the folder and gathered his keys and badge from the catch-all basket at the end of the counter.

"But, Dad, it's Saturday. Sam's old enough. She can watch Maddie. Or if you don't trust her, why don't you go ahead and pay the sitter? It's not like we are broke or anything."

"Why don't y'all just hang out here?" He tucked the folder under one arm, reached into his pocket, and pulled out his wallet. "I'll spring for pizza."

"Right. Like I want to flaunt Sam the gorgeous in front of PC."

"Wait. Didn't you just tell me he doesn't like her, but he likes you?"

"But Dad…"

"But nothing. Listen, Aubree, I'm in the middle of a big case here. People are depending on me. I have to work. You have to stay here with your sisters. End of discussion."

Bree stomped her foot. "But that's not fair."

Tucking his wallet back in his pocket, he said, "Honey, life and fair are both four-letter words, and that's about all they have in common. Get used to it."

"Oooh!" Bree threw her soda can in the sink. Brown, fizzy liquid splashed everywhere. "You always say that. Why does your job always come first? When do we get to come first? When do *I* get to come first?"

Running a hand through his hair, he said, "Aubree, I know it's hard on you, but you're the oldest, and as the oldest, you have responsibilities. One of those—"

"I didn't ask to be the oldest. I didn't even ask to be born. They're your children, not mine. I shouldn't have to raise them. I'm supposed to be a kid, too, you know. I have no life because of your job."

Rhyden's cell phone rang.

She glared at him. "Go ahead. Answer it." *I dare you.* Bitterness coated her next words. "I hate your job. And I hate you, too. No wonder Mom left."

****

Noah walked down the hallway to his office, humming to himself as he thought back on last night's dinner and his plans for the upcoming evening. *I can't wait to see the smile on her face when she sees the ring.*

Chatter from the CID squad room caught his attention. He popped his head through the door and counted seven sheriff's investigators kicked back and relaxed. Several reclined in desk chairs with their boots propped up on top of their desks. A heated discussion appeared to be taking place at the front of the room between the chief investigator and the three most senior investigators.

"What's up, guys?" Noah asked. "New case?"

"Nah, just talking about the Renner trial over in

Atascosa County."

"Renner? The guy who shot the SAPD officer?"

"Yeah, that's the one. The officer pursued him from San Antonio into Atascosa County and was shot through the windshield. Witness testimony starts tomorrow. A bunch of us are going over to the courthouse and lend moral support to the family."

Noah nodded. "So what's the argument about?"

The CI rolled his eyes. "I think we should wear blue and these yahoos want to go with yellow. Really? I go out in that color, I'll look jaundiced."

"As if that's all you need to worry about," one of the investigators called out. "The hat you're wearing looks like you fell in a pointed hole. Of course, it could be you needed it to cover up your cone head." The room erupted in laughter.

"Seriously?" Noah rubbed at the stress headache threatening to blossom behind both his brows. "A capital murder trial and y'all are arguing about what to wear? You going to court or prom? I thought they were joking when they called you peacocks, but I guess they were serious."

"Peacocks?" Several voices popped up in protest. "Who called us peacocks?"

"At least we're not rabbit rangers," another added.

"Smooth, dude, real smooth. Neither am I. I'm a Texas Ranger, not a game warden." Noah backed out of the room. "Sorry, guys, some of us have real investigating to do. Talk to you later." He paused in the doorway, tipped his hat to the investigators, and said, "Have fun at the prom."

Wads of paper and hoots of laughter followed him into the hallway.

Noah continued through the building to Rhyden's office, reaching the door just in time to hear a telephone handset slammed into its cradle followed by a stream of curse words that would turn a sailor blue.

He peered around the corner of the doorjamb. "Is it safe to come in? What's up?"

Rhyden ran his hand through his hair, causing it to stand on end. Shaking it back down into place, he glowered at Noah. "Today has been a total shit show. Everything I touch falls apart."

"Take a breath. It's only nine; it can't be that bad."

Waves of tension rolled off Rhyden. Popping his knuckles, he asked, "Want to bet on that?"

"What's going on, bud?" Noah dropped into his favorite chair and leaned forward. "I'm all ears."

The muscle in Rhyden's cheek jumped as he ground his back teeth. Nostrils flaring, he slammed his hands on his desk. "Am I a bad father?"

Didn't see that one coming. Noah sat up straight. "Not that I can tell. Of course, I don't exactly have the best role model to compare to. What the hell are you talking about?"

Rhyden looked like he had been sucker punched. "I'm losing them, Noah. The girls. They're growing up, and I'm missing it all."

"Wait a minute, bud. What brought this on? Your daughters love you."

Rhyden snorted. "You might ask Aubree about that. This morning, before she ran away with that punk loser, she informed me she hates me. She blames me for Cara leaving."

"Aw, man." A sour taste flooded Noah's mouth. "Where is Bree? What are we going to do?"

"I don't know where she is." He fished a piece of a torn envelope from his shirt pocket. "But I do know how to find out. My patience is shot."

"What's that?"

"The license plate of the vehicle she and the loser drove off in." Rhyden picked up the handset of the telephone on his desk and punched in the extension for the sheriff's office dispatchers. "Hey, Michelle, can you run a plate for me? Yeah, Texas plate. Boy-Robert-Nora-six-eight-two. Should come back to a red Mustang. Can you print a copy and leave it in my box, please? Thanks."

"One problem down," Noah said. "Why were you trying to kill your phone when I walked in?"

Rhyden's nostrils flared. "You will not believe the complete and total line of bullshit the paving company just tried to hand me. Utter lack of concern for the murdered girl. Un-freakin-believable."

Noah rubbed his hands together. "Do you have a physical address for the place?"

"I do now."

"What are we waiting for? Grab it and your hat, and let's go. I'll drive. I brought my Ruby Lee today."

Chapter Eleven

A swirl of red dirt from the county road chased Noah's octane red Challenger Hellcat into the parking lot of the green metal building. He remained behind the steering wheel, keeping his head on a constant swivel while scanning the location. The first thing he noticed, even through the closed window, was the odor of hot asphalt. An eighteen-wheeler tractor trailer hooked up to a flatbed trailer sat at the edge of the parking lot. Paving equipment, roofing tools, and supplies covered the top of the trailer. A large machine shed huddled between two dump trucks. The sheet metal gaped open on the far side, rendering the padlock on the front door useless.

Random patches of weeds pushed up through cracked and patched asphalt that led to a gravel-covered parking area in front of the metal office building. The glare from the midday sun bouncing off the double glass doors temporarily blinded him. A white vinyl banner with blue lettering proclaiming "Paving and Roofing" dangled beneath the corrugated, charcoal-gray tin roof of the office. No company name. No telephone number.

Knee-high dried grasses and stunted mesquite trees filled the lot behind the parking lot. A thin trail of trampled weeds and brush led from the back of the office building to a dilapidated wooden barn that peeked out from the trees at the far end of the property. Everything on the half-acre lot, apart from the ramshackle barn, could be loaded up and hauled away in a heartbeat. The easy "pick up and go" vibe of the yard brought back memories of doing just that—loading up and moving away before an angry crowd caught up to him—many times while growing up.

A fist-tight knot formed in his stomach.

"Looks fly-by-night, doesn't it?" Rhyden asked.

Noah pulled Ruby Lee to a stop next to an older-model, faded-silver, one-ton work truck. He caressed the custom leather seat, relishing the feel of the butter-soft fabric beneath his palm. Ruby Lee, named after her gorgeous crimson color and paid for with blood, sweat, and tears, was his personal symbol of overcoming a less-than-stellar childhood.

Rhyden pulled out a pen and miniature spiral notebook and started jotting down the license plate numbers of every vehicle in the lot. He grabbed his cell phone to call dispatch. While waiting, he pointed out a super clean, ancient custom pickup, lime green in color. "You don't see many of those in that good a condition very often these days."

Noah studied the truck through the windshield of his muscle car. The vehicle sparked fuzzy images at the edge of his brain.

Can't be. Paddy's truck never had dark, tinted windows. Or Texas license plates. As he wondered whatever happened to his father's old truck, a premonition of dread crawled up his spine.

Rhyden hit the speaker function on his phone. "Hey, Brooke. Can you run some 28s for me, please?" He rattled off the make, model, and license plates of the cars and trucks scattered over the parking lot. Within minutes, they would know who each of the vehicles was registered to, and whether any of them had been reported as stolen or involved in a crime.

After a moment, her voice floated from the speaker as she rattled off the requested information. One, in particular, caught Noah's ear. "Can you repeat the last 28, please?" he asked.

"Sure. 1969 Ford F-100, new lime color, registered to Gorman, Patrick C. of White Settlement, Texas. No wants or warrants at this time."

Noah's hand tightened around the steering wheel, knuckles turning bone white. *Impossible.*

He opened his car door and unfolded his lanky frame from the driver's seat. He walked woodenly toward the truck, acid churning in his gut. Cupping his hands against the tinted glass, he peered through the windows. The cracked black leather covering the seat curled up around the splits to reveal the crumbling yellow foam cushions beneath. A rusty spring poked through the driver side, guaranteed to stab the unwary as they climbed in and out. An empty gun rack hung on the rear windshield. Dirty rubber floor mats collected crushed, empty beer cans and wadded-up fast-food wrappers. The pristine exterior contrasted sharply with the trashed interior.

Exactly like the man who once owned the truck. The man now sitting on death row.

His knees buckled, but he caught himself on the bed of the truck. A memory surfaced and grabbed him, thrusting him back to the past. Suddenly, he was four years old again.

Gravel pelted the windows on the side of the house

as Daddy's truck roared into the driveway. Mommy raced to the door with her mad face on. She slid the security chain in place before kneeling beside him, bringing them face-to-face. She smiled, but he could tell it wasn't her happy smile. Rubbing her hands up and down his skinny arms, she said, "Honey, let's play hide and seek. You go hide really good now, okay?"

"Okay, Mommy." He giggled and ran away. After spinning in a circle, looking around the living room, he darted to the far corner of the room. He crawled behind the brocade sofa.

Daddy pounded on the front door. He shoved the door open as far as the chain would allow. "Open this damn door. Now." Growling, he kicked the door. It shuddered in its frame but wouldn't open any farther.

Noah scooted deeper into the shadows behind the sofa, tucked his head beneath his arms. Sometimes Daddy scared him.

"No, sweetie, I can still see you." She took him by the hand and led him to the hallway. Hands shaking, she propelled him into the closet. "Stay here. Lock the door and stay in here no matter what."

"But it's dark, Mommy, and..."

She gave him a little shake. "No matter what. Do you hear me? No. Matter. What. Stay put and don't make a sound. Not one sound."

He stuttered, "Y-yes, ma'am."

She slammed the door shut, trapping him in the darkness, except for a tiny splash of light sneaking in through the gap at the bottom of the door. "Lock the door. Now."

He twisted the shiny new lock Mommy had added to the closet door a few weeks ago and slid down the door to the floor.

Bam!

The front door burst wide open, crashing against the wall. Voices raised in anger. His heart raced. Blood pounded in his ears, muffling the words. Sliding his hand across the wooden floor, he found his teddy bear, the one he thought he was too old to play with now. He grabbed the bear and clutched it tightly against his chest. The voices got louder. He curled into a ball, burying his face in the bear's soft fur.

Daddy's home. Mommy called him Paddy. She only called him that when he was scary mad, and she was trying to make it better. What was happening? He had to see. He lay down on the floor and peeked through the crack under the door. Daddy drew back his hand and punched Mommy in the stomach. His voice grew louder and louder. "Why can't you be like the other wives? Is it really that hard?" He dragged her nearer to the closet. "Do you realize what the family says about me? The snide comments about how I can't even control my own wife? How am I supposed to take over the clan when Grandda passes if I can't even control one woman and a four-year-old boy? Don't you see I'm doing this for us?" He shoved her away.

The door rattled as Mommy fell against it. The boy jumped back. His stomach hurt. He couldn't swallow. She stood, had to lean against the door for balance. He saw her feet and Daddy's giant, mud-caked, steel-toed boots as he came closer.

"Is that where you've hidden him?" Daddy dragged Mommy away from the door.

The doorknob rattled. He rocked back and forth, trying not to make a sound.

The door rattled again, but the lock held. Mommy screamed at Daddy and jerked him away from the door. Glass shattered. He lay back down and peered under the door and saw Daddy backhand Mommy in the face, knocking her into the rock fireplace. As she fell, he leaped upon her. "Get up, whore," he screamed. "I'm not done with your sorry ass yet."

She didn't move.

"Are you in here, boy?" Daddy rattled the closet door again, but the lock wouldn't open.

The boy pressed even farther back into the dark corner. He covered his ears with his hands and buried his face in his lap. Eyes squeezed closed; he held his breath. Please don't find me. Please don't find me. Please don't find me.

A door slammed. The pickup truck screamed out of the driveway. Silence fell.

Hands trembling, the little boy cracked open the closet door and peered out. Mommy still lay on the floor. He peeked around the corner of the door. "Daddy?"

When there was no answer, he opened the door a smidge wider. "Daddy?"

Tick, tick, tick. The clock was the only sound breaking the silence of the house. The boy sagged in relief. Daddy was gone. Shivering with fear, he crawled through the sticky, red pool to Mommy. She lay so very still. Maybe she was pretending to be asleep so Daddy would go away. He patted her arm. "Mommy?"

Her head rolled to one side. He didn't know what to do. Her eyes were open, but she didn't talk. "Mommy!" he yelled. "Daddy's gone. You can wake up now."

He didn't remember laying his head down beside his mother. He didn't remember falling asleep, but when he woke up, his Grandda and Nana were there to carry him away.

****

"Hello-o-o-o-o-o-o-o?" Rhyden snapped his fingers in front of Noah's face. "Hey, man, snap out of it. You're freaking me out here."

After releasing the breath he didn't realize he was holding, Noah surveyed the parking lot in an attempt to regain his bearings. Slowly, he unfolded his white-knuckled fingers as he turned the death grip he held on the bed of the truck loose and shook the tension out of his hands.

"Buddy, are you okay?" Rhyden asked. "I was starting to get worried."

"Sorry." He forced a chuckle from his chest. "I was a million miles away. Didn't mean to scare you. My grandfather had a truck like this one. He got it from my dad after he…left. I was just remembering the day he showed it to me. He wanted me to check out his white pickup truck. It was the first time I realized the old man was color blind."

Rhyden shot him an expression that said he wasn't buying the bullshit Noah was shoveling.

Before he could ask any more questions, a young man in his early twenties and dressed in tar-stained blue jeans, sturdy work boots, and a heavy-metal T-shirt with the sleeves cut off be-bopped out the front door of the metal building. Shaggy, brown sable hair framed deep-set, narrow blue eyes. Sun-kissed streaks in his hair contrasted with nearly black lashes and brows. White wires ran from the earbuds in his ears down to clutched in his stained fingers. He und to the music coming from his phone.

olf whistle split the air as he loped toward the ers. “Nice wheels, dude,” he said, tugging the earbuds from his ears. “Is that a Hellcat?”

Noah met the young man at the car, placing a protective hand on Ruby Lee’s roof, stroking it gently. “Challenger Hellcat SRT coupe with a Redeye upgrade.”

The boy’s eyes widened. “A Hennessey Redeye? Aww, man! Is it true they embed the washers with crushed diamonds?” He held up his cell phone. “Hey, mind if I take a picture? I want to show my dad what I want for my birthday.”

Rhyden snorted a laugh. “Careful, son, don’t get too close. He might bite your hand off if you try to touch the car. He’s mighty possessive of his baby, Ruby Lee, there. I’m surprised he even lets me ride in her.”

“You named her after a girl? Was she your girlfriend? She had to be hot, right?” The young man slid to a stop in the gravel parking area a few feet from the front of the car. A slight scent of weed clung to his clothing. His eyes widened in awe. “Who can blame him for being protective? Eight hundred and eighty rear wheel horsepower from a supercharged 6.2-liter V-8? Eight hundred six pound-feet of torque? I’ve died and gone to heaven.” He ogled the car and with a tone bordering on reverence asked, “Six-speed manual transmission or eight-speed automatic?”

“Manual, of course,” replied Noah in his most “duh” voice, “as if that was ever even a choice.”

“Of course,” the boy echoed. “It’s all about control, isn’t it?” He tossed a quick peek over his shoulder at the creepy old barn barely showing through the brush on the edge of the property. Lost in thought, he rubbed his chin and lower lip with three fingers. He murmured almost to himself, “It’s always about the control.”

Noah and Rhyden both glanced toward the barn, then back to the boy. Rhyden raised an eyebrow; Noah just shrugged. *No clue, dude.*

Noah cleared his throat to regain the boy’s attention. “Who are you?”

“Oh, I’m…uh,” he stuttered. Sapphire eyes flicked up and to the right. “…Um, Patrick Gor…Collum.” He nodded his head a couple three times. “Yep, I’m Patrick Collum.”

“Okay, Patrick, do you work here?” A tinge of worry niggled at the back of Noah’s mind. *Not an uncommon name but not that common either.* The coincidences were starting to pile up, and Noah didn’t believe in coincidences.

“Yeah, for now anyway,” Patrick said. “I’m studying to be a taxidermist, though. Lot easier work than paving driveways and not nearly as hot as slaving away on a rooftop in the middle of a Texas summer.”

Rhyden stepped forward and held out a hand for the boy to shake. “I’m Texas Ranger Rhyden Trammell. This is Ranger Noah Morgan. We’re from F Company. Can we come in and speak to you for a moment?”

“Um, well, I’m supposed to be…uh, um…” He waved toward the parking lot.

Rhyden stepped closer and put a hand on the boy’s shoulder. He motioned toward the office. “Just for a moment. Is the office air conditioned? You’d probably like to cool off a bit, right?”

The boy shrugged and headed back toward the

metal building. “Sure, I guess.” He cast one longing-filled last look back at Ruby Lee. “Didn’t realize rangers made enough money to drive Hellcats. I may need to rethink my career path.” He stopped and laughed. “As if Da would really give me a choice.” He shook his head and led the way into the office.

Once inside the thankfully air-conditioned building, Rhyden continued questioning Patrick. “Who handles your scheduling? And your materials procurement?”

“Well, my Great-Grandda, Declan Gorman, owns the business but my Da, Seamus Gorman, pretty much runs things nowadays, so probably Da.” A tinge of bitterness crept into Patrick’s tone of voice. “I’m just the slave labor who does all the actual physical work around here.”

“I thought your last name was Collum? But your dad is named Gorman?” Rhyden asked.

All the blood in his body drained straight to Noah's feet. Icicles of panic pierced the knots lingering in his stomach. His heart pounded like a bird of prey trying to escape a cage. Before the boy could answer, Noah jumped in. “Declan Stuart Gorman?” He forced the question through a throat that was trying to snap closed. The words sounded strangled.

Rhyden tilted his head a bit. “You okay, buddy?”

Noah waved the question away. He cleared his throat and tried again. “Is your great-grandfather Declan Stuart Gorman? From Murphy Village, South Carolina? What are you doing in Texas?”

Patrick’s expression broadcast doubt. “How do you know Grandda’s middle name? And where he’s from? Do you know him?” His eyebrows drew together as he gave Noah a close inspection. "I didn't think Grandda had anything to do with the *peelers.*"

At Noah's narrowed-eyed look, crimson crept across Patrick's cheeks. "No offense intended," he said. "I just didn't know Grandda knew any Texas Rangers." The boy walked to the back of the office and shouted down the hallway. "Da? Grandda? Couple *guarda* here wanna talk to you."

Spinning on one heel, Noah couldn't get to the exit fast enough. *Why did I think moving twelve hundred miles was far enough to escape my past?*

"Can you handle this, Rhy? I need to… uh…" Coherent thought was impossible; his worst nightmare had come true. "I gotta…uh, take care of something."

"Sure, I've got this. I'll call one of the patrol deputies to pick me up and take me back to the office when I'm through." Rhyden slid a worried gaze up and down Noah. "Are you sure you're okay to drive? You look a little green around the gills."

"I'm fine." *Repeat a lie often enough, it becomes the truth, right?* "Just need air. Got to get out of here… for a minute."

Voices echoed down the hallway.

Get out. Get out now!

Noah glanced at the hallway that presumably led to other offices occupied by Declan and Seamus Gorman. Sweat formed on his face despite the cooled air in the building. His heart rate accelerated. His stomach turned.

"On second thought, I think I am going to be sick." He dove toward the front door and fumbled with the doorknob. His sweat-slicked hands slipped on the knob.

Rhyden reached past him to open the door. "Why don't you head on home? Are you sure you can drive?"

"Just need air, that's all."

"Get home and have your paramedic girlfriend perform another examination on you. You really don't look good. I'll call dispatch and catch a ride with one of the deputies. This shouldn't take long. Catch you later."

Noah stared longingly at freedom a few feet beyond the door before turning back to face his partner. "Are you sure?"

"Yeah, sure. I've got this." Rhyden took his phone out of his pocket and called the office. He spoke a few words and hung up, giving Noah a thumbs up. "Deputy Miller is right around the corner. He'll be here in three minutes. Go on, get out of here before you upchuck all over the carpet. I'll call you later." He examined Noah's face. "Or do you need me to drive you home? We can always come back here later."

The last thing Noah wanted to do was come back here. "No, I can drive. Probably just something I ate."

"Well, if you're sure—"

Come on, come on, come on. Let me go.

The sound of footsteps drew closer. "I'm sure." Gratefully, Noah escaped the office just as Rhyden turned back to face the counter. As the door swung closed behind him, Noah heard Rhyden say, "Good afternoon. Mr. Gorman, I presume?"

"Aye, I'm Declan Gorman."

Chapter Twelve

As Noah headed to his car, movement near the old barn caught his attention. After scanning the area to make sure no one was watching, he eased down a beaten path in the overgrown grass that led to the barn. Dried weeds crackled beneath his feet; stickers clung to his jeans. With thoughts of discovery stretching his nerves piano-wire tight, he kept his head on a continuous swivel.

He crept forward, his skin steaming from the heat. The closer he came, the more insistent his internal radar pinged. Within a few feet of the building, his danger meter went off the charts. Adrenaline mixed with fear had the hair on his arms standing straight up—just like walking through an electrical storm. Dropping into a crouch, he duck-walked to one of the dirt-encrusted windows. After rising to peek in, he discovered the inside of the windows blacked out, likely from spray paint. He tried squinting through tiny scratches in the paint but saw nothing in the darkened interior. The putrid, sickly-sweet odor seeping from the barn triggered his gag reflex.

One step at a time, pausing and stopping to avoid detection, he worked his way around the corner of the barn toward the door. Just as he stretched his hand out to grasp the door handle, a voice from the past rose up. And paralyzed him.

"Boy, are you still screwing around out here? I told you the other day, work comes first."

Though Noah couldn't see the speaker, he recognized the voice of Seamus Gorman. From his left, footsteps crunched through the dry grass, coming closer, heading directly for the barn.

No. No way. He dropped flat to the ground and, using infinitesimally small movements, belly crawled toward the tree line. *I can't let him see me.* After what seemed an hour, he reached the cover of the brush. Standing, he wiped dried grass, red dirt, and sand burrs from his clothes, ignoring the sharp pain from the burrs.

Working to remain undetected, he slowly and carefully made his way back to his car. He fumbled the key fob when he tried to open the Hellcat, almost dropping it in the dirt. After finally getting the door open, he folded his long frame into the driver's seat. Ignoring the seatbelt, as usual, he threw the transmission into reverse.

No way. No way. No way. I had to be imagining that voice. Plenty of other people have Irish accents.

Who happen to be named Seamus?

And work for a fly-by-night paving company?

His stomach rolled. After doing a fast K-turn, he shifted into drive, dumped the clutch, and stalled the Hellcat. *Damn it!*

He slammed his hands against the steering wheel, took a deep calming breath, and restarted the car. Methodically, he put the car in gear. He swallowed hard and scanned the parking lot before pulling out onto the county road. In the rearview mirror he saw the kid who just a few minutes ago drooled over Ruby Lee heading toward the derelict barn.

Something about the young man, and the blacked-out windows on the barn, gave him the heebie-jeebies. His skin crawled just thinking about them. He wasn't sure what, but there was something horribly off about that kid. Much more than the fact that he lied through his teeth about his name.

His mind set up a running argument with his gut. *What the hell am I going to do if this is my Declan?* His mind said, *it can't be the same one. Travelers trade names like they change socks. Hell, how many names did you have over the first twenty years of your life? Really, what are the odds they would end up here? You chose this part of Texas because it wasn't clan territory. Not even close.*

You wish, his gut taunted. *You knew that voice. There are too many coincidences for it not to be who you fear it is.*

Realizing he was still idling at the end of the parking lot, Noah scanned left, then right, and then left again before pulling out onto the deserted county road. Mood darkened by ugly memories and conflicting thoughts, he accelerated, then cursed as the car bounced on the washboard surface of the road. Shifting rapidly through the gears, he drove way too fast for the road conditions. The car fishtailed, sliding sideways in the loose rocks on the county road. He didn't care. He had to get away.

A cloud of red dust followed him as he sped down the road. Gravel pinged against the dust shield beneath the car. By the time he arrived at the main highway, his breathing had returned to normal; his heart rate slowed to normal range. The urge to vomit no longer tickled the back of his throat. His hands steadied on the wheel.

Maybe he'd regained some bit of control.

For the next hour, he drove mindlessly, paying little attention to where he was going, following the whims of the road. Eventually, he found himself on the highway outside of Devine, a small city that featured the Triple C, the best steakhouse around. Seeing the signs for the restaurant reminded him of Cat. They had met at the Triple C, a blind double date set up by Cat's paramedic partner, Jim, and his flavor of the month who just happened to work for the sheriff's office. They'd had an amazing time. Jim's date, however, moved on long ago, no big surprise.

Cat.

His breath caught in his throat. *What would she do if she knew the truth? Broken toy, broken, toy, broken toy.* The taunting chorus echoed inside his head.

His heart sped up again. Sticky patches of sweat formed beneath his arms, staining his shirt. Beads of sweat rolled down his spine, creeping beneath the waistband of his jeans. He could smell his own fear.

A homeless man sat on the concrete embankment with his back leaning against one of the graffiti-covered pillars supporting the overpass of IH-35. Long, greasy gray hair covered his face. Noah braked to a stop next to him and rolled down his window. The rumble of traffic thundering overhead echoed in the darkened space. He held his badge out the window for the man to see and motioned for him to approach the car.

The man rolled to his feet and stumbled over. The smell of old, cheap whiskey and unwashed body assaulted Noah as the man drew closer. The scent overpowered the smell of fear.

"Sir," he asked, "what are you doing here?"

The man shrugged, not making eye contact with Noah. In a raspy voice rusty from lack of use, he said, "Staying away from people." He tossed rapid glances over his shoulder in each direction while rubbing his hands in a washing motion. "It is not safe."

"What's not safe? Are you in danger?"

The man briefly met Noah's eyes. A shrill giggle escaped him, echoing off the concrete walls of the underpass. He glanced away quickly. His agitation increased. "No, not me. Safety is an illusion. Not safe for me to be around people right now." He shifted his weight from one foot to another. "Not safe. Not safe for them. Too many big bugs. Demons and metal monsters. And the crying, always with the crying." The man peered up at Noah, bloodshot eyes filled with sadness. "It never stops."

"Do you have any identification on you, sir?"

"No, sir. I was riding a wooden rocking chair with my gringo porch monkey until those big-eyed metal locusts from the bottomless pit buzzed down and chased me off." He kept his head bent low, avoiding eye contact. His hands tugged at his hair, making it stand out at weird angles. He resembled Albert Einstein—if Einstein didn't bathe and lived under a highway bridge in South Texas. A low rumble issued from the man's stomach.

Noah's stomach replied with a grumble of its own. "Are you hungry?"

The man raised his chin and tilted his head to the side in a curious bird-like listening motion. He finally made eye contact, studying Noah for a few minutes before replying. "Guess I could eat."

"Stay here. I'll be right back."

Across from the steakhouse stood a convenience store/gas station with a fast food joint attached. Noah passed through the drive-through and ordered several large cheeseburgers, a couple of large fries, two sodas, and two large chocolate shakes. He returned to the underpass with the food and parked the Hellcat on the shoulder.

The homeless man stared at him in wide-eyed awe as he approached with the bags of food. “Huh.”

“Huh what?”

“You returned.”

“Told you I would.”

Noah handed him the bags of food and drinks and one of the shakes. He kept the second shake for himself and sat on the concrete embankment to drink it. Ignoring the rough surface beneath his somewhat bony butt, he propped his elbows on his knees and watched as the homeless man fished a napkin from the bag and spread it primly over his lap before lifting out a box of hot, greasy French fries.

The man noticed Noah watching him. “Mother always said one cannot eat unless one has one’s napkin properly covering one’s lap.” He took a drink of the chocolate shake. An expression of rapture illuminated his face. He folded his paper napkin as if it were made of the finest linen and placed it on the ground to his left. He stood and offered Noah a courtly bow, then extended a grimy hand. As if just noticing how dirty it was, he pulled it back and wiped it on his shirt before extending it again. “Arthur J. Panzer the Third, at your service, sir.”

“So, Mr. Panzer, what did you mean it’s not safe for you to be around people?”

"Please, sir, call me Trey."

"Okay, Trey. Is someone after you?"

"Eggs have no business dancing with stones."

Panzer dropped back onto the concrete embankment. He picked up the napkin and ceremoniously draped it across his lap. He ate a few more fries and several bites of burger as he appeared to contemplate the question. Glancing at Noah from the corner of his eyes, he said, "No, sir. I do not mean it is unsafe for me. I mean it is not safe for all the others trapped in a prison of flesh."

"Care to explain that statement?"

"Not particularly," Panzer said and returned to his meal.

"You know you can't stay here under this bridge, right? Devine has an anti-vagrancy ordinance. They can and will put you in jail. Do you have a place to go? Anyone I can call for you?"

Mr. Panzer thought for a moment. "I am uncertain. Those hellish locusts bearing the faces of men and tails of scorpions keep buzzing my home. The screaming and crying from the haunted house keep me up at night. I am afraid the aliens will vanquish me if I return to my domicile."

What the hell does that mean?

"You know the old saying, right? You don't have to go home, but you can't stay here."

"I suppose if those dubious characters referring to themselves as Travelers can make movies and the ghosts do not hamper them, then I shall be safe enough. Correct? If only the aliens will refrain from visiting. And those damn insects, noisy, noisy, metal dragonflies. Bright lights and noise, I swear.

Grandfather always declared one cannot skirmish inanimate objects successfully, so I have refrained from engaging them in a melee. I vacated the premises prior to the metal insects discovering my existence. Tell me, sir, who creates bugs that loud, anyway?"

Travelers, again? Really?

Panzer exhaled heavily. Slowly, he gathered the refuse from his meal and placed it neatly back into the paper sack. "But I digress. To answer your question, yes, I surmise it will be safe enough for me to proceed home. After all, my presence is required no other place. Based on the cycle of the moon, the aliens should not return for a week or more. Father always said if one must be stupid, one must be tough. Time enough to test the theory, eh?"

"And where is home?"

"Over in Bennett County, of course. Redus Crossing to be exact."

Finished with his shake, Noah stood up and brushed off the back of his jeans. He thought about the pristine black leather interior of his precious Hellcat, then surveyed Mr. Panzer's filthy rags.

"What the hell? It will clean," he muttered, half out-loud. "At least black doesn't show dirt." He gestured to the passenger side of his car. "Climb in. I'm headed that direction and will give you a ride."

Panzer rubbed his hands together before clasping them prayer-like in front of his chest. "Perhaps we could stop along the way and pick up some brown bottle bravado? I mean, after all, why not? A miniscule portion of liquid courage to help me make it through the frightful night?"

Noah rolled his eyes. "Why not indeed?"

****

A tap on the door drew Noah's attention. He looked up from the stack of files on his desk. "Hey, bud, you feeling better?" Rhyden lounged against the door frame, a white bangora hat dangling from the fingers of his left hand. Noah shrugged as he sorted through the papers in the top file folder. "Yeah, I guess. Must have been something I ate." He closed the folder and leaned back in his chair. "Get anything helpful talking to the pavers?"

"Other than this Patrick kid is obsessed with your ride? Not really. I got the impression the old man Declan character was hiding something, but I don't know what. Never did meet the kid's father. I think he's the one I probably need to talk to. The old man just wanted to know if I was there investigating a complaint about his crew's work."

"Since when do Texas Rangers handle labor disputes?"

"That's almost verbatim what I asked him. I did discover he claims to use a quarry down near Carrizo Springs, maybe the one up near Von Ormy. Of course, he also claimed they could have used material left over from previous jobs. He really had no way of knowing what they used where."

"Convenient."

"That's what I thought."

"You do know the chances of the kid's name actually being Patrick Collum are slim to none, right?"

"I picked up on that, too. Kid was lying through his too-white, too-bleached teeth. Man, he reminds me of someone. Haven't figured out who yet but there's just something about him. Something familiar." Rhyden paused as if thinking, then shook his head as if to clear it. “On the way back to the office, I called the quarries the old man Declan mentioned and guess what? Neither of them knew anything about this paving company nor are they familiar with a Declan Gorman nor a Seamus Gorman for that matter.”

“No surprise there,” said Noah. “What did the old guy look like?”

“I don’t know.” Rhyden shrugged. “Like an old man. What does his appearance have to do with anything? You don’t suspect him of being the secret boyfriend, do you?”

“Was he a blond about six foot tall? Scar over his left eye? How old was he?”

Rhyden advanced into the office and leaned his hip against the edge of Noah’s desk. “Okay, what’s going on? Since I’ve seen some of the things you eat, I know for a fact you have a cast-iron stomach. I’ve never known you to skip out on an interview before. It’s kind of hard to play good cop, bad cop with only one cop and not look schizophrenic—which by the way is not at all helpful in the grand scheme of interrogations.”

Noah spun in his chair, reaching for another folder on the credenza behind his desk. Fear tied another knot on top of the one already in residence inside his stomach. “I don’t know what you’re talking about. I told you I had another lead to check out.”

“Uh, no, you didn’t.” Rhyden raised his right eyebrow. “What was the lead?” When no answer came, he continued, “Seriously? You are a lousy liar. How long have we been friends? Who was there for me through the whole Edwards fiasco? Something’s wrong. I’d have to be blind not to see it. It’s my turn to be there for you." He paused. "If you'll let me."

The memory of Rhyden teetering on the precipice of self-destruction as his world fell apart around him surfaced. At the time the poor slob got slammed with one knock after another. Like the partner who turned on him during an undercover sting and having to shoot same partner in self-defense. Then having his wife, Cara the bitch, abandon Rhyden and the girls before getting herself murdered. Not the best times in his friend's life considering. Rhy even spent a few days in jail under suspicion of murder.

Noah turned back to face him. "You haven't mentioned Edwards in a really long time. How are you doing with all of it? Still seeing Dr. Napoli?"

"Oh, no, you don't. Don't try to change the subject. We're talking about you, not me."

"Hey, you brought it up."

"And I'm shutting it down. I'm fine, and yes, Dr. Napoli is still helping. End of discussion. Now what the hell is going on with you? Spill it."

Noah rubbed a hand over his eyes. He squeezed his temples as if to force a migraine out of his head. "I've just got some shit going on right now. Personal stuff. I'll try to keep it from spilling over into work."

"No, I don't know," Rhyden said, "because you won't talk to me, won't let me help you."

"Rhy, I appreciate it. Really, I do. But this is something I need to handle on my own."

Noah grabbed his keys off the desk, stood, and headed for the door. As he walked out, he said, "Give me a little space, okay?"

Chapter Thirteen

With his father at his side, Patrick tugged the right-hand door of the metal shipping container open. A shriek of rusty hinges split the humid air. Whimpers and scampering noises echoed from the shadows within. Patrick flipped on his flashlight. The batteries were weak, and its sickly, yellow gleam did little to cut through the gloom. Darkness lurked in every corner.

He unlocked the left-hand door and with a grunt shoved it open, banishing all except for the farthest shadows. A dozen steel cages with plywood floors lined the walls. The stench of urine, feces, and fear exploded from the space. Huddled at the back of each pen, except for one, sat a disheveled, frightened child.

"…ten, eleven." Seamus slowly counted the children. He stopped at the last, empty kennel and turned on his son with a scowl. "I see you still haven't found me a replacement."

Patrick bit the inside of his cheek and silently counted to five. Between clenched teeth, he ground out, "I'm working on it."

"Work faster. We're almost out of time. And clean this place up." He gestured at the cages. "None of our buyers would want something like this in his bed."

Behind his father's back, Patrick glowered.

"Don't glare at me." Seamus turned to face his son. "The auction is in ten days. We need this merchandise ready to sell, and we're still short one. Are you going to be able to find me a replacement in time?"

"As far as I know, yes."

His voice deceptively calm and cool, Seamus asked, "As far as you know?"

Disregarding the telltale muscle tic in his father's cheek that warned Patrick he needed to be careful, the boy replied, "Well, I can't know any further that that, now can I?"

"Boy," Seamus growled. Raising a fist, he closed the distance. "Don't make me strike you."

"Sir, yes, sir," Patrick barked and mock-saluted his father.

Seamus' features tightened. His fists clenched at his sides. "I really don't need any of your smart-ass shit right now. Do you not realize what is at stake here? Do you know who these buyers are? Ever hear of the *Hijós de Yucatán?* They make MS-13 look like pussies. Do you really want to piss off people like that? Because I sure as hell don't. Pull up your socks and find a replacement. Today."

Patrick followed his old man as he stalked from the container. After locking the door behind him, the heat and humidity swamped his lungs. *Damn, I hate South Texas. I could drown just standing here.*

When considering his father's parting words, a lazy smile turned up the corner of his lips. *Maybe I don't care if your buyers get pissed off. Maybe they will make you disappear for me.*

****

For a change, Noah beat Cat home and did his best to shake off the shitty workday. *Tonight's the night.* Excitement tinged with a touch of fear fluttered in his chest while the same old refrain echoed in his brain. *Broken toy, broken toy, broken toy.*

He shook off the fear and jumped into a hot shower. There was a lot to do and a noticeably short time to accomplish it in. After toweling off, he dressed in a pair of soft, well-fitted denim jeans and her favorite shirt—a faded chambray with pearl snaps. Moving quickly through the house, he shut off all the lights and lit candles. Soon the scent of birds of paradise, her favorite, filled the air.

Headlights carved a path up the driveway. The engine shut off, and the lights faded to dark. No car door opened. Soft music flowed from the surround sound speakers in the living room. He waited near the front door. And waited. And waited. No one came to the door. He cracked the curtain and peered outside.

Yes, it was Cat's jeep sitting in the driveway, but she didn't climb out. *Maybe she's on the phone.* More time passed. She made no move to exit the vehicle, but he didn't see the glow of a cell phone either. She appeared to just be sitting there. Finally, as he was about to step out the door, she opened her car door.

Noah smiled. He took in the way her cinnamon espresso hair escaped from the braid she twisted it into each morning before leaving for her shift. The tendrils drifted down, framing her face, drawing attention to her high cheekbones. His eyes caressed the curves the tactical shirt and pants of her paramedic uniform couldn't hide. *How did I get so lucky?*

Cat paused on the sidewalk in front of the house, her jump bag filled with emergency medical supplies slung over one shoulder. Scanning the front of the house, she waved at him, letting him know she'd caught him spying on her through the crack in the curtains. A tired smile flitted across her face. She straightened her spine, thrust her shoulders back, and headed to the door.

Before she turned the knob, Noah flung the door open and swept her into his arms. Her jump bag slid from her shoulder and landed on the porch floor with a heavy thump. He kissed her in greeting. The taste of her kiss sent excitement sizzling through his veins. His nerves lit with pleasure. Heat raced through his entire body. He deepened the kiss. It had been too long since they had really spent any time together. He planned to remedy that tonight.

She pulled back. Noah dropped a kiss on top of her head before he reluctantly released his hold on her. His voice lowered like molten chocolate. “You’re home.”

“Yes, goofball, I am. Now let me come in and shut the door before the mosquitos carry us away. I need to get off my feet. I’m exhausted.”

Before she could take a single step, Noah swept her up and carried her into the house, kicking the bag into the living room in front of him. He shouldered the front door shut behind him before depositing her on the sofa and propping her feet on a throw pillow. He stepped back and gave a little bow. “Stay put,” he said as he headed into the kitchen. “Do you want a glass of red or white wine?”

“Um…no wine. I…I don’t think it would be a good idea.”

He stuck his head back around the corner. “No wine?” Surprise tinged his voice. “You always want wine after a long day.”

She placed a hand on her stomach. “Not tonight. Maybe a ginger ale or a lemon-lime soda?”

"Your wish is my command." Noah returned to the living room and handed her a bottle of soda and a glass of ice with a straw, just the way she liked it. He took time to really look at her. "Are you okay? You look a little pale. Beautiful, but pale."

"Just a little queasy," she murmured. "Noah, I need…"

"Hold that thought." He dropped her feet onto the couch as he hopped up. "I'll be right back." He dashed out of the room.

In the bedroom, he rummaged through the top drawer of his dresser, searching for the engagement ring. It wasn't there. He opened the second drawer. Tossed T-shirts around. No ring. Starting to panic, he jerked open the third drawer. The tiny blue box, snuggled in the corner of the drawer beneath his rolled socks, winked up at him. His shoulders sagged in relief. He reached in, grabbed the box, and opened it.

Empty. No ring.

Oh, crap. Where is it? His eyes darted around the room. He dashed to the laundry basket, flinging dirty clothes left and right as he dug for the last pair of pants he wore. Images of the diamond ring devoured by the washing machine flooded his mind. His pulse pounded. He collapsed to the floor as his fingers brushed the hard, circular object in the front pocket. *Thank God, I didn't wash it.*

When he returned to the living room, the engagement ring nestled safely in the bottom of his front jeans' pocket. He tugged a drowsy Cat to her feet to stand before him. He took both her hands in his. *Here goes nothing.*

"Cat, sweetheart, you light up my world. You are

my universe. I can't imagine my life without you in it. Do you know where I want to be at the end of this year?"

She tugged her hands from his grasp to cover a yawn. She ran her hands through her hair, releasing it from its braid. Befuddlement shone from her face. Her eyebrows squished together, and she cast her gaze around the room as if searching for the answer. "Where do you want to be?" She shrugged. "I don't know. Out of debt?"

Noah snagged her left hand. "Put your hand in my pocket." The diamond ring weighed a ton where it waited for her at the bottom of his pocket. He tried to guide her hand.

"What?" She snatched her hand away. "Babe, I'm exhausted. Too tired to play one of your perverted games. It's been a really long day. And I feel like crap."

"Please?"

Cat sighed. "Fine." As she reached for his pocket, an alarm tone split the air. She turned and tugged her radio from the waistband of her cargo pants.

The radio crackled to life. "All units, on duty and off, respond to 1292 FM 473 outside of Bigfoot. Structure fire. Mass casualties. Repeat all units respond to 1292 FM 473 outside of Bigfoot. Explosion and structure fire with multiple injured. Air life helicopters en route."

She shoved the radio back onto its clip, slid her feet back into her boots, and grabbed her jump bag. As she twisted her hair back into a braid, she dropped a quick kiss on Noah's lips. "Sorry, babe, gotta run."

****

"Put your hand in my pocket?" Noah banged his

head against the wall. Really? What the hell kind of marriage proposal was that? No wonder she ran out of here. She thought he was a pervert. She even said so.

"Way to go, dummy. Scare off the love of your life." *Useless broken toy. You can't even propose right.*

A memory of another almost proposal flooded his mind. He turned and slid his back down the wall. Sitting on the floor, he wrapped his arms around his knees and curled his shoulders inward. Throat bobbing, he swallowed rapidly, fighting off the memories to no avail. They transported him back in time.

The memory of prom lingered in the back of his mind. The lights, the music, Maeve Byrne's unique scent of incense over amber and pine. The feel of her curves pressed against his chest. Long, strawberry-blonde hair curled about her shoulders, fell to the middle of her back. Her laughing eyes of sparkling green flecked with gold danced with mirth. Pale porcelain skin, high cheekbones dusted with pale freckles—his Maeve. Noah could still hear her breathless "I love you" as it brushed the inner shell of his ear. She was the center of his teenaged world. He whistled a cheery tune as he policed the shop parking lot for cigarette butts, picking them up and putting them in the rusty, old coffee can.

"Hey, String Bean." His older cousin waved him down as he walked back into Grandda's shop. "Got a message for you. The girl wants you to meet her at the lake tonight. Who knows? It might be your lucky night."

Snorts of raucous laughter filled the room. Heat crept up Noah's cheeks. The blush made his cousin and his cousin's buddies laugh harder.

He didn't think the day would ever end. He drove

up Edgefield road to the parking area near the lake. Before opening the door of his muscle car, he dragged his hands down his blue jeans, wiping sweat from his palms.

Grabbing the flowers off the passenger seat, stepped out of the car. The sharp corners of a small ring box poked his leg through the pocket of his jeans. Inside the box rested a tiny, opal and diamond-chip promise ring. His heart fluttered, almost skipping a beat. In two years, when he turned eighteen, he would buy Maeve a real diamond, an engagement ring. For now, the promise ring would have to do.

Walking down the path to the lake, he spotted a trail of clothing. His hands tingled. Heat rushed up his neck into his face. The thought of going all the way for the first time, especially with the girl he loved, stole his breath. The flower stems made his palms itch. His pulse raced.

Slowly, he followed the trail of clothing, thinking Maeve left him a map to the treasure. He continued on the path, picking up pieces of clothes as he went.

The sun was dropping beneath the horizon. The trees became silhouettes. He opened the gate, slipped through. With each piece of clothing he'd collected, his jeans grew tighter. Walking became uncomfortable, but he picked up the pace. As he approached the lake, he heard the splash of water. Maeve's lilting laughter split the air, calling to him.

Noah rounded the final curve in the path and skidded to a stop. His knees buckled. Her clothing dropped from his right hand. Flowers tumbled from his left. Maeve's naked body glimmered golden in the setting sun.

But she wasn't alone.

Bile boiled up the back of his throat. His cousin, Seamus, smirked at him over her shoulder as he continued to plunge into her. Noah turned and fled; his heart broken.

Noah forced himself from the past. Cat was nothing like Maeve. Cat loved him. He walked through the house, blowing out candles while heading for his in-home office. He turned on the light and sat down in front of his laptop. *May as well do some research on the case.*

Before pulling up his current case file on Alyssa Sanders, he gave in to curiosity. Logging into the Texas Crime Information Center, TCIC for short, he typed in the name Seamus Gorman followed by a date of birth. The picture that came up on the screen matched the image that haunted Noah's dreams. The man was a little older, a bit more worn, but the same face, the same mocking grin, sneered at him from the computer.

He quickly pushed aside the images of Seamus with Maeve at the lake and scanned the available information, noting the current address to be White Settlement, a town northwest of Fort Worth, a good five and half hours away from Bennett County. Noah exhaled noisily in relief. They were no longer in South Carolina, but they weren't in South Texas, either.

Congratulating himself on his good luck, he read on—and was soon cursing the air blue. Right there in black and white: Seamus Gorman received a speeding ticket two days ago, issued by a Bennett County deputy. The Travelers—his Travelers—were here.

"What the hell am I going to do? If Seamus finds me, I'm done—kaput, through, finished. My life will be over—my job, my home, Cat—all gone."

Noah reached into the bottom drawer of his desk and drew out a dark green glass bottle and grabbed a lone highball glass he kept stashed in the drawer for circumstances such as this. "Fuck it." He shoved the glass back in the drawer and opened the Irish whiskey, drinking straight from the bottle. *How many times had Seamus tried to kill him? Three? Four? Seven? Yeah, lucky seven.*

The last time, Noah let him believe he had succeeded. For a fleeting time, he almost had. If it hadn't been for his lucky spark plug, he would have. He let the alcohol sweep him back to the last attempt, back when he was known as Ferrell Gorman.

Bright lights speared his eyes. Metal shrieked. Glass shattered. The jacked-up truck pushed him over the embankment. Water rose over his head. Darkness swallowed him. Pulse pounding, his chest ached. Colored spots danced in front of his eyes. He was drowning.

Grabbing a fouled spark plug from the morning's tune-up that he hadn't taken the time to throw away, Noah smashed the porcelain against the vehicle's windshield, shattering it. He kicked his way out the broken glass, clawed his way to the surface, and sucked in a whooping, painful gasp of air.

Laying on the muddy bank, spark plug still clutched in his fist, he watched as flames flickered on the surface of the water. The boy known as Ferrell died in that river. In his place, Noah Morgan was born.

And now, Noah was in danger. Worse than that, all he'd worked for, all he'd become, and all those he loved were in danger.

Chapter Fourteen

Bree stared out the kitchen window. A storm rolled in. Lightning flashed in the distance, splitting the night sky. Too busy reliving the last fight with her dad, she didn't see it. Behind her, Sam entered the room and went directly to the refrigerator. "I'm hungry, and there's never anything to eat here." She slammed the fridge door closed.

"I feel for you," Bree mumbled. "I just can't reach you."

Sam tilted her head to one side, a puzzled expression on her face. "What?"

Bree turned away from the window. "Nothing, okay, just nothing."

"Where's Dad?"

"Who the hell cares? He's probably at work. Isn't that where he always is?"

"Whoa. What's wrong with you?"

"There's nothing wrong with me. Why don't you mind your own damn business?" Outside, the wind picked up, rattling the windows. Raindrops drummed against the roof.

"Hey." Sam walked over to stand beside Bree. "You're my sister. You are my business."

Bree turned away. Her eyes filled with tears. "Dad grounded me." She plopped into a kitchen chair and dropped her head on the table. Tears fell.

"So? Dad grounds me all the time." Sam joined Bree at the table and shrugged. "I just do what I want anyway. It's not like he's ever home to find out."

Bree brushed the tears from her cheeks. *Why the hell not?* She threw her arms around her sister. "Thank you, Sam. You're brilliant."

"Of course, I am." Sam winked and grabbed a bag of chips out of the pantry. Plastic rattled as she pulled them open.

Bree picked up her phone and began texting.

—Meet me at the corner in five?—

Her phone dinged. *—What corner?—*

Her fingers flew across the keyboard. *—Duh, our corner. Maple and Redbud—*

—Thought your dad grounded you—

Bree growled. *—Do you want to meet or not?—*

A few minutes passed before the response appeared on her screen. *—Okay but 'Stang in shop. Driving uncle's Buick—*

Bree grabbed a chip from Sam's bag.

"Hey!" Sam protested pulling the bag away.

Bree grinned and asked Sam, "Will you keep an eye on Maddie for me? And cover for me with Dad if he should ever come home? Just tell him I'm spending the night with Jenn."

"Why should I? What are you going to do?" Grabbing a soda and a glass of ice, she dropped back into a chair at the kitchen table.

Bree folded her hands, begging. "Please? I didn't tell Dad about your weed. I'm going out."

"All night?" Slouched in the chair, she cracked open the soda and poured it over the ice. "Don't you have exams tomorrow?" She grabbed her bag of chips, then sat straight up. “Wait a minute.” She narrowed her eyes, pointed at Bree with a chip. “You’re not going out with that two-timing asshole, are you?” She slammed the bag of chips down on the table. “Bree?” A warning frosted her tone of voice.

Heat creeping up her neck, she dropped her gaze. “Aren’t you the one who’s always telling me to get a life? I’m getting a life.” She turned to face her younger sister. Her eyes pleaded. “Please? I’ll be at school in the morning. No one will ever know. Cross my heart.”

“You promise?” At Bree’s nod, Sam said, “Okay, but you are going to owe me one. A big one.”

****

“Come on. Let’s go. Pick up the pace.”

Seamus gestured toward the cattle trailer waiting to be hooked up to a stolen three-quarter ton pickup. Smears of mud obscured the license plate on the truck. Sheets of plywood lined the inside of the trailer, blocking out any prying eyes who might try to get a look-see at the cargo inside. “Load them up. With any luck, people will think we’re hauling blackbuck antelope or some other exotic animal.”

Patrick paused in mid-stride, an unconscious eleven-year-old girl in his arms. He raised his chin. Icicles dripped from his tone. “And what exactly, Da, does it look like I’m doing? Picking daisies?”

“Do it faster. I had to guess at the dosages. The sedation could wear off before we get them all loaded.” As if in response to Seamus’s words, the child in Patrick’s arms stirred, moaning lightly. Patrick continued to the trailer. He carried the girl inside, then returned to the shipping container for another captive.

Seamus circled the truck and trailer, checking

lights. "When you're done, get over here and help test these turn indicators. Last thing we need is for an overzealous *peeler* to stop us."

Patrick dumped the last child unceremoniously onto the floor of the trailer. "There." He stepped out and brushed his hands against his jeans before shutting and securing the trailer gate. "That's the last one."

"Good. Come on. Check these lights. I want out of here before those rangers come snooping around."

An evil chuckle escaped Patrick's lips. He opened the text messaging app on his phone. The cursor blinked, waiting for his message to Roc.

With one hand, he typed —*Now*— and hit Send.

He tucked his phone in his pocket and met Seamus' eyes with a smug grin. "I wouldn't be too worried about the rangers, or any other law enforcement, for the next few hours." His gaze turned inward. *All that time sucking up to that pathetic loser is going to pay off.* A sly smile slipped across his features. "I have an inkling they will be a wee bit too busy to worry about turn signals on a livestock trailer."

****

Killough High School consisted of a two-story, red brick central structure with sweeping wings that had been added on at various times as the population of Bennett County grew.

English and history classes were taught in the main building. Theatre, arts, music, and the gymnasium were in the right-hand wing. Science and math classes took place in the left-hand wing. These wings were connected by covered, paved walkways passing through the courtyards between them.

Directly behind the main structure stood the

cafetorium—a combination cafeteria and auditorium. Next to that was the band hall and practice field for the marching band. Across an open field stood the athletic compound consisting of the football field, baseball and softball fields, and the fieldhouse. A sense of urgency blanketed the parking lot of Killough High School, ramping up Noah's heart rate. Heat reflected from the cracked, black pavement seeped through the soles of his custom boots. Car doors slammed. Exhaust drifted from the tailpipes of running vehicles.

Noah and Rhyden raced toward a knot of men studying a set of blueprints near an armed, tactical assault vehicle. The huge clock on the front wall of the center of the building read 1:39 p.m.

Rhyden scanned the groups of students already evacuated, his focus jumping from group to group in search of Bree and Sam. "I don't see my girls."

Noah's knees buckled. *Not the girls. Please, Lord, not the girls.* "What do we have here?" he asked Sheriff Preston.

"So far it appears to be a hoax. We received a call about several suspicious packages in the gym, but we haven't seen or heard anything yet. We started evacuating the students and staff from the classrooms closest to the gym."

The area swarmed with first responders. County deputies, city police officers, constables, and state troopers wrapped in Kevlar vests scurried to and fro. Radio chatter filled the air. Firefighters and medics hovered on the outskirts of the lot, restrained from entering the scene by Incident Command personnel. Air life helicopters swooped across the football field. Waiting.

****

"Okay, kids, pop quiz." Mr. Routh, Bree's biology teacher, grinned. "On the front lab tables, I have stations set up. Ten in total. In each tray you will find an internal organ from a fetal pig. You must identify the organ and give a brief description of its function. Working in pairs, you have one hour to finish."

Bree checked the clock hanging on the wall above Mr. Routh's desk—1:29 p.m. Chairs scooted over the floor as students paired up.

Ding! Ding! All over the classroom text notifications began ringing. "What's going on here?" Routh asked. "Haven't I told you not to have cell phones in class?"

Ding! Mr. Routh's cell phone notification rang.

"Hey, Mr. Routh," Malcolm, a junior with attitude, popped off, "aren't you supposed to turn your cell phone off in class?" The class erupted in laughter.

"Funny, Malcom. Is this some kind of joke?" the teacher asked.

All the students in class had their cell phones out, comparing text messages. Every phone said the same thing. —*Boom!*—

The room erupted in chatter.

"Okay, folks, calm down. Put your phones away. You're wasting time."

Bree gathered her paper and pen and met her best friend, Jenn, at station number three where a grayish-green gelatinous mass lay in the silver specimen tray.

Jenn poked it with the end of her pen. It wiggled. "Gross."

Bree giggled. "Quit playing with it. Large intestine, right?"

Her friend poked it again. "I think so. It's supposed to absorb water from the undigested food and get rid of waste."

"Sounds good to me." Bree scratched the answer down on her notebook paper before she and Jenn stood up to advance to the next station.

"Tick-tock, people," Routh reminded them. "You now have forty-five minutes to complete the quiz."

Pop, pop! Pop, pop, pop!

As screams echoed down the hallway, the fire alarm shrieked.

"What's going on out here?" The biology teacher opened the door. Bree watched in stunned disbelief as dark red blood and gray brain matter sprayed from the back of his skull. He collapsed, falling to the floor to the sound of singing.

Pop, pop, pop! Boom! Boom! Her stomach clenched. Bile boiled at the back of her throat.

Richard, a senior Army JROTC cadet in the class, grabbed Mr. Routh. A bullet flashed past his head. Two more bullets plowed through the open doorway. The girl standing next to Bree screamed and clapped her hands over her ears to block out the sounds of the gunfire.

Richard dragged the teacher into the classroom; a trail of blood and brain matter smeared the floor. He slammed the door shut. "Down! Everyone get down." Twisting the lock on the doorknob, he shoved the teacher's desk in front of the door. Several other students rushed over and helped pile furniture in front of the door, blocking the path of the shooter.

Bree rushed to Mr. Routh's side. His skin was cold to the touch. No pulse. No respirations. Tears clogged her throat. She raised her frightened gaze to Richard and shook her head.

Bullets pounded against the door. One passed through, hitting Richard in the leg. He screamed. A loud thud hit the door, jarring it in the frame. The shooter tried to bulldoze into the room. Several boys pushed back. After several unsuccessful attempts, the shooter's footsteps echoed off down the hallway.

Keeping low to the floor, Bree scrambled closer to Richard. She eased him to the floor. Hands shaking, she grabbed a wad of paper towels and applied pressure to the wound. Warm, slippery blood pulsed through her fingers. The coppery odor flooded her senses. Saliva filled the back of her mouth. Her stomach roiled. Swallowing back a sob, she called out, "I need help here." She tried to breathe through her mouth to keep from vomiting.

"Here." Another student ripped off his T-shirt. "Use this."

Bree plucked her pocketknife from her boot and cut strips off the t-shirt. She wrapped the strips around Richard's leg. Color faded from his face. Another student grabbed a wooden dowel and helped her twist the shirt into a tourniquet. "Come on, Richard. Stay with us."

He passed out.

The shooter returned. Another barrage of bullets pounded into the door, followed by a physical assault. The barricade could not hold against this kind of pressure. Bree grabbed her phone. It slipped from her bloody fingers. She wiped her hands on her jeans and grabbed it again to dial her dad. It went straight to voicemail. *Damn it.*

She switched to her text app and thumbed down to her dad's number. Her fingers flew across the screen.

—Active shooter. High school. At least one fatality, multiple injuries. I'm ok—

Her throat tightened with tears as her fingers trembled over the keys.

—I love you, Daddy—

****

"A hoax?" Noah asked. His pulse settled a tiny bit.

Rhyden cut in. "I don't see my girls. Where are they?"

"Not all the students are out. We started on this side of the campus." The sheriff pointed to the gym. "The basketball coach discovered a couple of suspicious packages beneath the bleachers around 1:15 p.m. They looked like pressure cookers. About the same time, a custodian found a few more hidden under the lunch tables in the cafeteria. While they were reporting their findings to the school resource officer, half the student body and most of the teachers received a one-word text Boom. Principal Harkness activated the fire drill procedure and contacted us. We got here within six minutes but so far, nothing."

Students and teachers trickled from the front central doors of the school. Officers lined the sidewalks, herding them to a secure location a safe distance from the school where they could be searched and questioned.

The sheriff continued, "No one, so far, recognized the number the text came from."

"Burner?" Noah asked.

"Most likely. We think it's a prank…senioritis and all that, but we're evacuating all the students before we send the ATF bomb squad and their dogs in."

"I don't see Sam," said Rhyden in a tight voice. He resumed scanning the parking lot. "Or Bree."

Ding! Rhyden's text notification sounded. He looked down at the screen. "Fuck!"

Before he said another word, muffled shots rang out from the far side of the school. "Bree texted me. Active shooter. Science building. Injuries. I've got to get over there."

While Rhyden rushed toward the far side of the school, responding officers hunkered behind their vehicles, rifles resting on the hoods, aimed at the school. Noah chased after his friend. More shots sounded. Screams echoed from inside. The trickle of students exiting the front double doors became a flood.

And chaos erupted.

****

A couple of students huddled in a corner, hysterical. Bree crawled over to them. "Hey, shhh. We need to keep quiet." She surveyed the room. "And we need to get out of here."

Outside the building, lights flashed, and sirens wailed. Cop cars and ambulances flew into the parking lot. Malcom pried the classroom windows open and began helping other students out. "Stay down," Jenn whispered as she and Malcolm boosted others through the window. "Stay down."

Students raced across the lawn toward the waiting first responders. SWAT officers waved the teenagers to take cover in nearby ditches. The shooter began taking potshots at them as they fled, pinning the remaining students down.

Crouched next to the unconscious Richard on the

floor in the classroom, Bree texted her boyfriend.

—Trapped. Shooter at school. Love you—

The response was instant. *—Get out of there—*

—Trying—

****

Noah, along with the sheriff, several Bennett County deputies and investigators, and other first responders, charged toward the building, weapons drawn. Students fled the building, some elbowing and shoving their way out, some helping those who had been trampled get back to their feet, dragging them to safety.

"I still don't see my girls," Rhyden said when Noah caught up to him.

"We'll find them. I know this school inside out. Every nook and cranny."

The two men separated from the main force of officers and slipped into the left wing of the school through a side door. Weapons at the ready, they swept down a deserted hallway, clearing abandoned classrooms as they went.

Radios crackled. "Anyone have eyes on the shooter?"

"Negative, no eyes on."

"Negative."

"Nothing on the south end of the school."

Noah added a negative response to the chatter. A noise from the classroom on the right drew his attention. Using hand motions, he indicated to Rhyden that he would enter the door high. Rhyden would go low. Moving quickly but quietly, they rushed the room. A metallic rattle came from beneath the teacher's desk in the far corner.

The rangers exchanged a tense stare. Rhyden pointed to himself and gestured to the left.

Nodding, Noah rolled his footsteps to avoid making noise and cut to the right. He dropped into a duck walk as he crept toward the desk. Weapon at the ready, he swept the chair away. “Come out. Now. Hands where I can see them.”

Rhyden covered his partner from the other end of the desk. More scraping noises came from beneath the desk. The smell of ammonia permeated the air. Noah gestured toward the desk with his head. He holstered his gun and held up three fingers.

His partner nodded in agreement.

Muscles tensed, Noah folded his fingers down…three, two, one. When the last finger folded, he blew out a quick breath, grabbed the top of the desk with both hands, and flipped it onto its side.

Before the rattle of metal against tile stopped, Rhyden stepped in and pointed his pistol at the figure huddled on the floor. A mass of red curls shook in fear. Rhyden slipped his gun into his holster and held a hand out to help the young woman cowering on the floor to her feet.

Ignoring his outstretched hand, she scrambled backward away from him, much like a blue crab scuttling across the sand. Back up against the overturned desk, she whimpered, clutching at her throat. She whipped her head from side to side, searching for an escape.

“Easy now.” Rhyden gentled his voice. He kept his hand extended and kneeled to her eye level. “We’re here to help. Are you hurt?”

The girl shook her head no. Visibly trembling, she

placed her hand in Rhyden's and allowed him to help her to her feet. Keeping his voice soft, he said, "Let's get you out of here. What do you say?"

The girl released a muffled sob and buried her face in Rhyden's chest. He placed a comforting arm around her shoulders and guided her to the classroom door. As he did so, calls of "all clear" rang out from the radio followed by "we're sending in the dogs."

Chapter Fifteen

After Bree left Richard with the EMTs, she overheard another girl telling a paramedic the blood covering her wasn't her own. She looked down at herself. *This isn't mine, either.*

An ambulance raced out of the parking lot past her, lights flashing and siren wailing. Another zoomed in to take its place near the triage area. Life flight choppers swooped into the parking lot, slinging up dust and dirt everywhere, loaded up the next patient, and took off again.

She stumbled blindly toward the tent erected to shelter the students from the rain just beginning to fall. Richard's blood soaked her clothing. As it dried, the cloth had stiffened. She scrubbed her hands together, trying in vain to eradicate the bloodstains.

Media swarmed all over the campus. "Miss. Miss!" A journalist and her camera operator rushed toward her. "Can you—"

Bree shook her head. "Please." Her voice cracked. An urge to smash the camera shoved in her face raced through her. She stepped back. "Just leave me alone."

She turned away and ducked behind the walls of the tent to hide from the cameras. Someone handed her a sign-in sheet. By this, she knew authorities were attempting to get a list of everyone. Students and teachers huddled together, some praying, others weeping. Some stood silent in shock. She searched for Sam and her dad. She spotted her dad and Noah still helping students from the building. No sign of Sam. *God, please, don't let my sister be hurt.*

Chatter overwhelmed the tent. Everyone speculated on who could have done this horrible thing. No one seemed to know. One girl, crying into her phone, kept repeating, "The shooter's hiding with us."

Bree's heart dropped. *No way. She's just panicking, that's all.* Rumors flew. The shooter was a former graduate who blew out his knee in the final football game last year, losing all his scholarships and getting hooked on opioids. The shooter was one of the janitors who had been having an affair with a student. The shooter was a girl. Suspicion filled the tent. No one knew what to believe. No one knew who to trust. She scrutinized other students. *Could it be? Who?*

Her phone dinged. *—Have to see you—*

She read the text from her boyfriend, and milling around the edges of the holding area, she texted back.

—Waiting to be released—

—Meet me behind the gym?—

Bree looked around, found her father and Uncle Noah. They'd be busy for a while yet.

—K. Just for a minute—

—In uncle's truck—

—Not the Buick? What color?—

—Green pickup, older model—

—K lu—

—lu2—

All of a sudden, rain dumped from the sky in buckets. Bree's pulse kept pace with the rapid rhythm of the rain hammering on the roof of the tent. She slipped out and headed toward the gym. She passed a huge bus with "AMBULANCE" stenciled on the side.

A pickup truck pulled around the corner of the building. She sped up to catch it, but the truck turned right and continued driving. Impatiently, she shifted her weight from foot to foot as she sheltered in the doorway, wishing she had clean clothes to change into. Bree slipped her phone from her pocket, checking for new messages. Her phone was blowing up but no new messages from her boyfriend or her sister.

Where is he?

Headlights crept up the road in her direction. The vehicle slowed to a stop half a block from the gym. Bree squinted at the truck but couldn't make out the color through the downpour. The truck crept closer. *Green!* She dashed to the corner as the old truck slid to a stop. Water dripped from her hair into her eyes, blurring her vision. She jerked the door open and jumped in.

"Damn, it's nasty out here. Oh my God, you can't imagine how scared I was." She shook her hair out of her face and glanced up. "Wait, you're not—"

A coarse voice, like sand on glass, replied, "No, *acushla,* I'm not."

Bree scrambled out of the truck. She pivoted and ran only to slam into a wall of muscle. She spun back the other direction. Beefy hands wrapped around her upper arms from behind, lifting her off her feet. *No!*

She squirmed in his grasp, trying to free herself. *I did not escape being shot to be kidnapped.* She smashed her head backward into his nose. *Ow!* She swung her legs, hammering her boot heels into his knees.

The man dropped her. "Bitch!"

Her feet hit the pavement. The impact shot pain up her shins. She stomped on his instep, hard. Frantically, she glanced around for help. Everyone was still at the front of the school sorting out the shooting aftermath. No one else was out in this storm. He grabbed her. She jammed her elbow into his solar plexus, knocking the wind out of him.

"Help!" she screamed. No one responded. Remembering her training, she yelled, "Fire!" People afraid to get involved in the problems of others responded more quickly to threats to themselves, but there was no one around to hear her shouts.

The driver circled around the front of the truck. Bree made her move. She exploded forward, drilling her shoulder into his sternum. He doubled over. She drove her knee into his groin—and ran.

Her boots slipped on the wet pavement. The first guy grabbed her by her ponytail, stopping her in her tracks. He transferred his iron grip to the back of her neck, shaking her like a rag doll. Spinning her around to face him, he drew back a meaty fist. His punch caught her in the cheek, snapping her head back.

Agony slammed through her face. Tears flooded her eyes.

The driver winced and straightened up. Grabbing his partner's wrist, he stopped the next strike before it could be launched. "Not in the face." He stepped closer, crowding Bree's personal bubble.

A sharp pinch on the neck caused her to jump. Fire raced through her veins. The world began to spin. She felt clumsy. Her arms and legs refused to respond to her brain. *What's happening?* Bree collapsed into a puddle on the sidewalk.

As if underwater, she heard the driver say, "Gotta love Special K. Load her up."

The big man popped the lock on the aluminum toolbox in the back of the truck. He scooped Bree from the ground and unceremoniously dumped her in.

Chilly rain pelted her in the face. Jumbled thoughts and images raced through her mind, competing with her pulse. A primal scream built in her throat, but her muscles refused to cooperate. No sound escaped. *Gotta move. Eyes. Keep eyes open.* Bree tried to fight, tried to climb out of the toolbox.

The passenger laughed at her uncoordinated attempts. "Just relax. No use fighting it. Ketamine always wins." He slammed the toolbox lid closed, blocking out the light.

****

Hot. So very hot.

Searing pain tore through Bree's head. Her eyes fluttered open. Pitch black darkness surrounded her. *Can't breathe. Where am I?*

A rotational vibration lulled her back to sleep. A sudden bump jarred her neck, lifted her, and slammed her head into the surface she rested on. Her eyes popped open. Featureless faces leered at her from the gloom, fading in and out. Hands grabbed at her. She screamed.

She tried to scramble away, but her limbs were too heavy to lift. An invisible force pinned her in place. She squeezed her eyes closed. The hands and faces kept coming. *Not real, not real, not real.*

A panicked, hollow sensation filled her chest, too tight for air to enter. She inhaled sharply. Gasoline fumes burned her lungs. Still, the faces kept coming.

Reason fled, along with the contents of her stomach. Her stomach clenched, and she heaved until nothing was left inside.

Light-headed, she struggled to breathe. Her eyelids weighed a ton. Thankfully, the shadows pulled her back under.

****

Patrick pulled up in front of the shipping container. His dad stormed over to the truck before he and his buddy could climb out. "Where the hell have you useless gobshites been? I've got trouble enough without having to wait on your lazy asses."

Patrick ignored his father and walked around to the toolbox. He propped it open, examining the contents. He squished up his nose and made a face of disgust. *Damn, that stinks.* Stepping away, he leaned against the tailgate of his truck. A self-satisfied smirk lingered on his lips.

An oilfield tanker idled in the pasture next to the tank batteries. The driver paced near its open door. He fiddled with the top button of his shirt. Rubbed the back of his neck.

Seamus glared at the driver. He stalked away from his son. Stopped. He cracked his knuckles. His gaze bounced from his son to the tanker back to the driver. He clenched his teeth. The muscle in his cheek jumped as he ground his molars together.

"Da, over here."

Seamus joined Patrick at the back of the truck. He tugged at the collar of his shirt. Dragged his hands through his hair. "Fooking thief. I hate thieves. Just got the livestock unloaded and now we have to move again. Immediately." He glared at his son. "You better not have messed anything else up, boyo."

"What's going on?" Patrick asked. "What's wrong?"

"Damn tanker driver snuck out here to steal oil and stumbled into our operation. Caught us unloading." Seamus glared across the pasture at the driver. "To top it off, we lost another head of livestock. Couldn't handle the heat." Seamus turned on Patrick. "Didn't I tell you to take care of the merchandise? Now we're short two and have another body to dispose of."

A slow burn of anger rolled over Patrick. *Now I'm supposed to control the fucking weather?* He pushed it down. "Da, I have an idea about that."

"I don't fooking think so. Your last disposal sicced the Texas Rangers on us. What the fook were you thinking, putting a body in a driveway?" Seamus raised his fist. "I ought to knock the crap out of you."

It would have worked, too, if you didn't do such shoddy work. He swallowed the rebellious thought and raised his hands in a submissive gesture. "Da, please. Wait a minute, okay? Just listen to me." He waited until his father lowered his fist. "I have an idea to take care of the driver and the body."

Casting another glare at the idling eighteen-wheeler, Seamus said, "Go ahead. I'm listening."

"Drop the body in the tanker and have the driver haul it away. What's he gonna do? Tell the cops 'hey, I was out stealing oil and stumbled across these people selling kids, and oh yeah, they gave me a dead body to get rid of.' He can't say anything. He's involved. Two birds, one stone."

Seamus rubbed his chin, a thoughtful expression crossing his face. Nodding slowly, he said, "Not a bad idea, boyo. Not a bad idea at all."

Yes! "Can I show you my other good idea? Remember that *gorger* kid we hired for the paving jobs? His dad fired him, so we hired him? He left his cell phone in the work truck at lunch today."

Seamus threw his hands up in the air. He shook his head in apparent frustration. "And I care why?"

"His girlfriend texted him during the…uh…let's say 'distraction' at the school."

"What happened at the school?"

Patrick chuckled and waved the question away. "Anyway, I dug back through his texts. She sent him several pictures over the past few days. Quite a looker so…" With a dramatic flourish, he gestured to the contents of the toolbox. "Ta-da."

He crinkled his nose. "Well, she cleans up good."

His father stepped closer and peered in. He patted Patrick on the shoulder. "She's a bit older than our normal, but she'll do. Good job, boyo."

He raised his chin, excited to share the details of the girl's capture with his dad. "I texted her back and had her slip away and meet me—well him—during the confusion at the school. It will be a while before anyone even realizes she is missing. Name's Aubree Trammell."

Seamus stared down at the unconscious girl in the toolbox. "Who cares what her name is? What did you do with what's his name's phone? The one you were texting her with?"

"Pulled the sim card. Took out the battery. Dropped them off three different bridges into the San Miguel creek. Did the same with the girl's phone."

"Good. Get her out and hose her down. Get the

vomit off her. Whose blood is that? Never mind. Don't care. Clean her up and put her in the trailer with the others. Get 'em moved."

He started to walk back over to the truck driver, then stopped and reached into his pocket, pulling out a business card. He studied it for a moment before turning back to Patrick. "Wait a minute. Did you say Trammell?"

He handed a Texas driver's license to his father. "Yeah, the boy called her Bree, but her license reads Aubree Nicole Trammell."

Tapping the plastic card against the palm of his hand, he said, "Well, well, well. What are the chances? Boyo, you may have hit a gold mine this time. The ranger that came sniffing around the shop was named Trammell, too. What do you want to bet they are related? We can back off the *peelers* and make a pretty penny all at the same time. Maybe you're not as stupid as I thought you were." Seamus patted his son on the back. "I'm actually proud of you, son. You might even have earned yourself a bonus."

Shoulders back and chest out, Patrick bounced on his heels. He dug his cell phone from his pocket and pulled up a photograph of the ranger and his Hellcat. Already feeling the leather steering wheel beneath his hands, he turned the image to face his father. "Enough of a bonus to buy one of these?"

As Seamus studied the picture, he felt the blood drain from his head. He grabbed the phone. Enlarging the photo, he squeezed the phone until his knuckles whitened. "No, he's dead. I killed him."

"What did you say, Da?"

He shoved the image into his son's face. "Where

did you take this photograph? When did you see this man?"

Flinching, the boy stammered, "A-at the sh-shop. He was one of the rangers who came to see you. He—he said he knew Grandda."

Patrick watched as telltale signs of ice-cold fury swept across his father's features. Nostrils flaring, the vein on his forehead pulsed. He tightened his jaw and ground his teeth. Talking to himself, he murmured, "Yeah, I bet he does know Grandda. Nana, too. Son of a bitch. Bastard must have nine lives."

Curiosity overcame fear of his father's anger. "What's going on, Da? Who is that man?"

Seamus blew out a deep breath. "Nothing. Nothing at all. Did you catch this guy's name?"

"No, just that he's a ranger. Didn't you see him? He was with that other *peeler* that came to talk to you."

"I didn't talk to any *peelers*."

"They must have talked to Grandda then. He was asking about some job and where we got the materials for it."

"Oh, you mean the job you fucked up by burying a body in it?"

Patrick averted his eyes. He bit his lip. "Um…"

"Never mind." Seamus waved his son away, but continued mumbling. "A ranger, huh? What name are you using these days? How the hell did you go from being a grifter to a Texas Ranger? Now that's the ultimate long con." He almost sounded proud of the stranger.

"Da, who is he?"

Patrick's partner approached carrying a dripping wet, still unconscious but half-ass rinsed off Aubree.

Seamus gestured at the girl. “Put this one in the trailer and load the others back up. We need to get them transferred to the secondary holding location. Transport to the buyers should be here in a day, two at the most. Then go take care of the body and the driver.”

Patrick hesitated.

“What?” his father snapped.

“Can I have my phone back? Please?” Taking the cell back from his father, Patrick studied the photo as his mind raced a hundred miles an hour, trying to discover who this stranger was and why he had the power to upset his father so much. Anyone who could scare his father that much was someone he wanted to get to know.

Chapter Sixteen

Back in the school parking lot, while Rhyden turned the girl over to the paramedics, Noah returned to the mobile command center. “What’s the sit rep?”

Sheriff Preston shook his head. “Not sure what’s going on. No one can find any sign of the shooter. No one saw anyone. At least, no one alive saw anyone. The explosive dogs hit on two of the packages. Bomb squad’s in there now. We should be getting more information soon.”

About that time, the front door of the school opened again, and a bomb tech wrapped in protective black armor minus the face shield and helmet carried an open package out. He placed the package on the sidewalk in front of the school. Noah, the sheriff, and a few investigators joined the bomb tech.

“It's a fake,” he said. “The package contained a pressure cooker loaded with shrapnel and a dusting of fertilizer. Just enough fertilizer to make the dog hit on it but not enough to make a boom.” The tech wiped his sweaty forehead on his arm. “Scene’s clear.”

The sheriff turned to his investigators. “One of you find the principal or the school resource officer and see if you can get your hands on surveillance videos. We need to find out who the shooter is, now.”

Rhyden rushed up. Panic flared in his eyes. “The girls are missing.”

"Missing?" Noah scratched the base of his neck. "What?"

"You heard me. I can't find Bree or Sam. No one's seen Sam at all today. Bree hasn't been seen since the shooting stopped. She helped patch up one of the injured students and got him to safety and then just vanished. Hasn't been seen since."

Has the entire world lost its collective mind? Aloud he said, "What the fuck is going on?"

"Neither is answering her phone either."

"You try Sam again. I'll try Bree."

Noah dialed Bree. Straight to voicemail. He looked at Rhyden and shook his head.

Rhyden texted Sam. *—Call me—*

—Dad! R u trying to get me suspended—

—Call me ASAP—

—Can't. In class. It was a harmless prank. Why do I have to call u? It's not like I shut the school down this time. U r gonna get me ISS!!—

*—ANSWER THE DAMN PHONE—*he bellowed in text speak and hit send.

Without waiting for a response, he redialed Sam's number. When she answered, he hit the speaker button so Noah could listen and asked, "Where the fuck are you?"

"Dad," Sam hissed, "I'm in class. Are you trying to get me suspended—again?"

"Samantha Elaine, now is not the time to lie to me. Where are you?"

"In class." Muffled voices giggled in the background.

"No one is in class. There's been a shooting at the school. Where are you, and where is your sister?"

“Shooting? What shooting? Oh my God, is Bree okay?”

“I don’t know. We can’t find her. We couldn’t find either of you. Where are you?”

“I’m at the beach.” Sam started to cry. “I’m sorry, Dad. I didn’t know. Last night, she just said she was going out with PC.”

“When was the last you saw her?”

“Last night about seven. Is she okay?”

“I don’t know. Get home and wait for me. I’ll be there as soon as I can.” Rhyden disconnected the call. He turned Noah. “Any luck?”

Noah ran a jerky hand through his hair. He tapped his thumb against his leg. He shook his head no. His gaze danced across the parking lot, bouncing from vehicle to vehicle. He returned his attention to Rhyden. “Let’s go to the office. Maybe we can download her text messages from your cell carrier.”

****

Noah leaned over Rhyden’s shoulder as he logged into his cell phone account. As he waited for the messages to download, he chewed the hangnail on his thumb. “Where the hell can she be? Where would she have gone?”

Messages from Bree’s phone finally popped up on the computer. Rhyden sent them to the printer.

Noah nodded to the computer screen as he snagged the pages off the printer. “Anything helpful there?”

“I think she’s with that PC creep. They exchanged messages right before she disappeared. That damned…”

The muffled sound of a cell phone ringing cut short Rhyden’s response. The phone rang and rang before stopping. It rang again. “You going to answer that?”

“Don’t look at me,” Noah said. “Not my phone.”

The phone stopped, then started ringing again. The rangers realized it originated from inside a FedEx package on the corner of Rhyden’s desk. “What the hell?” He grabbed the package and ripped it open. Out fell a cell phone and an unmarked, silver DVD in a plastic case. As he answered the phone, he put it on speaker.

“Ranger Trammell, top of the evening to you.” An exaggerated Irish accent flowed over the telephone lines. “I see you received my care package. Have you had time to watch my sweet little movie yet? It’s a special production just for you and your partner. What name *is* he using these days? Ranger Morgan, is it? Your communications department is so immensely helpful.”

Noah flinched. His grip tightened on the papers he held. Acid churned up his esophagus, burning into his chest wall. “Who is this?”

“Ah, let’s not distract ourselves with labels, shall we? The names change so easily these days. Don’t they, *Noah?* Please, take a moment to enjoy your movie. It’s short. I so look forward to hearing your reactions in real time. Go ahead now. I’ll wait.”

“Look, Mister whoever you are, I don’t have time for games—”

“Ranger Trammell, for your family’s sake, I must insist.”

Rhyden gave his partner a questioning look as he popped the DVD into his computer.

Noah shook his head, eyes widened, and mouthed, “No clue.” His hand tightened around the spark plug in his pocket. He stepped around the desk to see the monitor. A screen opened with the image of an unconscious teenager lying in a wire animal cage. Various tools and five-gallon buckets of chemicals littered the background.

Rhyden inhaled sharply. "You son of a bitch. Where is she? What have you done with my daughter?"

Low chuckles ranged out from the telephone speaker. "I see you recognized my newest star."

"Where is she, you cocksucker?" asked Noah.

"Now, now, Ranger Morgan, no need for such profanity. What would your mother say? Oh, wait, your dear sainted mother's dead, now isn't she? Perhaps I should ask what your dear old Nana would think of such language? Would she still be reaching for that bar of lye soap?" Light-hearted peals of laughter filled the room. "This is such fun. Tick-tock, gentlemen. I do so hope you and Ranger Trammell enjoy the hunt. Ta-ta."

"Wait, where…" The call disconnected.

Rhyden flung the phone across the room. The screen cracked on impact.

"Hey, easy," Noah said. "We may need that."

Rhyden grabbed his own phone and glared at his partner. "Don't you *easy me.* I didn't see your daughter in a cage. What do I do now?"

Noah hesitated. *If that voice is who I think it is…who I know it is, he would want easy access to his captives. Could Seamus' son, Patrick, be this elusive PC?*

"I think I know where she might be."

"Well, spit it out already."

"The boyfriend worked for a paving company, right?" Noah asked.

"He did?"

Fuck! "Uh…yeah, that's what Bree told Cat," Noah lied. Mentally, he kicked himself. *Quit giving away information you shouldn't have.* "Where's the information on those plates we ran the other day? The boyfriend's muscle car?"

"Wait a minute. Patrick Collum. PC. You think he's the boyfriend, don't you?" Rhyden started rummaging through the files on his desk. Papers flew everywhere. "But the car was registered to a Fred Durham."

Sarcasm dripped from Noah's lips. "Yeah, because someone who kidnaps girls would never register a vehicle under a false name." *And Travelers don't lie about their names.* Noah heaved a heavy sigh. "I'm sorry. I just don't know."

"Here's the address. Let's go."

"Fine," Noah said, "but let me drive."

****

Scuffed square-toed boots and faded blue jeans with tattered hems poked out from under the meticulously restored muscle car parked haphazardly in the driveway. Rhyden stormed over to the car, grabbed the boots, and yanked. A lanky, sandy-haired teenager with a sunburned face and laying on a red mechanic's creeper rolled free of the vehicle.

"What the fuck, old man?" The boy glowered up at Rhyden, blinking against the sudden sunlight. He clutched a box-end wrench loosely in his fist.

Noah let out a quiet sigh of relief. *Not Patrick Collum.* "Fred Durham?"

The sullen teen clambered to his feet, tapping the wrench against his thigh. "Who wants to know?"

Rhyden grabbed two fistfuls of the boy's shirt, twisting it tightly around the kid's throat. He lifted the boy from his feet and slammed him against the door of the vehicle. The wrench clattered as it fell to the pavement.

Noah stepped in and murmured, "Hey, easy."

His partner snarled over his shoulder at Noah. "What? I'm lifting with my knees." He turned back to the frightened teenager, using the grip on the T-shirt to keep the boy balanced on his tippy toes. He gave the boy a sharp shake. "Where is she?"

The young man trembled in fear. "Wh-wh-who?" he stammered.

"My. Daughter." Rhyden punctuated each word with a slam of the boy's head against the side of the car. "What have you done with her?"

Tears formed in the corners of Fred's eyes. He tried to shake his head. "Dude," the boy choked, "I don't know who your daughter is."

Switching to a one-handed grip on the teen, Rhyden jerked his pistol free from its holster. He held the gun tightly against the boy's temple. "Aubree Trammell," he said. "Do you know who she is now?"

"Whoa, buddy. Whoa, whoa, whoa." Noah grabbed Rhyden's gun hand. "Back down."

The distraught father turned wild eyes on Noah. "Fuck off."

"Sir," the teenager squeaked. "Isn't Bree at school?"

Rhyden dropped his gun back into its holster and released the boy with a shove. "If she was at school, would I be here?"

"I haven't heard from her since this morning, sir."

Fred rubbed a hand across his throat. He swallowed audibly. "She snuck out, and we spent the night here." He raised his hands quickly. "Nothing happened, sir. I promise. Nothing at all. My parents were here. We fell asleep in the living room watching movies. When I woke up, she was gone. I tried calling her a few times, but her phone went straight to voicemail. I figured either she didn't answer because she didn't recognize my number or that you caught her sneaking back in and had confiscated her phone."

"Text her. Now."

Fred hung his head. "I can't. I lost my cell phone. That's why I've been calling her from my parents' landline."

Rhyden climbed back into the passenger seat of Noah's pickup. "Fuck!" He slammed his hands against the dash repeatedly. He turned to his best friend, anguish painted on his features. "Now what?"

Noah put the truck in gear. "Let's check out the dilapidated barn behind the paving company. I tried to see what was in it when we were there the other day, but that weird kid was holed up in it. Something's off about that place."

****

Rhyden and Noah arrived at the paving company shortly before sunset. Heavy equipment ringed the parking lot, interspersed with work trucks loaded down with tools. Deepening shadows ratcheted up the eerie factor. They parked as far away from the office as possible just in case someone lingered inside. The darkened hulk of the barn was barely visible in the gloom. No lights or signs of life could be seen.

Anxiety battled utter exhaustion as Noah reached

for his door handle. Before he could open it, the radio screeched to life. *Shit!* He lunged forward to silence the radio but paused when Officer Lopez's voice, an octave higher than usual, blared over the airwaves speaking so fast he was hard to understand. State troopers and county patrol deputies were in pursuit of an oilfield tanker truck. Just before he shut off the radio, he heard the officer tell dispatch the truck hit the spikes and crashed through a fence, rolling over in the field. The officer was requesting an ambulance just as Rhyden and Noah exited the truck.

Shadows deepened as the sun slipped from the sky. Hands resting on their weapons, they waded through the thigh-high grass leading to the barn. They paused frequently to make sure no one spotted them. As they approached, Noah signaled for Rhyden to go around to the back.

He crept to the front of the building, keeping a low profile. He tried to peer through a cracked window, but once again the spray-painted black glass defeated him. He rattled the doorknob. Unlocked. Cautiously, he opened the door a sliver. Stifling air rushed out. The smell of rotting flesh and old blood slapped him in the face.

Please, God, no.

A rustling in the brush to his right caused him to slip his cocked and locked 1911 from its holster. Easing the door closed, he stepped back against the building, hiding in the shadows. A twig cracked. He tightened his grip on his weapon. Stepping into the fading light, he said, "Hold it right there."

Rhyden popped out of the brush. "It's just me. No entrances anywhere on the building but here."

Noah exhaled. Tension eased from his body. He stepped back and re-holstered his weapon. He remembered the odor from the barn. “Wait here.”

“Bullshit. I’m not waiting anywhere. If my daughter is in there, I’m going in to get her.”

“Rhy, please. Just let me check it out first. I’m begging you.”

Trammell ignored him and jerked the door open. Fetid air rushed out. He paled and shoved Noah out of the way before charging into the darkened interior.

A crash followed by the sound of breaking glass and cursing pulled Noah through the doorway. He flicked on his flashlight. The intense blue-white beam cut through the dismal murkiness. The hair on the back of his neck stood up. *Someone’s watching me.*

He whipped the light up. All around him, glittering glass eyes leered from the walls. A shiver tore through him. “You okay?”

“Yeah, knocked over some kind of aquarium. Freaking bugs went everywhere.” Rhyden slid his own LED beam around the space. Roach-like insects burrowed into the sawdust shavings scattered among pieces of broken glass. Several beetles crawled out of a partially decomposed hog’s head.

Noah played his light over the hog’s head. Long and yellow, wickedly sharp tusks shone in the beam of his flashlight. Bits and pieces of rotting flesh and hide clung to the skull.

As the partners advanced deeper into the building, the stench of old blood grew stronger. A trickle of sweat rolled between Noah’s shoulder blades and puddled beneath the waistband of his jeans. The flashlight illuminated dried spatters and puddles of blood. A glint of silver flashed.

"No!" Rhyden fell to his knees. He scooped something off the floor. Fists clenched, he pounded the floor. Tears tracked down his cheeks.

"Stop." Noah reached for him. "We don't know that's Bree's blood. We don't know if it's human."

Desperation painted on his features, Rhyden raised his head. "It's human." Torment colored his voice. He opened his fist to show Noah a silver locket drenched in blood.

Noah's breath caught in his throat. *Please, Lord, no.* "Still doesn't mean it's Bree's."

Hopelessness deepened the shadows in Rhyden's eyes. "The boyfriend gave her one just like it a few days ago."

Noah's cell phone shrilled before he could respond. "Morgan here." The back of his throat began to ache, a feeling similar to his reaction to the bee sting. He turned away from Rhyden and lowered his voice. A sour taste filled his mouth. "Are you sure?" A pause. Cold fingers punched through his chest and squeezed his heart. "On my way."

Rhyden leaped to his feet. "What?"

"We've got to go."

"What's wrong?" Rhyden grabbed Noah by the shoulder. Turned him to face him. "What the fuck is wrong? Did they find her? Did something happen to Sam? Maddie? I can't lose any more of my girls."

Noah shrugged out of Rhyden's grip. He stalked toward the truck, shoulders stiff, fists clenching and unclenching. "Please. Just get in the truck."

"Not until you tell me what that telephone call was about."

Cracking his knuckles, he said, "When the tanker they were chasing crashed out, it flipped. The top hatch popped open." He swallowed hard, shook his head, and continued walking to the truck.

Rhyden's glare hardened. He crossed his arms over his chest and stepped in front of Noah. "And?"

Noah slumped forward. His shoulders dropped. Arms wrapped tightly around his abdomen, he looked anywhere but at Rhyden. The words fell from his mouth. "And a body fell out. Soaked in oil, no identification, no clear description. It—it could be anyone." Guilt flattened his voice. "All they can tell is that the body was small in stature…"

He choked on his grief. "…and female."

Chapter Seventeen

Noah grabbed for Rhyden as he jumped from the truck, but he wasn't fast enough. Rings of flashing red-and-blue lights surrounded the overturned tanker. A motor whined as the wrecker driver struggled to winch the eighteen-wheeler back onto its wheels. Yellow crime scene tape fluttered in the breeze.

A man, arms cuffed behind his back, sat against the rear wheel of a marked Bennett County patrol unit. His sweat-stained ball cap and mirrored sunglasses lay on the ground beside him. A large, purple-blue bruised knot covered the right side of his forehead.

Rhyden fought his way past the crime scene perimeter with Noah tight on his heels. "Where is she? Where's my daughter?"

He shoved through the circle of officers standing over a body. A photographer snapped images of the girl's body. Rhyden knocked him out of the way. He kneeled next to the girl. Hands shaking, he gently rolled her face up. Wiped the oil residue from her slack features. He inhaled sharply. He pressed a hand to his mouth. Blinking up at Noah, he said, "It's not her. It's not my Bree."

Noah sagged in relief.

Rhyden stormed up to the man on the ground. Grabbing him by the throat, he jerked the suspect to his feet. "Where is she? What did you do with her?"

"I—I—I—uh…" the man stammered, his voice heavy and filled with smoker's phlegm.

He slammed the man against the side of the sheriff's department's vehicle. "Where. Is. My. Daughter?" The enraged ranger emphasized each word with a sharp jab to the driver's stomach. He released his hold on the man.

The driver doubled over and collapsed to the ground. He curled into a protective ball, wheezing for air. "I don't know anything. They just put her in the tank and made me leave."

Rhyden reached down and jerked the man back to his feet. He drew his fist back again.

Noah grabbed his wrist. "Whoa, man. He can't talk if you knock him unconscious."

Rhyden shoved the man away, spun, and jerked his arm from Noah's grasp. His eyes narrowed on his partner's face. Noah tensed, bracing for the punch he could see coming.

With trembling hands, Rhyden grasped Noah's shoulders. "It's not Bree. I have to find her."

Noah drew him into a hug. "That's a good thing, brother." The men clung together for a brief moment before he released his grip. "Bree's tough. She's smart. She's alive. And she's going to stay that way. We'll find her. You have my word."

Rhyden stumbled back a step. He nodded his head, bleak pain filling his eyes. He pleaded, "We have to, man, we have to."

The partners turned to the driver. Noah opened the back door of the marked unit and helped the man inside. "His daughter is missing. Most likely taken by the same people who gave you that girl." He gestured toward the body now inside a black bag and being rolled on a stretcher to the waiting hearse. "If you don't want me to turn him loose on you again, you better start talking. Fast."

The driver swallowed convulsively. Sweat poured down his face, dripping into his eyes. He blinked rapidly. "I-I-I have nothing to say."

"Choice is yours, buddy. I wouldn't be surprised if he wanted you to suck start a pistol." Noah started to step away from the vehicle. Rhyden advanced, eyes narrowed, hands fisted at his sides.

He scooted backward over the vehicle seat away from the door. The tendons on his neck stood out, his rapid pulse visible. He shook uncontrollably. "Wait," he croaked, his voice laden with alarm, "I can tell you where I picked up the girl, but they won't be there. They were already moving out." He dropped his head. His voice lowered to a whisper. "What else do you want to know?"

Noah grabbed Rhyden by the shirt sleeve, tugging him toward the pickup truck. "Come on. Let's go see where the driver picked up the body."

A text notice chimed from Rhyden's phone. One glance at the screen buckled his knees. The phone slipped from his hands.

Noah caught it before it hit the ground. He read the screen and swore viciously.

—Did you find my driver? Did you like his present? Tick-tock, rangers, tick-tock—

Seamus was taunting him again.

****

Her eyelids felt like they weighed a ton. Bree forced her eyes to open, but they simply didn't want to remain that way. She fought to compel the world into focus. And lost. Her eyes drifted closed. *Too tired to breathe.*

"Five more minutes, Dad," she mumbled. "Just five more minutes." She rolled onto her side. The room spun. She flung an arm out to stop it. Her arm wouldn't move. The room continued to whirl.

"Daddy…" She squeezed her eyes shut tighter. Her stomach clenched. Spikes of nausea stabbed her abdomen. She tried to pull her knees up, to curl into a fetal position. Her legs were slow to respond, but they did shift.

Heat flashed on the back of her neck. Bile flooded her throat. She gagged. She gulped air in an attempt to keep her stomach contents on the inside where they belonged. An overwhelming odor of urine and feces overlaid with sour gas slapped her in the face. Sweat dripped from the ends of her hair. She squeezed her eyes even tighter as her stomach heaved.

Please, I don't want to throw up. Not again.

Pained whimpers crept into her consciousness. *I'm not alone.* "Who's there?"

Ever so slowly, she cracked her eyes open. Gloom surrounded her. Everything appeared blurred, distorted. Black lines caged her in. *Bars?* She narrowed her eyes, focusing. She tilted her head and scanned the space surrounding her. She bit her lip. Fear tightened her dry throat, squeezed her chest. Hazy, nonsensical images danced at the back of her mind. Bars did indeed surround her. *Where am I?*

She wriggled her toes. Lifted her arms. Slowly, she regained control of her limbs. She lay on a plywood floor. She sat up. Her head swam. A whimper escaped her lips. She pressed her hand to her mouth, silencing herself. Dried blood, too much blood, coated her clothing. Clung beneath her fingernails. She clutched her throat. Straightened her back. Whimpered. A quick inventory of her body parts reassured her the blood wasn't her own. She sagged in momentary relief.

Memories of the shooting and consequent kidnapping rushed into her consciousness. For a moment, she was back in the classroom. She could hear bullets pounding against the doorframe. A shiver of fear raced through her as she remembered the feel of Mr. Routh's cold flesh against her fingertips. She remembered Richard's blood coating her hands, still hot, pulsing, slipping through her fingers as she fought to save her classmate. Shoving a fist in her mouth and biting down, she choked back her sobs.

Breathe, two, three. Inhale, exhale.

She slowed her breathing. Regaining a semblance of control, she took in her surroundings. Welded metal bars formed the walls of the hog trap confining her. It resembled an oversized dog kennel but made with thicker metal. It reminded her of the traps her hog-hunting buddies used. She peered into the darkened space surrounding her. All around her sat similar cages, each except one containing a young child or teenager—girls and boys, both.

Tiny shafts of light beamed in from ventilation holes in the ceiling, adding to the gloom rather than illuminating her surroundings. At the far end of the narrow, corrugated steel box, a slim seam of light outlined the place where two doors met. The other end was bathed in darkness. The light dimmed.

The sun is setting. How long have I been here?

"Hey," she called out, her voice scratchy and barely audible. She swallowed, clearing her throat. Fear gnawed at her like a coyote chewing on bones. "Where are we? What's happening?"

"Shh." A tremulous voice tinged with dread from the depths of the hot, humid blackness called out. "They'll hear you and come back."

"Hello?" She shook the walls of the trap, trying to escape. *Must get out of here. Can't breathe.* "How do we get out of here? What's going on? Why are we here? Who are they?"

No answer.

She tried again. "Who are you?"

Still no answer.

Her eyes darted around the cage, searching for anything to use as a tool to escape. A keyed padlock held the door closed. Two bottles of lukewarm water and an empty bucket rested in the corner near the lock. Her eyes lingered on the bucket in disgust.

She shook the bars harder. Nothing gave. *Trapped.* Bree drew her knees up to her chest and wrapped her arms tightly around them. Tears pooled in her eyes. The tops of her boots dug into the backs of her thighs. She shifted uncomfortably. *Boots. Knife. Oh please, God, please.* Holding her breath, she slid her hand into her right boot. Her fingertips scraped the tip of her pocketknife.

Thank you, Jesus. She exhaled in relief. She scrambled over to the door of the hog trap. She inserted the blade of her knife into the keyhole of the padlock and tried wiggling it around.

Was that a click? She grabbed the base of the lock and tugged hard. Nothing. She re-inserted the blade point and tried again and again. Sweaty palms made the knife slippery. Sweat rolled down her spine, tickling the crack of her ass.

A feeling of being watched scratched the back of Bree's neck. She turned to her left. Large, luminous green eyes glowed in the murk. A tiny, blonde girl with dirt-smudged cheeks clung to the bars of the pen.

"I'm hungry." The plaintive whisper echoed in the darkness, shattering her heart.

She can't be any older than Maddie. "Oh, baby, I'm so sorry." Bree thrust her arm through the bars, trying to comfort the child. Her fingers fell a few inches short. "I'll get us out of here."

"Promise?"

Hesitating, she rubbed her fingers across her heart. Forcing a confidence she didn't feel into her voice, she answered, "I promise."

Determined, Bree turned back to the lock. She inserted the point of the pocketknife back into the keyhole. She wiggled the tip around but the blade slipped and and sliced her hand. *Fuck!* She wrapped her hand in her shirt to slow the bleeding. She switched the blade to her left hand and renewed her efforts. *Just one more twist.* Plink! The tip of the blade snapped off. Hope disintegrated, crumbling to dust.

Crawling back to the farthest, darkest corner of the cage, she curled up into a tight, little ball. Panting, she rocked back and forth. Bree shoved her fist against her mouth as she tried to stop herself from bawling. She failed.

Daddy! I want my daddy.

****

Dreams of car crashes, drowning, and oil-soaked

bodies haunted Noah's sleep. Bree's image danced just out of reach. He chased her and chased her and could never quite catch her. Behind it all, Seamus laughed and laughed.

Noah tossed and turned. The sound of his text notification startled him awake. Beside him, a steady, gentle snore indicated Cat slept soundly. He grabbed for the phone, quickly silencing the repetitive beep. Fumbling in the dark, he pressed his thumb to the lock screen and swiped on his text app.

The screen glowed, but he couldn't decipher the words. Rubbing sleep from his exhausted eyes, he tried to focus. The message from a blocked number flared to life on the screen.

—Hey, cuz. Long time no see—

Noah's fingers flew across the keyboard.

—Who's this?—

—Don't play stupid, Ferrell. It doesn't become you—

Ferrell? Noah buried his head in his hands.

Ding! *—Still there, cuz? Or should I call you Noah now? How did you like the little present we left you? Not that I expected you to find her. Damn oilfield trash—no guts. Too bad she wasn't strong enough to handle the heat. Sure hope this new one is stronger—*

Noah sat straight up in bed. Next to him, Cat moaned and rolled over to snuggle deeper into the quilt. Using both thumbs, he worked the phone rapid fire.

—Where the hell is she?—

—She calls you Uncle Noah. Isn't that sweet? Guess that makes me her uncle, too. Or just a cousin, hmmm, I wonder?—

—If you hurt her...—

Silence. Noah tapped the screen on his phone. He climbed out of bed and walked into the darkened living room, shutting the bedroom door quietly behind him. He re-sent his last text and waited. No response. He tried once more.

—Hello?—

Again, he waited. Minutes ticked by. No response. "Son of a bitch!" He flung his phone across the room. It hit the wall with a solid thump.

Noah sank onto the sofa, his head buried in his hands. *I'm going to kill him. I'm going to track the cold-hearted bastard down and beat the shit out of him until he tells me where Bree is, and then I am going to put a bullet right between his eyes.*

"Babe?"

Wearing an ancient Department of Public Safety t-shirt, hair tousled, eyes swollen with sleep, Cat stood in the doorway between the bedroom and the living room. The light from the bedside lamp cast a golden glow around her. She noticed his phone laying on the floor several feet away. "What's going on?"

His stomach lurched. "Nothing."

She tilted her head to the side. "Nothing?"

He crossed the room and wrapped her in his arms. Holding her tight, he said, "You know I love you? Right?"

She pulled away. "Too tight. Can't breathe."

"Sorry." Stepping back, he stared intently into her eyes. He nodded. "You know I love you more than anything?"

Cat rested her hand on his cheek. Her eyebrows drew together. "Noah, baby, you're scaring me. What's happening?"

He hugged her close again, burying his face in the loose hair surrounding her neck. He held her close, inhaling her jasmine scent. His voice shook with emotion. “I just need you to know I love you.”

Chapter Eighteen

Seamus carried his tackle box and pole to the surf. He turned at the sound of his grandfather's voice. "What?"

"Why didn't you tell me?" Declan repeated, his voice tight. The tails of his untucked, vented fishing shirt flapped in the ocean breeze.

What the fook is the old fool blathering on about now? Schooling his features into a neutral expression, he asked, "Tell you what, Grandda?" He continued rigging up his hook and leader before reaching into the cooler for a piece of live bait.

Face flushed, the old man's eyes bulged. "Tell me what? *Tell me what?*" he snarled. He raised a hand and rubbed his chest just below his breast pocket.

"Grandda, you're losing it. Do we need to look for a nursing home?" He dragged a rugged workman's hand across the back of his leathery neck and turned back toward the surf.

"Don't you turn your back on me. All that nonsense about wearing a dead man's boots." Declan stepped closer to be heard over the sound of the waves crashing on the sand in front of them. "You couldn't tell me Ferrell was still alive?"

"I…" Seamus swallowed hard. "I…" His mouth opened and closed, but no words emerged.

The older man surged forward. His fist tightened,

knuckles cracking. "You *knew*? Knew my grandson was alive, trapped in the car slipping beneath the surface of the river?" His words bounced off Seamus' chest like hot pellets of lead. "Alive beneath the flames burning on the surface of the water and you left him there to die a slow, hellish death?"

The younger man retreated, stumbling over a piece of driftwood. He fell, landing hard on his ass in the damp sand. "How did you find out?"

The old man barked a short laugh. He rubbed his chest again. "How did I find out he was alive? Your stupid gobshite son showed me his picture on his phone and asked me who he was. How did I find out you tried to kill him? You just told me."

"I'm going to skin that boy alive."

"Maybe you should have answered his questions instead." Declan loomed over his grandson as he scrambled backward to the water. He plucked a desert tan pistol from the waistband of his shorts.

Seamus stared up at the black hole at the end of pistol's barrel. It wavered slightly as the old man's hand trembled. The closer the gun came, the harder it shook.

With a sudden moan, Declan collapsed to his knees. The gun fell from nerveless fingers.

Seamus scooped the gun from the sand and turned the barrel on his grandfather. The old man didn't move. The younger man's lips turned up in a narrow sneer. "You never suspected. I played the grieving cousin so well. I missed him like a brother, or so you thought. Never suspected I caused the wreck in the first place, did you? Never dreamed I was the one who forced his flashy little hot rod off the road and into the river."

Seamus kneeled beside his grandfather and leaned

closed to the old man's ear. His voice dropped to a faux-honeyed tone. "Here's something else no one will ever suspect, old man. I'm going to sit here and watch you die. After you take your last breath, I'm going after your precious Ferrell again. And this time, I'm going to finish the job I started all those years ago."

Chapter Nineteen

Think, Morgan.

Overwhelmed by so many questions with no answers, Noah tapped his fingers against his desk in time to the music playing on the radio. “Get Back” by the Beatles segued into “Sweet Home Alabama.”

Even though the music was upbeat and totally out of sync with his current mood, it isolated him into his own little bubble, slowing the random thoughts bouncing through his brain like a pinball. The melodies helped him to shut out any distractions and focus.

He stood and paced around his office. *What do I know?* His fingers beat the rhythm of the song against his jeans. *I know Bree is missing. Why?*

I know the boyfriend is not Patrick, and he did not do it.

I know Seamus did. But why now? And the bullshit text about slowing down the investigation is just that, bullshit. He knows involving Bree, involving the rangers, is just going to turn up the heat on the investigation, so why does he want us focused on Bree? What are we missing? What are we being distracted from?

I know of at least two other girls who have now been found dead: Alyssa Sanders, the hip implant, and Jane Doe, the girl from the overturned tanker.

His stomach rolled at the thought of finding Bree’s

lifeless body. *Nope. Not going to let that happen.*

How many of the reported missing can be pinned back to Seamus?

Even more worrisome, how many children that haven't been reported missing does he have?

He circled back to his desk where he flopped into the leather desk chair. He picked up a number-two yellow pencil, made sure it was sharp, and grabbed a legal pad. He needed to find the pattern. "Brown-Eyed Girl" poured from the speakers hidden in the acoustical ceiling tiles of his office. He twirled his pencil between his fingers before bouncing the eraser off the pad.

Grandda always taught him everything always boils down to "why." He said his father and his father before him taught him that if he could find the why, he could figure out the rest.

What in the hell does Seamus want with these children?

Deciding it was time to start a list, he spun in his chair, allowing his head to fall back against the cushioned headrest. He made a visual search of the dingy ceiling tiles, casting for answers he still couldn't find. The words of the song circled in his head like an earwig burrowing ever deeper. *Brown-eyed girl?*

Sitting straight up, he dragged the legal pad closer and stared the list with "appearance" and followed it with a question mark.

All three girls shared a similar build—petite, slender with curves. No other similarities, though. One redhead, one blonde, one brunette. Eye color varied. Bree was a whisper older than the other two girls, seventeen to their fourteen and fifteen. Briefly, he considered going through the files of the additional missing children, but he lacked enough information to know which files to include in his lists and which to exclude.

Okay, moving on. What do the girls have in common besides being female?

Fragments of a long-forgotten memory whirled through his brain. Bits and pieces of a conversation tickled the edges of his conscious thought—one of the last conversations with his cousin before—well, just before.

A shudder danced down Noah's spine as the memory ran into a brick wall. He couldn't remember what happened after that conversation no matter how many times he tried. Seamus had been calling people sheep, something about livestock needing a master.

Livestock? Could he be keeping his captives on a ranch? Lord knew there were enough big places and empty hunting cabins in the area. It would take weeks to search them all. Time was something they didn't have. Still, he made a note of it on his list.

Why? Why is the key. Noah wrote "why" on his list, circling it multiple times before drawing harsh, black lines beneath it. It all came back to that one word. Why had Seamus grabbed Bree? It couldn't be as simple as wanting to slow down the investigation. Even the most simple-minded idiot would know grabbing a ranger's kid would turn up the heat, not turn it down. There had to be more.

Unless they hadn't known she was a ranger's kid when they grabbed her. But if that was the case, why not let her go? Why taunt them?

Noah forced himself to focus on the past he'd tried to repress, to think on the time growing up with

Grandda, Nana, and Seamus. He had to figure out what his cousin really wanted.

The scar on his lower abdomen twanged. Noah convinced Cat it was from an appendectomy. In reality, Seamus had wielded the blade that caused the scar. *Why does he hate me so much? Would he really use an innocent girl for vengeance against me? I went away. He's the one dragging me back.*

Noah dropped his head into his hands. *What did he say when he stabbed me? Why can't I remember?*

****

A furious wind howled, buffeting the metal container holding the hog traps. No light crept through the cracks; Bree had no way of knowing the passage of time. Just the wind, pummeling, whirling wind that threatened to rip the doors off their hinges. The constant roar made her teeth itch. She curled into a ball, tucking her head against her knees, swiping at tears tracking down her face.

Whimpers from the cage next to her added to her feeling of helplessness.

"Here, take my hand." Bree sat up and scooched to the edge of her kennel. She stretched her arm through the bars of the cage. Pinching and bruising it as she forced it through the narrow space, she took the young girl's hand in her own. "Hush now," she crooned, "it's all going to be okay." She cringed as soon as the words left her mouth. *How could anything ever be okay again?*

She gave the small hand another squeeze. "What's your name, sweetie?"

Sniffles answered her.

She tried again. "I bet you are five years old?"

"Nuh-uh. I'm six."

The outrage in the little voice made Bree chuckle despite the circumstances. "Oh, I'm sorry. My sister is five. I thought you might be her age. What's your name?"

"S-S-Sarah."

"Hi, Sarah. Where do you live?"

"I'm scared." Sarah laid her head against the bars. She raised her face, a pale oval in the darkness. "I want my mommy."

"It's okay, sweetie," she said, struggling to keep her voice light. "My name's Bree, and my dad is a Texas Ranger. He and my Uncle Noah will find us and get us out of here."

"What's a Texas Ranger?"

Bree smiled for the first time in days. "A ranger is a police officer only better. He always gets his man. He will move heaven and earth until he finds us. He won't ever stop."

Please, God, let him find us. Soon.

****

Noah cranked up both the speed and incline on the treadmill, pushing himself harder and harder. Sweat dripped onto the control board. He jabbed at the buttons, forcing the machine to its maximum capabilities. Inside his running shoes, the soles of his feet burned as he pounded the belt.

From her perch on the sagging second-hand sofa across the room in their home gym, Cat asked, "You okay, babe?"

Gulping oxygen between words, he replied, "Just…hunky…dory."

My best friend's daughter has been grabbed by my

psychopathic cousin. I have information that could find her, but I can't share it because I don't have a logical reason for having the information. I'm hiding everything, including who I really am, from the woman I love. And I'm probably going to lose my job. If my cousin doesn't kill me first.

So yeah, hunky dory.

"Babe, you can't keep pushing yourself like this. You can't keep working eighteen, twenty hours a day. You're not eating. You're not sleeping. You're going to make yourself sick."

"Bree is missing."

"I know, babe, I know, but you can't help anyone if you work yourself to death." Cat patted the worn cushion of the ratty sofa. "Join me for a minute? We need to talk."

"That sounds ominous."

She grabbed her Saint Michael's pendant and slid it back and forth on the chain. A wan smile faltered on her face. When she met his eyes, the smile faded.

"Uh-oh." He shut off the treadmill, grabbed a towel, and mopped the sweat from his face and neck. Dropping the towel across the handrail of the machine, he walked over to join her. He placed a kiss on top of her head before slouching onto the seat beside her.

He lifted the medal from her fingers, rolled it between his own. "St. Michael, patron saint of police officers, paramedics, firefighters, and the military. Do I need his help?"

Silence.

"Hey." He placed a gentle hand on her cheek. "I was teasing." He searched her eyes. "Is everything okay?"

"Why don't you want to have children?"

Everything inside him stilled. "Cat." He stood and stepped away from her. Looking at his watch, he said, "I don't have time for this discussion right now. I need to get back to work."

She reached for him. "I need—"

He brushed her hand away. "Not now. I'll be home late. Don't wait up."

****

The squeal of rusty hinges on the shipping container split Patrick's already pounding head. Squeezing his eyes shut didn't help. Rubbing his temples—forget that.

Fuck! Will I ever learn? Beer before liquor, never sicker. Semi-sweet air competed with the overwhelming odors of captivity. The stench turned his already rebellious stomach.

The captives scooted to the backs of their cages, moving as far away from him as possible in their tight, confined spaces.

"Clean the cages." With an ugly twist to his mouth, Patrick mimicked his father's voice. "Water the livestock." He snorted. "Do this. Do that." Reverting to his own alcohol-soaked voice, he muttered, "Why don't you do any of the work yourself, huh, Da? What am I? Your whipping boy? Your slave?"

He set the beer can down and withdrew a syringe and glass bottle from his pocket. He inserted the syringe and measured out a dosage of the fast-acting sedative. Holding the syringe up to the light, he pushed the plunger just enough to squirt a bit of liquid from the tip of the needle.

Armed with the needle, he unlocked the first cage.

Grabbing the child by her arm, he dragged her to the door of the cage and injected her. Within moments, she collapsed in his arms. He scooped her up, threw her over his shoulder, and carried her out into the sunlight where he laid her on the grass. He then picked up a hose and rinsed the accumulated dirt and filth off the unconscious child.

He tugged the hose inside the storage container. With a flick of his wrist, he whipped the kink restricting water flow out of the hose and washed out the now empty cage. Still muttering to himself, he carried the girl back to her cage, placed her inside, and re-locked the padlock on the door. He tugged on the lock to make sure it was secure.

****

Bree cowered in the corner of her cage. Her fingers traced the message she carved into the wooden floor. As the angry young man stomped closer, Bree froze, regulated her breathing, and squeezed her eyes shut. *Damn it. Pretending to sleep won't get me out of here.*

Through eyes barely opened a slit, she watched the young man repeat the process cage by cage, moving steadily closer to her own. The closer he approached, the faster her heart beat. *I must get out of here—whatever it takes.*

Stomach churning, she bit her lip. Her throat convulsed. *I'm going to be sick.* Closing her eyes, she steadied herself. *Whatever it takes.* Concealing her movements, she slipped her pocketknife from her boot. The missing tip wouldn't make much of a difference. The edge was razor sharp. She wiped her sweaty palms on her filthy jeans. Surreptitiously, she opened the blade and clutched the knife tightly in her right hand.

Still muttering to himself, the sullen boy worked his way through the shipping container, cleaning cages and children. He approached Bree's cage. He reached through the bars of the cage and fingered a lock of her hair. "Aren't you a pretty one?"

She didn't react. Didn't so much as twitch. *Breathe. Stay still.* She moaned, shook her head listlessly, pretending to be in the twilight stage of consciousness.

The fucktard yanked her hair sharply.

Her jaw ached from biting her tongue, but still she controlled her outward response. *Bastard.* She slowed her breathing even more.

He readied the syringe and unlocked the padlock.

Panic threatened to sweep over her. Muscles tensed, she prepared to lunge at the young man holding the needle. Before he could grab Bree, the girl in the cage he had just finished started gagging. Then she vomited. Still semi-unconscious and laying on her back, she began to choke.

"No. No, no, no, no." Her captor abandoned Bree's cage and rushed to the choking girl. "Da will kill me if I lose another one." He fumbled with the lock before jerking the cage open and tugging the girl out. He turned her on her side. He swept two fingers through her mouth, clearing her airway. He held her on her side until she could breathe easily on her own. Carrying her outside, he laid her in the sparse grass. He grabbed the hose and started washing her down again.

Bree crawled to the door of her cage. *Unlocked!* She readied her weapon and shoved through the kennel door. Unused to standing, she fell to the floor. Scrambling to her feet as fast and as quietly as she could, she forced her way to the opening of the metal shipping container, blinking when the harsh daylight sun hit her eyes.

"Fuck!" The asshole grabbed at her. His fingertips brushed her filthy t-shirt as she twisted out of his grasp. Carrying the other girl back inside, he shoved her back into her cage and secured the padlock. Quickly, he spun around and chased after Bree. He launched himself at her from the doorway of the container.

Together, they tumbled to the ground. She jabbed her elbow into his stomach. Wriggling out from under him, she struggled to her feet. He grabbed her again. Slammed her to the ground, knocking the breath from her lungs. His hands wrapped around her neck. He squeezed. Tight. He pressed his thumbs against her carotid artery. A high-pitched ringing began in her ears. Everything blurred. Blackness swirled at the edges of her vision. Her feet drummed against the ground. Life was slipping from her grasp.

Bree slashed out at him. Again, and again. Slashing and stabbing. Her blade slid across his face, missing his eye by a fraction of an inch. He howled in pain. Releasing Bree, her captor clasped both hands to his face. Crimson blood pulsed through his fingers.

Life-giving oxygen rushed to her lungs. Bree raised her knees and kicked the wailing young man off her. She snagged the cell phone from his shirt pocket, clambered to her feet, and ran. Her chest tightened. Dark spots encircled her vision. Still she ran until the stitch in her side doubled her over. She dropped to her knees, gasping for air.

Trees rustled to the left of her. She rammed her fist into her mouth and bit down to block her cries. She held her breath. Rising to her feet, she backed farther from the patch of underbrush, hiding in the shadows.

"When I find you…"

Her captor crashed through the brush, cursing. He swung a large stick, poking into bushes and cactus, moving mesquite branches out of the way.

Stifling a whimper, Bree slunk away from him. She tripped and fell into a crevice in the ground, landing hard on her butt. The phone fell from her white-knuckled grasp. She rolled deeper into the shallow depression in the ground, scrambled farther under cover. She burrowed beneath the fallen branches and foliage, listening as the young man trampled on.

Gathering her wits, she belly-crawled toward the edge of her cover. Raising her head a few inches, she spotted the boy silhouetted against the horizon. She swallowed a sob and wiggled back into concealment. She waited. And waited.

After Bree was certain he had moved out of range, she searched for the cell phone. *There.* She grabbed for the phone. Hands shaking, she dropped it—twice. She slid her finger across the screen. *Thank God, no password.* She dialed her dad's number. Voicemail. *Damn it.*

She dialed again. When a live voice responded, she croaked, "Uncle Noah?"

"Bree? Is that you? My God. Where are you? Are you safe?"

Tears flooded her voice. She was so tired of being brave. "I—I—"

"Calm down, sweetie. Take a deep breath and look around. Tell me what you see."

"Pasture and brush. Cactus. We have to save them,

Uncle Noah." She wriggled from her hiding spot. "I think I see…" Beep. Beep. Beep. The call dropped. Frantically, she redialed. Nothing. She looked at the screen. *No service. Damn it all to hell!*

****

"Rhyden," Noah yelled into the phone. "Where are you?"

"At the jail. Interrogating the driver of the tanker truck, again."

"Meet me in your office. *Now.* I heard from Bree."

****

"What do you mean you lost the girl? Which girl? You fookin' idiot." Seamus pounded a fist into Patrick's jaw. "How in the hell did you let her get away? You outweigh her by at least a hundred pounds. One simple chore. That's all I asked of you."

Patrick spat fresh blood onto the ground. "I. Don't. Know." He slid a hand across his jaw to wipe away red-tinged spittle. "Maybe your sedative was faulty. I gave her the shot. She attacked me. With a knife!"

"Are you sure you gave her the drug? Where the hell did she get a knife? Didn't you search her before you locked her in the cage?"

The boy shrugged. "I need a doctor."

"I need to clean up your mess. Where did you last see her?"

Chapter Twenty

Bree shoved the useless cell phone into her jeans pocket. She knew she had to find an area with better service—after checking herself for injuries. Luckily, she only found a few minor scrapes and cuts, and hot, angry bruises circled her neck. Her throat began to swell from the need to cry.

Suck it up, buttercup. You've got to hold it together.

She'd never been a crybaby and wasn't about to start now. She had made a promise to Sarah, and she planned to keep it. Working her way out of the brush, she searched for landmarks. Every miserable roughing-it camping trip taken with her family in the past now felt like a treasure as survival tips and methods of primitive navigation flooded her mind.

Thank you, Daddy.

Dotted across the pasture were piles of dead mesquite trees and cactus shoved there by bulldozers attempting to clear the pasture for cattle grazing, burn piles waiting for the latest drought to end—if it ever did. In the distance, she spotted a row of rusty tank batteries originally intended for storing oil. These looked abandoned. She ran toward them, weaving from brush pile to brush pile. She stopped and took cover. Listened. Nothing. Peeking around the last burn pile, she scanned the open pastures for signs of pursuers.

The memory of Sarah's big, sad eyes and the whispered promise of rescue haunted her. She needed a way to mark this location. A way to bring back help. To keep her promise. *If only I had cell service, I could drop a GPS pin.*

She peered around again. *Maybe higher ground would help.* Taking a deep breath, ramping up her courage, she jumped up and ran for the tank batteries. She scrambled up the ladder, the rungs wobbly beneath her feet. She made it to the top and crouched down on the inspection platform at the top of the tank. The rickety grate supporting her swayed in the breeze. She checked the cell phone. Still no service.

Heart racing, she forced herself to stand. Fear of heights shoved her adrenaline levels sky high. Her legs shook. Her knees locked. Bile crept up the back of her throat. Clinging to the corroded railing, she caught her breath. Consciously, she focused on slowing her breathing and lowering her heart rate while she scanned the horizon. No sign of her captor.

From up here, things looked vaguely familiar. Maybe a quarter mile away she spotted a derelict airfield. Tall grass and tiny trees grew in the middle of the runway, but two helicopters with round glass cockpits sat on the helipad. *That's weird. I thought Dad said the oilfield company abandoned that airfield three years ago.*

A grinding of truck gears reached her ears. She looked to the north. In the far distance, a cloud of red dust followed a dump truck racing down a dirt road. The road ended in a parking lot filled with heavy equipment and a couple of metal buildings. *Civilization!*

Bree inched back down the ladder, not breathing again until her feet hit solid ground. She sat down on the bottom rung. She rested her forehead on her knees. Inhaled deeply. Exhaled strongly. Raising her head, she scrubbed her face with her hands. *Okay. One step at a time. I can do this. Easy.*

She began walking.

****

Limping slightly from the blisters rubbed on her heels by her boots, Bree staggered into a dusty parking lot. She ignored the pain as she skirted around several large piles of gravel. She licked her dry, cracked lips. What she wouldn't give for a tall glass of ice-cold water. *There!* She rushed past the dump truck she had spotted from atop the tank batteries, now parked next to a road grader, toward a metal office building sitting at the edge of the parking lot.

"Hello?" She tugged the smudged glass entry door open. A bell tinkled as the door shut behind her. "Is anyone here?"

No response.

She tugged the cell phone out of her pocket. Still no service. She stepped into the office and sneezed. Dust danced in the sunbeams flowing in through the small window in the back wall. A counter split the room in half. Behind the counter, a hallway led to offices hidden behind closed doors. Bree didn't care if she was breaking and entering because sitting on the far end of the counter sat a telephone. An honest to goodness landline. *Thank you, Jesus.*

She rushed to the phone and picked up the handset. No dial tone. *No!* She sagged against the counter, still clutching the handset. Her eyes grew hot. Hands shaking, she replaced the handset in the cradle. A light went on in her brain. *You dummy. Push the button.*

She raised the handset back to her ear and selected a line on the telephone. Dial tone! With shaking fingers, she dialed her father's number. A sob escaped her throat as the phone rang.

****

"Damn it!" Noah shoved away from his desk. "This isn't working. We need the van." He picked up the phone on his desk and dialed dispatch. "Morgan here. I need the mobile cell phone tracking van. Can you set it up?" He listened for a moment. "No, we haven't found her yet. That's why we need the van. Yeah, thanks. We're on our way there. Tell them to be ready."

****

After riding in circles for nearly an hour, Noah jerked the headphones from his ears in frustration. "Nothing. All we have is the last tower the cell phone pinged on." He sighed. "I don't know what to tell you. We lost the signal when the call dropped."

He slammed his fist against the interior wall of the van. "Stop the van." He looked at his partner. "Let's get out of here. I need air."

The driver pulled the van to the side of the road. The rangers scrambled out, gratefully escaping the claustrophobic interior smelling of stale coffee, old sweat, and fear. Rhyden met Noah's eyes. "What do we do now?"

Heavy dread settled in the pit of Noah's stomach. They were so close. He could feel it, but he couldn't find that final clue that would give them Bree's location. Not even his past insider recollections of Seamus' operations could help with that. "At least we know she escaped. Trust her, okay? She's a smart girl."

"But…" Rhyden's cell phone rang, an unfamiliar number flashing on the screen. "Trammell here."

A sob echoed from the other end of the phone. "Daddy!"

His knees buckled. He caught himself before he fell and tapped the speaker button so his partner could hear the call as well. "Bree! Baby girl, are you okay? Where are you?"

"I don't know. Please, find me, please. We must save them. I promised."

"Save who, baby? Where are you? Are you safe?"

"The other kids. We were all caged, locked up. Daddy, please, come get me."

Noah took over. "Bree, take a deep breath. Look around. What do you see? Is there anyone you can ask for help?"

"I'm in a building, a metal building. It's deserted. No people here." A high-pitched beeping issued from the phone, a familiar, repetitive beep.

"Go to the window. What's that noise?"

He heard footsteps clatter across a floor. "A dump truck," she said. "It's a dump truck backing up."

"Bree, careful now. Describe the building. Tell me everything you see. Every detail."

"Um, there's a gravel parking lot, dumpsters everywhere, piles of gravel, and a lot of trucks. Some heavy equipment."

"Did you see a company name? A telephone number?"

"N-nooo, no name or number."

"This is important, Bree. Was there a sign on the building? A blue banner? Did you see an old green pickup in the parking lot?" Noah's heart raced. *God, you couldn't be that cruel.*

"Yeah, a blue sign with white letters. I don't remember what it said. No green truck, though. Wait, someone's coming." The phone clattered against the countertop. "Sir?"

Noah screamed into the phone. "No, Bree, no. Run! Hide!"

Sounds of a struggle came across the speaker followed by a heavy click as someone dropped the handset back into the cradle. Silence.

****

Lost in angry thought, Seamus stalked toward the office. *How did that fookin' idjit let a wee bit of fluff escape him?*

The door flew open. "Sir?" a young redhead called out to him.

You have to be kidding me? Really? A smile split Seamus' face. "Well, well, well, what have we here?"

He grabbed the girl, jerking her close, twisting her arm behind her back. "And I thought I would be scouring the countryside to find you. Welcome to my office, Miss Aubree Trammell."

"How do you know my name?"

"I know many things about you." He reached into his pocket and pulled out the driver's license his son had given him. "Aubree Nicole Trammell, driver's license number 08746…well, I'm sure you know the number." He tossed the driver's license on the counter.

She struggled, kicked, and scratched, but he was too strong. She couldn't escape his grasp.

Seamus hit her with a brachial strike designed to knock her out. The flat edge of his hand caught her neck just below and to the front of her ear. She dropped like a stone. He scooped her unconscious body from the floor and tossed her over his shoulder.

Whistling a jaunty tune, he strode to his chrome laden dually pickup truck. He tossed her in the backseat, securing her hands and feet with green plastic cable ties. Grabbing a dirty rag off the floorboards, he fashioned a gag and shoved it into her mouth, securing it with duct tape. “That should hold you.”

Bree glared daggers at him as she struggled against her bindings.

“Now you’re going to be hurting my feelings, wee one. I’ll be thinking you don’t want to spend time with me.” He chuckled. “Good thing looks can’t kill, isn’t it, *a leanbh?*” Seamus slammed the rear door of the truck closed, walked around, and climbed into the front seat. He started the engine. “Let’s go visit some new friends, shall we? It’s almost time to make you famous.”

****

“We know where she is.” Noah climbed back into the van. “Come on, let’s go.”

“What do you mean we know where she is?” Rhyden asked.

“Metal building, heavy equipment, a blue banner?”

“The fucking Traveler paving company?”

Noah typed furiously on the laptop keyboard, summoning up an aerial map. He pinpointed the paving company. “Okay, we need to block off everything within a five-mile radius. No, better make it a ten-mile radius.”

Rhyden grabbed the radio. “819, Bennett County,

my daughter has been located but is being transported by suspect. I need roadblocks now."

"Bennett County, 819. Where do you need them? Do you have a vehicle description?"

"No vehicle description. Let's block off FM 140 at Mill Lane, 97 at Kyote Road, Dawson and Edwards, and Hindes Boulevard at Bigfoot Road."

"Don't forget Trimble Lane at Highway 173," said Noah.

Rhyden relayed the additional location to dispatch. For the first time in days, Rhyden smiled. "We've got the son of a bitch."

****

The mechanical female voice from the navigational unit said, "In three-quarters of a mile, turn left on Kyote Road."

Seamus hummed to himself as he drove. He glanced at the clock on the dashboard. Six forty-five. Plenty of time before he had to meet his buyers.

"Continue on Kyote Road for five miles."

Headlights on the oncoming car flashed him. *Cop ahead.* He instinctively glanced at his speedometer and eased the weight of his foot off the accelerator. Looking in the rearview mirror, he saw the girl lying in the back seat. She had finally given up trying to squirm out of her bindings. Another oncoming vehicle flashed its lights, too. He lifted his foot completely off the accelerator. He steered the truck to the shoulder, letting it glide to a stop.

Who had been on the other end of that telephone call? His brain said if he drove on and stayed below the speed limit, there was no reason a *peeler* should stop him. His gut disagreed. Listening to his brain, he eased back onto the road. A mile passed. Then another. No sign of a cop car. Another mile passed. Two more vehicles signaled him with their headlights. The hair on his neck stood up. *Something's not right.*

Seamus jerked his truck back onto the shoulder of the road. He turned on his hazard flashers and climbed out. He waved down the next vehicle that came toward him. The SUV with a young woman at the wheel swerved away from him and kept driving. So did the next two vehicles.

Frustration, anger, and a tinge of fear fueling him, Seamus pulled his truck diagonally across both lanes of the road. He tugged a gun from his waistband and stepped into the middle of oncoming traffic, forcing the approaching pickup truck to stop, run off the road, or hit him.

The driver slammed on his brakes, smoke boiling up from the rear wheels. He idled in the middle of the road. Seamus tapped on the driver side window with the barrel of his pistol.

The man reached for his gearshift.

Seamus shook his head, tapped the window harder.

The man lowered his window.

Seamus gestured down the road with his pistol. “What's going on up there?”

“R-r-road block of some sort. Cops searching all the vehicles.”

Seamus's gaze darted down the road, then back the way he had come. Heat pricked up his spine. He swallowed hard. “Give me your cell phone. Now.”

Hands shaking, the man held his phone out the window. He snatched the phone, stepped out of the road, and waved the driver around his truck. “Thanks.”

The other driver nodded nervously, scrambling to roll up his window, and drove on, kicking up a cloud of dust and gravel from the shoulder of the road in his wake.

Seamus stomped back to his dually and ripped the door open. He climbed in and slammed his fist on the dash, cracking it. *Fuck!*

He grabbed his phone. Thumbs flew across the keyboard.

—Complications. Abort. Will be in touch. —

He tossed his cell phone onto the truck seat. A shiver of dread raised gooseflesh on his arms as he imagined the potential response to his text.

Turning the truck around, he spun his tires in the loose gravel. Pings of little rocks hitting the chrome running boards filled the air. Dust followed his truck.

Where to now?

****

"Go home. Take a break." Rhyden's voice cracked. "I need to check on Sam and Maddie. None of us are doing Bree any good if we don't take a short break to recharge. Meet you back here, five a.m.?"

Noah checked his watch. Four hours. "Yeah, you're right." He stifled a yawn. "It'll take that long to get a judge to sign the search warrant for the paving company. Damn! I just knew we had them with the roadblocks."

His partner rubbed his hands across his eyes. "Yeah." His voice dropped, exhaustion coloring his words. "Me, too."

****

Noah twisted the doorknob and walked into the house. Shoving away the fear for Bree, the frustration for the lack of answers, the worry that Cat was still angry for his avoidance of the children discussion, and plain old exhaustion, he called out, “Lucy, I’m home.” He slammed the door shut behind him.

No answer from Cat.

Well, it is one in the morning. “Hey, hon, you left the door unlocked—again. How many times do I have to remind you we live in a dangerous world?”

Still no response.

He walked into the living room. Fancy china, complete with a serving platter covered with a silver dome, adorned the table. Wax dripped down flickering white candles to pool on the tabletop. Polished family silver sparkled on linen napkins. A lace table runner graced the mahogany table, but there was no sign of his girl. *What did I forget now? I know it’s not our anniversary.* He wracked his brain trying to figure out what they could possibly be celebrating. His birthday was in February. Hers was July.

“Cat? Sweetie? Where are you?” He peered out the window. Her vehicle sat in the driveway, so she had to be somewhere inside the house. Even if she'd gone to bed, she wouldn’t have left candles burning. “Honey?”

The taunting texts from Seamus combined with the unlocked door rose to the surface of his racing mind. His stomach lurched; the muscles in his legs spasmed. Tugging his service weapon from its holster, he methodically swept through the house. Light on his feet, soundless, he slipped from room to room searching for signs of what he wasn’t certain.

He nudged the bedroom door open. A large manila envelope, legal-appearing papers, and photographs lay scattered over the bed and floor. Clothes exploded from the closet. He stepped closer and had to duck to avoid a pair of flying boots. He peeked into the closet. Tucking his gun back into its holster in relief. "Hey, sweetie, what are you doing?"

Cat glared up at him from her position on the closet floor. An open suitcase lay beside her.

Noah dropped to the floor beside her. He put an arm around her shoulders and tried to draw her close. "What's wrong? Is it your mom?"

She struck out at him, punching and slapping. "Don't you touch me."

Noah jerked back, startled by the vehemence of her response. "Baby, I'm sorry I'm late. I didn't realize I was missing a special dinner."

Without a word, she stood and stalked from the closet, dragging her suitcase and carrying an armful of clothing.

Dumbfounded, he asked, "What's wrong?"

She flung the suitcase on the bed and shoved clothing inside it.

"Is this because I didn't want to talk about starting a family?" Noah turned to exit the closet. After one step, photographs pelted him in the face. He picked one up. *Fuck!*

He stared at a booking photo, himself at seventeen, complete with the date, his social security number, and his name. His real name. He gathered more photos and documents from the floor. All contained identifying information which did not correspond with the name Noah Morgan. "Where—"

"These were waiting for me on the front porch when I got home from work." Cat grabbed another handful of paperwork from the bed and flung it at him.

"Who the fuck are you?" Before he could answer, she stormed back to the bed. She threw more belongings into the open suitcase. "I'm going home."

"Sweetie, you are home."

She stopped, facing the bed, shoulders shaking. "Am I?" Slowly, she turned to face him, betrayal in her eyes. "I thought you were having an affair. All the secret texts, the unexplained late hours." She whirled away, made a sweeping motion at the incriminating documents. "Now, I don't know what to think."

She straightened her spine, squared her shoulders, shoved the last of her clothing into the suitcase. Pain sliced her words. "Now I actually wish it was an affair."

Noah stepped up behind her. He spun her to face him. She refused to look up. Placing a hand beneath her chin, he gently raised her head until their eyes met.

Before he could say a word, she shrank away from him. She held up a hand. "Don't. Just don't." Brushing past him, she hauled her luggage after her down the hallway.

Stunned, he stood in shocked silence. He crumpled the photographs still clutched in his hand. In the distance, Cat's car door slammed, the engine fired up, and the wheels spun out on the concrete driveway.

"Fuck!"

Blind rage swept through him as he stormed through the house, knocking over chairs, kicking over the trash can, punching holes in the walls. *If I tell them, I can maybe save Bree, maybe. But I will lose everything else—Cat, my job, Rhy, Sam, Maddie...my life. Hell, I've already lost Cat. Can I save Bree? Is it worth the risk?*

Noah made it to the dining room. *Is it worth it?*

Did I really just ask myself that? What the fuck? Who am I? Bree's life depends on me.

With one sweep of his arm, he flung the china, silver and the now-defunct candles to the floor. *What am I going to do? Why did I think I could have a life? Why did I think I* deserved *a life?* His cousin's taunting chant echoed in his head. *Broken toy, broken toy, broken toy.* The pressure increased.

Seamus. Noah's teeth clenched. *This was all because of Seamus.* Rage spiraled, growing and festering, consuming his very soul. His heart raced in an ever-tightening chest. It pounded like a jackhammer crushing concrete. His hands fisted, opening and closing. *I can't continue like this. Something has to give.* Fear slithered in, adding to the volatile emotional mix.

He dropped to his knees in the middle of the destruction. Great heaving sobs tore from his chest.

****

Clouds of blue-gray cigarette smoke swirled beneath neon lights. Tinny music blared from the man-sized speakers surrounding the disc jockey. Noah shoved through the crowd of people to reach the bar. He tapped two fingers on the scarred wooden bar top. Everywhere he turned, couples leaned against each other, swaying to the slow country music. Pain squeezed his chest. He looked away.

The bartender, a dingy white towel draped over one narrow shoulder, leaned forward. Pungent breath slapped Noah in the face. "What's your poison?"

He laid a twenty-dollar bill on the sticky bar. "Irish whiskey, straight up."

A water-spotted glass tumbler appeared. Golden

liquid from a dark, emerald bottle splashed into it. Noah slid the twenty forward and nodded his thanks to the bartender. He picked up the glass, rolling the liquid inside it, watching it cling to the sides before slipping back to the bottom of the tumbler. He closed his eyes and lifted the drink to his lips.

The odor jarred his memory. Images of his father's scarred fists, bleeding knuckles, danced behind his closed eyelids. *What am I doing? I'm not him. I didn't run two thousand miles to become him. I moved to Texas because I thought I'd be safe. When I looked at that map, I thought I'd found the perfect place, as far south as I could get and not leave the country. No one would ever think to look for me here. Not that I figured they'd ever look for me. Why look for a broken toy?*

Setting the untouched drink back on the bar, he turned and walked away.

"Hey, bud," the bartender asked, "what about your drink?"

Noah glanced back over his shoulder as he headed to the exit. "Thanks, but no thanks."

He stepped out the door into the night. Moonlight shone down on him. Brisk night air brushed his face. He closed his eyes and took a deep breath. "Well, looky here," an alcohol-soaked voice with a heavy Hispanic accent slurred from the darkness. "Not so tough without your gun and buddies, now are you, Mr. Ranger Man?"

Noah whirled.

A figure stepped from the shadowed edge of the parking lot. A dragon tattoo circled his neck. Noah recognized him as the thug from court last Thursday. W*as that only a week ago?*

The man bounced the end of a hickory ax handle

repeatedly off the palm of his left hand. He made a come-hither gesture with the wooden handle. A silhouetted stepped out of the shadows. Followed by another, and another, and *another…*

Six gang bangers surrounded him, all sporting macho, in-your-face attitudes. They spread out, circling like a pack of coyotes. Each held a weapon—a club, a knife, a chain.

Well, this isn't going to end well. He reached for his holster. His fingers brushed empty air. *Right. Bar. No gun. Well, hell.*

He spun to face the leader. He rolled his shoulders and his neck, loosening up tight muscles. His vertebrae cracked. *This is gonna hurt.* He widened his stance and opened his arms. "We gonna do this thing or what?"

The leader swung his bat.

Noah dodged.

The leader swung again, this time connecting with his head.

Noah's bell rang. His balance disappeared. So much so he didn't see the punch coming from the second thug. Or the third.

He stumbled. Fell to one knee.

Thug number four swung a boot at his jaw. Noah grabbed the boot and twisted, jerking the thug off his feet, slamming his head to the pavement. The thug didn't move.

Noah scrambled back to his feet, his ears still ringing. He wobbled from side to side. Finding his footing, he stepped into the leader's personal space. He led with an uppercut to the jaw, slamming the man's teeth together with a sharp crack. He followed with a solid punch to the underbelly, one that vibrated all the way through the spine. A left hook finished the job.

The remaining gang members jumped into the fray. Fists, knees, feet flew. Noah went down, overwhelmed by sheer numbers. Metal thudded against flesh. Blood spattered.

With Noah pinned on the ground, sucking air, the leader staggered back to his feet and waved everyone else away. A feral grin crossed his face. He pulled a small, matte-black pistol from his waistband. Squatting next to Noah, the gang member leaned forward. "Your cuz says to say hi…and bye." Grin widening, he stood and pointed the barrel of the gun right between Noah's eyes.

Squeezing his eyes shut, he inhaled deeply before opening them and locking his gaze with that of the gang leader. Sirens split the air. Red-and-blue lights flashed in the distance, minutes away from swarming into the parking lot. Minutes Noah could not afford to wait. The bangers scattered, leaving him alone with their leader.

Noah tried to stand. His legs folded beneath himself. Stabbing pain surged through him from his ribs. It hurt to breathe. He crumped onto his back on the ground.

The leader thumbed off the safety. His finger tightened on the trigger.

Noah's focus locked on the round, black barrel staring him down. *Well, it's in your hands, Lord.* His muscles tightened. He thrust his chin up and glared at the gunman. "Well? You waiting for an engraved invitation?"

Anticipation glittered in the thug's dead eyes. His lips curled up in a cruel smile. He squeezed the trigger.

The flash was blinding. Huge splotches of shadow

danced in Noah's vision, afterimages of the gun's muzzle flash. The noise, inches from his head, deafened him. The bullet slammed into the ground beside his head. The shooter collapsed on top of him, crushing the breath from his lungs.

A grimy, calloused hand stretched down to help Noah to his feet. "You okay, sir?"

Noah shook his head to clear it. "Trey? Is that you?"

"Yes, sir." The vagrant gave a slight bow. "Father always said a man must at times be as hard as nails and do what he must—in spite of personal consequences and ought to carry himself in the world as an orange tree would if it could walk up and down in the garden swinging perfumed things." A sock swung from his right hand.

"What?" Trey's words confused Noah. He grimaced and tugged on his ear. It didn't help with his confusion or the ringing from the gunshot. "Never mind. What's in the sock?"

Trey shook a chunk of black-veined, green granite out of the sock and held it up for Noah to see. "My lucky rock."

The sirens grew louder. Law enforcement was coming closer. Trey grabbed the ranger by the wrist. "We need to vacate these premises, posthaste."

Noah scooped the thug's gun from the dirt. He hiked his jeans up on his hips and shoved the pistol in his waistband, untucking his shirt to cover it.

Chapter Twenty-One

Tap, tap, tap. A finger patted Bree's cheek. She brushed it away. The small hand returned. "Maddie, go away." Bree rolled over. She crinkled her nose at the sour smell of the threadbare blanket but pulled it over her head anyway to block out the stripes of sunlight torturing her eyes.

"Bree?" Sarah whispered. "Where are the Texas Rangers? Are they here yet?"

Texas Rangers? What?

Bree flipped the blanket down and swiped the sleep from her eyes. She sat up, and the room whirled. Memories rushed back. Frantically, she surveyed the room. A group of small children surrounded her. In another corner of the dirty, wooden room sat a cluster of teenagers. She directed her attention to them. "Where are we?"

Vacant eyes met hers briefly before dropping away. A girl with tangled, unwashed brown hair held her palms up and out, shrugging slightly, before returning her gaze to the floor. "Who knows?" she said, her voice cracking on the last syllable. A bruise, fading from green to yellow, graced her cheek.

Bree tried to stand. Her knees buckled, sending her plunging back onto the thin mattress. Wire coils poked her in the backside as she landed. She sat for a moment, catching her breath, her head held in her hands.

A petite, blonde child kneeled beside her. “Is your daddy here yet? Has he found us?”

Bree raised her head, schooling her features and holding in her tears. “Sarah?”

The girl nodded; hope glistened behind her fear. “Is he here yet?”

Choking back a sob, Bree gathered Sarah into her arms. She held her tight. “Not yet, sweetie, but soon. I talked to him. He’s coming. Soon.”

“When? I want to go home. I’m hungry.”

The rancid scent of sour gas floated into the room on a hot breeze. Bree rose and walked to the open window. The window wasn’t actually open, but broken, allowing the fetid air to waft in and out. Bars covering the outside of the window shut down her thoughts of escape.

She surveyed room, taking in the emaciated condition of the others trapped with her. The room itself offered no help. Wooden, dirt-encrusted floors covered with worn twin mattresses, sheetrock walls peppered with holes, surrounded her. A solid steel door with a deadbolt was the only thing from this decade in the place. Wadded-up fast-food wrappers redolent with old grease littered the corners. *At least they feed us…maybe.*

A loud clattering noise outside the room made the children jump. Bree wrapped her arms around Sarah, holding her tight. She wasn’t sure if she was comforting the child or taking comfort. The other young children darted behind Bree, attempting to hide. More thumping noises and a few voices came from the outer room.

A key grated in the deadbolt. The door swung inward. A large man holding a pistol in his right hand blocked the opening. With his left hand, he tossed a large bag of fast food into the room before slamming the door closed and relocking it.

The kids swarmed the bag, ripping it open and tearing into the lukewarm hamburgers. Bree grabbed a burger for Sarah and for herself. She took a bite. It tasted off, but she was so hungry she didn't care. She inhaled the entire burger.

Twenty minutes later, her head began to swim, and the room spun. In one moment of clarity, a thought occurred to her. *Damn it, they drugged the burgers.*

****

Seamus paced outside the metal door, watching the hairdresser and two makeup artists set up their workstations. He glanced at his watch. Thirty minutes had passed since they had fed the livestock. He nodded at his son. "Handle this. I've got to go."

Patrick opened the steel door and dragged out three of the younger children, handing them off to the hairdresser and makeup artists. The women went to work on the children, curling hair, applying makeup, and draping them in skimpy costumes.

"Hurry it up," he snapped at the photographer setting up lights and a background. He ran his hand over the bandage on his face. "We don't have all day. The drugs will wear off soon."

"I'm ready." The photographer adjusted the height of one of the lightstands. "Lead them over."

One at a time, the photographer took digital images of the children for the online catalog. As soon as he finished with one child, someone carried out another. Before long, all the captives were in the front room.

Patrick watched the man with growing disgust. He

understood getting excited about the older girls, but half these kids were just that—little kids.

****

Bree's mouth tasted like old gym socks. *Drugged again. Damn it!*

She blinked her eyes and shook her head trying to clear it. She realized they were no longer in the dilapidated wooden room where they'd been held. She scanned this new room, searching for an escape. Dizziness messed with her depth perception. She reached her hand for the door only to fall to the floor, landing on her face.

Rough hands dragged her to the other side of the room. They propped her against the wall like a rag doll.

Fight it. Push through. You can do this. She struggled against the drugs. Slowly, clarity returned. She stayed huddled in the shadows against the wall, keeping her head down and trying not to attract any attention. She touched her lips, smearing dark red lipstick across her fingertips.

Sarah sidled over and climbed into her lap. Bree wrapped her arms protectively around the tiny girl.

The photographer's assistant grabbed for Sarah, trying to tug her away from Bree, but the little one clung like a burr.

Bree tightened her grip. The photographer motioned to one of the men guarding the children. "Screw it. Bring me both of them."

The beast grabbed Bree around the waist and lifted her to her feet. He half-carried, half-dragged her in front of the cameras. The photographer's assistant carried Sarah. She dropped the child with a hard plop onto the backdrop.

The heat of the lights made Bree glisten with sweat. She fought to keep Sarah hidden.

"For heaven's sake, fix the girl's lips. She's smeared." The photographer threw his hands up in the air. "And give her a drink. I can't work like this. She's dripping sweat." He reached around and grabbed an open bottle of water sitting beside his camera. Shoving it toward the teenager, he commanded, "Drink."

She glued her lips shut. Shook her head no. She crossed her arms over her chest and thrust her jaw out. *No way. No how. Not gonna do it.*

The brute who had already manhandled her pinched her nose closed. As soon as she opened her mouth to breathe, he dumped the water down her throat, spilling it over her chin and shirt. Within moments, euphoria allowed giggles to escape her lips. The sensation of being swept away in a veil of light engulfed her. *I can fly.* She gathered Sarah into her arms and began stumbling around the room, believing she was waltzing on clouds. Bright lights flashed around her. Bree collapsed to the floor, her limbs like jelly. Sarah curled up in her lap.

"Beautiful. Magnificent. Little Madonna, perfection." Lights continued to flash. The photographer dashed around, draping fabrics over and around the two girls, posing Bree's arms and legs this way and that.

Bree faded away, drifting on clouds of nothing.

****

The key scraped in the lock as Noah re-entered his house. Broken dishes, splinters of glass, a shattered tea pitcher, debris from his temper fit, littered the dining room floor. A sharp spike of pain pierced his right eye.

A band tightened around the top of his skull like someone had stuck an oil filter wrench on top of his head and cranked it down. Bright flashes of light and dark spots intermingled in his vision. This migraine would finish the job started by the thugs outside the bar.

He stumbled to the bathroom and collapsed on the floor in front of the toilet. Clinging to the porcelain god, he emptied his stomach. It was way too late to take the triptan that might have broken the migraine before it reached this point. *Maybe I should have gotten drunk.* The fleeting thought danced through his aching head.

He opened the cabinet and blindly fumbled for a washcloth, wetting it with hot water. Laying on the bathroom floor, in a semi-fetal position, he draped the cloth over his eyes. Just before his eyes closed, an object on the floor caught his attention.

Pushing through the pain, he struggled to his knees and crawled across the floor. There, by the trash can he had kicked over earlier, lay a box. A box for a pregnancy test. Random images flashed through his mind—Cat turning down wine; Cat holding her stomach; the weird way she acted when he said he was glad they didn't have kids. He picked up the box. Rattled it. Empty. Headache forced to the background, he pulled himself to his feet using the bathroom vanity. *Where is it?*

Frantically, he gathered the garbage from the floor, placing it back into the trash container. Nothing. No sign of the test. He checked the debris on the bedroom floor. Still no test. He whipped his gaze from wall to wall. Where could it be? The fancy table setting popped into his memory.

Noah made his way to the dining room. Faster and

faster, he began cleaning up the mess he had made all while searching. He had to know.

He had to know now.

There. In a pile of shards of ceramic from the broken dinner plates, he spotted the white stick. He nicked his finger, drawing blood, as he grabbed the test, hands shaking. *Cat must have wanted to surprise me with it at dinner tonight.* He could see her presenting him with the dome-covered silver platter, whisking away the lid with a sultry voilà, a soft smile on her crimson lips, and then what? *How do I read this damn thing?*

Taking a deep breath, he turned the stick over. He fell to his knees. In the result window, he read one word—*pregnant*.

Everything faded away. His mouth felt like it was stuffed with cotton, dry as a desert. A stupid grin lifted his cheeks. He smiled so hard it hurt. He was going to be a father. His shoulders dropped back as his chest puffed out. Pride filled him. *I'm going to be a daddy.*

Suddenly, he felt like he could walk on water.

A moment later, reality slammed home. He folded in on himself, his heart racing out of control. A cold sweat dampened his hairline. His migraine returned with a vengeance. Cat was out there somewhere, running from him, alone—and pregnant.

****

Hours before sunrise, Noah paused in the doorway of the all-night café, gathering his courage. Cat sat in their favorite booth on the far side of the restaurant. Armed with his new knowledge, his gaze lingered on her, searching for hints or confirmation. Light from the streetlamp in the parking lot flooded in the window. It teased cinnamon sparkles from her espresso colored hair. *So beautiful.*

Noah inhaled sharply. Scents of dark-roasted coffee beans—*why does coffee always smell like week-old skunk spray? Why do I even care?*—competed with freshly baked bread. His stomach growled. Ignoring it, he slid across the hunter green vinyl bench into the booth opposite Cat. “Hey, you.”

She stared at the untouched cup of coffee sitting on the green-speckled laminate table in front of her, her face tight, and her expression closed. She refused to face him. She twisted her fingers together. “What do you want?”

He reached across the table, placed his hands over hers. “Cat, sweetheart, look at me? Please?”

She yanked her hands out from beneath his. Her gaze met his. Hurt and anger battled for dominance on her face. “Don’t.”

“Cat, sweetie…”

She scrambled out of the booth. “Don’t touch me and don’t sweetie me.”

He stood, blocking her path to the exit. “Please, sit down.” He sighed. “I won’t touch you.”

She remained standing, arms crossed protectively over her abdomen. “It's a little late for that, don't you think?” she scoffed than stepped back. “I have absolutely nothing to say to you. I don’t even know who you are.”

His shoulders slumped. He moved aside and motioned for her to walk past him. As she did, he leaned forward and whispered in her ear, “I know.”

She stiffened, started to look at Noah, but whipped her head forward, raised her chin, and swept past him, right out the door.

"Damn it." Noah slammed his hand on the table, splashing cold coffee from the full cup. He dropped back into the booth and buried his head in his hands.

"Hello, Officer. I hope you will forgive me for mentioning it, but you look like shit."

Noah lifted his head.

Trey Panzer stood beside his table. Gray hair neatly bound in a braid dangling over his shoulder, clothes and hands clean, he appeared more alert and saner than Noah had ever seen him. The older man gestured to the empty bench. "May I join you?"

Wearily, he waved at the empty seat. "By all means. After last night, I owe you at least a cup of coffee." He checked the time on his watch. He had an hour before meeting Rhyden at the office. "Probably even breakfast. Please, join me."

Trey dropped into the booth and immediately began rearranging the condiments. He lined them up by size, in a precise line on the back edge of the table. Next, he picked all the sugar and sweetener packets from their ceramic container and likewise straightened them by color and size, turning the labels so all the lettering faced the same direction. "So what rests so heavily on your shoulders this morning?"

What the hell? "Where should I start? My girlfriend hates me. I bought her a ring, foolishly believing we would be together forever. Last night she left me. And I just discovered she's pregnant. She didn't even tell me. I'm going to be a daddy and will probably never even get to meet my child." Noah looked across the table, evaluating his audience.

"The truth will set you free. Of course, according

to Garfield, first it will make you miserable. James Garfield that is, not the lasagna-loving cat." His hands still busy adjusting items on the table, his eyes clear and focused on Noah, Trey nodded encouragingly.

In for a penny, in for a pound. "It goes deeper than that."

"Doesn't it always?" Lining up the salt and pepper shakers, he nodded sagely.

"My life is crumbling all around me. The past I tried to escape is trying to ruin the future I've made for myself. I have so many holes in my memory it may as well be made of swiss cheese. I'm terrified those blank spots will destroy my life. That is if my cousin doesn't kill me first. I'm going to lose it all…every single important piece of my life.

"And the rage…damn it, the fucking rage. It's eating me alive. Consuming me from the inside out. I don't know how to deal with it."

"You know, Father always said, a man who has never angered a woman is a failure in life. I believe he was a big fan of Christopher Morley. I miss Father. Perhaps he could make the rolling beasts and metal locusts go away. I know for certain he would be able to dismiss the aliens and the ghosts. I, for one, certainly do not wish to feel the sting of the locust's scorpion tail. I doubt my domicile such as it is would survive."

Noah bit back a heavy sigh as he glanced at his watch again. He let Trey's words roll over him without registering.

Trey continued rambling. "What a dust-up yesterday afternoon when one of the ghosts escaped the aliens! It was a sight to see. Vastly different from the parties they normally host. You could come and watch if you wanted. They are sure to let the ghosts out of the metal box tonight. It's time, you know. Last night the flashes. Tonight, the aliens come and take the ghosts away before the next batch arrives." Trey folded his hands neatly in his lap. "Perhaps we could order breakfast now?"

Noah waved to catch the attention of the server. "Perhaps we should."

As the server took Trey's order, Noah surreptitiously dialed Cat's number. The phone rang in his ear, once, twice, click. She sent his call to voicemail. Again.

****

"Ranger Morgan?"

The tone of Sylvia's voice triggered an alert in Noah. He met her at the door of his office. "Sylvia, what is it?"

She twisted her hands together. Speech rushed, she said, "Ranger Trammell's not here. I tried calling him, but it went to voicemail. I need you up front. There's a girl waiting. Says she knows something about his daughter. Knows she is missing."

Wetting lips that suddenly dried up, Noah brushed past the receptionist, texting his partner as he went. "Where is she? The girl? Where?"

"In the lobby, sir."

Noah pushed through the glass door separating the employees-only area of the law enforcement from the public lobby. A teenage girl sat alone, arguing with herself, rhythmically tapping her thumbs against her fingers. At the sound of the door opening, the girl jumped to her feet. She was a tiny thing with stringy, mouse-brown hair, wearing a too-large long-sleeve shirt, baggy jeans, and scuffed, holey tennis shoes. She clutched an oversized hobo bag to her chest. She looked familiar, but he couldn't place her. He searched his memory for friends of Bree who might resemble this girl and found none.

"You're not Ranger Trammell. I know you." She searched the lobby. Her thumb bounced faster against her fingers. "Where is he? I need to talk to him. Now. Please."

"No, I'm not." Noah approached the girl. "I'm Ranger Morgan. Ranger Trammell is in the field. Do you know where Bree is? Can you take me to her?"

Her shoulders drooped. She appeared to fold in on herself, her petite frame shrinking even more. "But I really need to talk to Ranger Trammell," she whispered brokenly.

Noah moved closer, holding one hand in front of him, palm up. "It's okay, Miss…?"

No response. She seemed to be struggling with a weighty matter. Her eyes flicked back and forth across the floor as if she were foraging for answers.

A memory clicked in his head. She was the girl with the crappy parents who tried to have her arrested. "I remember you. The girl with the Honda, right?" He racked his brain, trying to remember her name.

She startled as if she had forgotten he was there. Her eyes held a world of hurt. She swallowed visibly hard, her throat jerking up and down. She shook her head. "He said he loved me." One hand slipped into her open bag. She drew a pistol from her bag, raised it.

"Gun!" Sylvia yelled, hit the panic alarm and scrambled behind the bulletproof glass.

Noah waved the receptionist off. "Get out of here."

He turned his attention back to the girl. Hand still outstretched toward her, each step precise and deliberate, he eased slowly closer, never losing eye contact with her.

The gun wavered in her hands. Tears cut a path down her cheeks. She gulped air.

Gentling his voice like he'd observed Rhyden do with a skittish, unbroken colt, Noah said, "Hold on there, darlin'. Why don't you give me the gun?" A tiny touch of Irish whispered through his words. "Ye don' wanna choose a permanent solution for a temporary problem, now do ye?"

Rochelle jerked away from him as if slapped. She steadied the gun in her hands. "Temporary problem? Who says it's a temporary problem? Don't you get it? I can't fix it. It can't be fixed. I killed people." Her voice broke. "I murdered people…for…a lying sack of shit. I thought we were changing the world. Making it better." She locked eyes with Noah. "I thought he loved me." Pain rolled off her in waves. "Why?" she whispered. "Why did I believe anyone could ever love me?"

Her words struck a deep chord within Noah. With infinite patience, he sidled another step closer to the girl. He caught movement in the corner of his eye. Other officers converged on the lobby. He signaled for them to stay back.

In one smooth, swift motion, Rochelle raised the gun to her temple.

Noah rushed her, slapping the gun from her hand. He slammed her to the floor. They grappled for the gun. The gun fired. Both stopped moving. A puddle of blood formed on the tile floor around them. Officers rushed into the room, screaming for medical assistance.

****

Sharp, stabbing pain and an incessant beeping forced Noah's eyes open. The thin fabric curtain surrounding the emergency room cubicle whisked open with a rattle of metal hooks in their tracks. A doctor wearing a white coat over bloodied green scrubs carrying a clipboard in his large hands approached the bed. A purple stethoscope looped around his neck.

Looking up from the chart in his hands, he squinted over his reading glasses at his patient. A smile wreathed his face. "Ranger Morgan. Are you trying to set a record for the most ER visits in one week? Don't you see enough of the lovely Cat at home?"

Beside him, Rhyden caught the doctor's attention. He frantically ran the flat edge of his hand across his throat in a cease-and-desist motion.

Noah glared at the doctor from the bed. The plastic ID bracelet chafed his wrist. Tubes and lines snaked around him, tying him to various monitors. The beeping of the equipment combined with the moaning cries and the vomiting noises from the bed in the next cubicle and the doctor's flippant attitude stomped all over his last nerve. "Not funny, Doc."

The doctor cleared his throat. "Okay," he said in a brisk, decidedly more professional manner. "Let me see what we have here." He nudged the readers farther up his nose. After skimming the chart, he snapped it closed and removed his glasses, rubbing his eyes. "You were beyond lucky today. The bullet passed cleanly through the soft tissue on your anterolateral flank…"

Rhyden interrupted. "His what?"

Seeing the blank expression on Noah's face, the doctor continued, "Err, um, your love handles…"

Affronted, Noah cut in. "I do *not* have love handles. Look at this torso. Fit as a fiddle."

Without missing a beat, the doctor continued. "The bullet missed all your major organs and blood vessels. Thank God. It's a good thing the bullet was a target round. Had it been a hollow point, we'd be having a completely different conversation right now, most likely with your next of kin." The doctor paused and asked Noah, "Is it true…err, well, I mean, a couple of the officers were saying you charged a suspect holding a loaded gun. You do realize this could have been a fatal wound, right? What were you thinking? Especially now, with Cat—"

"Doc…" A warning tone edged Noah's voice.

"Right. Sorry. Okay. We've cleaned the wound and closed it with absorbable stitches. They should dissolve in two to three weeks. Keep the dressing clean and dry. Change it daily. Gently clean the wound and treat it with antibiotic ointment. I recommend wrapping the bandages with plastic wrap when you shower."

He scribbled on a prescription pad, ripped off the top page, and scribbled on the one beneath it as well. He handed them to Noah. "I'm prescribing something for the pain and a general antibiotic for the next seven days. Based on our previous encounters, I don't suppose I can talk you into spending the night?"

"Don't even think about it."

"Yeah, that's what I thought." The doctor threw up his hands in an *I give up* gesture. He exhaled sharply. "All right, tough guy, wait here. The nurse will be in shortly with discharge instructions."

Noah nodded. "Thanks, Doc." He faced his partner. "What are you doing here? Have you found Bree?"

"You were shot. Why do you think I'm here?"

Noah scrubbed his hands across his eyes. He peered at Rhyden, taking in the dark circles beneath his eyes, the obvious weight loss. "I really don't know. Girl came in rambling on about murdering people, and she had a gun. She was going to shoot herself. I stopped her. Something else…something…important." He yawned widely and rubbed at his eyes again. "Damn drugs."

"Bree!" Noah shot straight up in the bed, grabbing the railing, eyes wide. "She said she knew about Bree." White hot pain shot through his abdomen. "Is the girl all right? Did anyone question her? Do we have Bree home?"

Laying a hand on Noah's shoulder, Rhyden eased him back to a prone position. "Easy, buddy. The girl's fine. Bennett County investigators interviewed her. She claims to be the school shooter. Some boy—we think it may be the same one the Sanders girl was mixed up with—convinced her shooting up the school would save the world. She kept calling him PC. Judge is holding her on an emergency detainment. We can't talk to her again until her parents are located, and they've vanished. She's being held up on the fifth floor in the psych unit with armed guards on the door while we search for them. She didn't know the kid's real name or where Bree was. She didn't even know for sure that he took Bree."

"What are you doing here? Shouldn't you be out searching for your daughter?"

Pain flashed across Rhyden's features. "Search where? We're at a loss. It's killing me, but there's literally nothing more I can do without new information except sit by the phone and pray. I can't stand to go home. Sam and Maddie follow me around the house, silent accusations painted all over their faces. Constantly asking if we've found Bree yet, when we're going to bring her home…as if I would hide her away from them. It's been almost a week now. I've never felt so useless in all my life." He paused, his Adam's apple bobbing as he struggled for control. "I was hoping the girl had told you something useful. Given us a new starting point."

Noah ripped the blood pressure cuff from his arm. He tugged on the IV needle where it slid beneath the skin of his arm. "Where are my clothes? I need to get out of here so we can interview her. She came looking for you. Maybe she will tell us something she didn't tell the detectives."

"Yeah, can't do that until we find her parents. Minor, remember?"

"Damn." He fell back against the gurney, ignoring the trickle of blood running down his arm. "How weird is it that I don't know whether to be furious with the girl or feel sorry for her? She just kept ranting and apologizing. I didn't really believe her when she said she had killed people. This tiny little waif with big, soulful eyes. She looked like a war orphan." Fatigue swept over Noah. Eyes heavy, his head drooped against the pillow. His arms weighed a ton. Even breathing became a chore.

"From the sounds of it, she lives in a war zone. The sheriff's office has had multiple calls to her residence for domestic situations. Dad beats up stepmom. Stepmom beats up dad. Sounds like stepbrothers have tried sexually assaulting the girl, too."

Rhyden's nostrils flared. He cracked his knuckles. "Don't know why CPS didn't yank her out of there years ago, but then again I don't know how much she says is real and how much is imagined. She's pretty messed up. She does know details only the school shooter could know, so yeah, I'm with you. Don't know whether to feel sorry for her or hate her. Poor girl is completely broken." He ran a hand across the back of his neck. "Have to wonder how much of it is the system's fault."

Rhyden fidgeted with the rolls of bandages on the stainless-steel rolling tray. He avoided making eye contact with his partner. "So," he continued, "on the subject of not knowing whether or not to feel sorry for someone, what happened with you and Cat? I've known her for a long time, and I've never seen her so shut down before."

Noah fake yawned. "Damn these drugs."

"Answer my question. I'm worried about you. You've just been really weird lately. What's going on?"

"Do we have to do this now?"

Rhyden tapped his fingernails against the tray. He stared at Noah without responding. Tap, tap-tap, tap, tap-tap, tap, tap-tap.

On top of the beeping, and the other hospital sounds, pain, misery, and that god-awful tapping pushed Noah over the edge. "Fine. I'll tell you. Just, please, stop that infernal racket."

Leaning back and folding his arms across his chest, Rhyden tucked his hands under his armpits. He nodded regally. "Please. Proceed with your tale of woe."

"Tale of woe? Really? Cat and I had a fight."

"Duh."

He dropped his chin, tilted his head, and aimed a venomous look at his partner. "Do you want to hear this or not?"

Rhyden pretended to lock his lips and throw away the key before he waved his hand in a rolling *go ahead* motion.

"It was bad. She left. I trashed the house. Huge mess. Holes in the sheetrock. The works. Then I headed to the bar."

Rhyden's eyebrows disappeared into his hairline. "You what?"

"Don't worry." Noah obviously hadn't shared specifics of his childhood with his buddy, but he had talked about growing up with an alcoholic and his feelings about drinking to solve problems. "I didn't drink. I sat and stared at the glass for an hour before deciding to go home and clean up the house."

He conveniently forgot to mention the altercation with the thugs. That would lead to too many other questions he didn't want to answer. He was good at skipping over things he wanted to hide.

"O-ka-a-a-y. What am I missing? Did Cat give you the black eye? I mean, y'all have fought in the past, but you've never gotten physical before."

"We didn't get physical this time either."

"Fine, you didn't get your ass kicked by a girl. I get it. This isn't your first rodeo, though. Y'all always make up. So what's actually going on?"

This time, he avoided Rhyden's eyes. He zeroed in on the whiteboard hanging on the wall across from his bed, the one with the smiley-frowny faces used to indicate pain levels. *What's my pain level? Physically or mentally? Cat ripped out my heart. I don't think numbers go high enough.*

"Hello?" Rhyden waved a hand in front of his face. "Where did you go?"

"I don't know what to do." He turned to face his best friend, despair radiating from his entire being. "Cat's pregnant…and she didn't even tell me."

"Excuse me?"

"Yeah. I found the test stick. Great big, bright pink letters spelling out P R E G N A N T." His voice shook. "I'm going to be a dad." *And I'm probably going to fuck that up, too.*

Rhyden scooted closer and patted Noah awkwardly on the leg. "Um, congratulations?"

Chapter Twenty-Two

There's only one way to solve this problem.

Noah tugged on latex gloves before he reached for the unregistered AR-15 he had picked up at a gun show. Lightweight and inexpensive, the locally built gun rested beside his binoculars on the seat of the rental car. He removed the magazine and checked his ammunition for the fourth time. Fully loaded.

One at a time, he flicked the bullets out of the magazine. Picking up a red mechanic's rag, he rubbed each cartridge down, ensuring no fingerprints existed on it. He wasn't going to prison because of a stupid mistake. Keeping the gloves on his hands despite the sweat building up inside of them, he reloaded each round one by one.

He inserted the magazine back into the rifle and racked the charging handle, chambering a bullet. Determined, he tucked the gun under the driver's seat within easy reach. He pulled off the gloves, wadded them up, and tucked them into his shirt pocket.

Eyes glued to the front door of the paving shop, he tapped a rhythm on the sticky steering wheel. His leg bounced. He hadn't slept in thirty-six hours. His stitches itched beneath the bandage. With one hand, he popped the lid off a bottle of pain pills. He tossed two in his mouth and swallowed them dry. He chucked the bottle onto the seat beside him.

Come on, come on, come on.

A light in the office went dark. The door of the shop swung open. A familiar profile, now creased by time, exited the building. Noah's chest tightened. *Grandda.* A flood of warm recollections swept over him. The man turned. Noah caught sight of him head-on. *Wait, that's not Grandda.* Cold hatred flooded through his veins.

Seamus. Let's go, you bastard. I'm gunning for you.

He saw his cousin lock up the office door, then amble across the parking lot to his heavy-duty work truck. His cell phone must have rung because he lifted it to one ear while he climbed into the truck, started it up, and drove out of the parking lot.

Hidden in the shadows of the dump truck, Noah cranked up his rental. Dust blew from the air conditioning vents in the cracked dash. A tinny rattle from a loose heat shield filled the cabin. *Guess they weren't kidding when they called the place Rent-A-Wreck.* He tugged the bill of his ball cap lower, hiding his face, hoping the darkly tinted windows would help conceal his identity. With a heavy clunk, the vehicle's automatic transmission ground into reverse. Noah backed from the parking space. Hands twitching with anticipation, he shifted into drive, ready to follow his prey. Hopefully, Seamus would lead him to the captives.

Why the hell didn't I think of this sooner?

Noah thought of the rifle nestled beneath his seat. *And if he doesn't lead me to the kids, well, I'll still solve one problem.*

Mile after mile, he followed Seamus down twisting

back roads, hanging far enough back to stay off his cousin's radar but close enough not to lose sight of him. The sun slipped toward the horizon, leaving a brilliant swatch of crimson in its path. The glare reflecting from the silver pickup blinded Noah. He wished the sun would hurry up and go down. He squinted before shoving his aviator shades over his aching eyes. Lack of sleep, anger, and the glare combined to give him a vicious headache. The pain pills couldn't touch it. Hell, with his luck, they probably even contributed to it.

Come on, you sorry bastard. Lead me to the kids. The silver truck drove farther into the South Texas countryside before turning off on a red dirt road. Mexican eagles picked at a swollen deer carcass lying partially on the roadway. As Seamus' truck approached, they lifted off as one, spiraling upward. As the truck passed, they drifted back down to finish their roadkill dinner.

Seamus turned right passing a yellow "no outlet" sign previously peppered by a shotgun. Rust formed at the edges of the pellet holes. Noah's eyes narrowed. *Got you now, you useless waste of human flesh.* He sped up, knowing the cloud of dust kicked up by his cousin's truck would keep him hidden from view. Red brake lights flared in front of him. Noah eased off the accelerator.

Ignoring the posted no-trespassing signs, Seamus left the county road turning into an oilfield lease. The easement he turned onto was a narrow, one-lane path with deep tracks embedded in the red dirt. An eighteen-wheeler carrying a full load had obviously traversed the thoroughfare shortly after the last heavy rain. Noah pulled to the shoulder of the county road, idling in the high weeds. *If things continue true to course, my muffler will start a brush fire.*

He watched as Seamus drove up the easement to a gate. The newfangled automatic gate blocking access to the property contrasted greatly with the leaning mesquite fence posts and drooping barbed wire. Seamus stretched his arm out of the truck window and typed a code into a keypad at the entrance of the lease. The gate slowly swung open. He drove forward and continued bouncing down the easement. He paused just long enough to ensure the gate closed behind him.

Noah placed the rental car in park and switched the ignition off. He picked up the binoculars and watched the silver truck until it came to a stop in front of a stack of rusty shipping containers. He scanned the area, watching for any other activity. To the left of the containers, he spotted a set of tank batteries used for storing oil and the saltwater waste pumped from the oil wells. Beyond them sat an empty helipad. Several hundred yards past the helipad stood a falling-down, centuries-old farmhouse.

Noah double-checked to make sure the overhead light was disabled before easing the door on the rental car open. He didn't want an untimely flash of light to attract Seamus's attention. A throbbing twinge in his side prompted him to pop another couple of pain pills. Reaching beneath the seat of the car, he grabbed his rifle. He hissed. A sharp pain sliced through his finger. *Damn rental car.* A loose spring hidden beneath the seat had cut into the meat of his trigger finger. He wiped the blood on his shirt as he stepped from the vehicle. He leaned back into the car, grabbed the binoculars, and placed their strap around his neck.

Another quick look around where he stood revealed no danger of anyone spotting him. The sun finished its silent slide into oblivion, shrouding Noah in darkness. Quietly, he eased across the bar ditch to the deteriorating fence surrounding the oil lease. He examined the fencing material. *Good, not electrical.* Raising the binoculars to his eyes, he searched for Seamus. *Too dark.* He let the binoculars fall, dangling against his chest. Picking up the rifle, he peered through the night vision scope. *Like looking through green cellophane.* He found Seamus still sitting in the driver's seat of his truck. The man appeared to still be focused on his cell phone.

Noah reached the fence and cautiously placed his rifle in the grass on the other side. Avoiding the cut on his finger, he carefully separated the strands of barbed wire and climbed through the fence. Clear of the obstruction, he dropped to a crouch, wincing at the pain from his wound. He used the rifle scope to once again scout for danger. Not seeing any, he allowed tunnel vision to take over, focusing all his attention on Seamus. He clenched and unclenched his fists. His jaw ached from grinding his teeth. Taking a slow, deep breath, he relaxed his jaw and shook the tension from his hands.

He scanned the area one more time. The shipping containers snagged his interest. His sixth sense tingled. *Secure. Isolated. Good place to keep captives.*

Beyond the containers, he saw the helipad and farther along, the decrepit farmhouse, all bathed in shades of green from the night vision. The helipad showed signs of recent use but was empty now.

Noah strained his ears. No telltale whomp, whomp,

whomp noise. He watched the horizon. No navigational lights so unless the helicopter was running dark, there wasn't one inbound…yet. He inspected the farmhouse through the scope, searching for movement. It sat several hundred yards beyond the helipad. Roof caving in on one corner, paint peeling, it appeared abandoned. His gut told him looks could be deceiving.

He slithered closer to the tank batteries. His skin steamed with sweat. The stench of oilfield gases stung his eyes, burned his lungs. He examined the tanks. Someone, probably the pumper, had left a hatch at the top of one of the storage tanks open.

An interior light flashed from the pickup. Seamus stepped out of the truck, glancing at his wristwatch before turning his attention to the night sky. Impatience boiled. He paced beside his truck. He rolled his neck and shoulders. His eyes flicked from the night sky to his watch and back again. Several times he paused and checked his cell phone.

Noah wasn't close enough to hear what he said, but it was plain from his expression and gestures that Seamus was complaining. After checking the security of the rifle strapped over his shoulder, he dropped to his belly and crawled closer. Sand burrs dug into his clothing, reaching all the way through to draw blood. His stitches pulled. He ignored the pain and crept ever closer. Even with the sun long set, the heat continued to rise. Sweat glued his shirt to his back, turned the dust lingering on his skin from the road to sticky, red mud. Still, Noah snuck closer to his target. Finally within range…

He snugged the rifle tight against his shoulder, laying his cheek against the cool, black polymer stock.

He zeroed the crosshairs on Seamus's temple. The image in the night vision scope wavered crazily. *Probably shouldn't have taken those last two pain pills.* He closed his eyes and held them closed for a ten count. Opening his eyes, he inhaled deeply, held it for a moment before blowing it out. He held his breath as he resettled the crosshairs on his foe. *Easy now. Steady.*

His finger tightened on the trigger. Seamus turned, his face plainly visible in the magnifying scope, staring straight at Noah but not seeing him in the darkness. The breath whooshed from his chest. He whipped the rifle down. He could not pull the trigger on an unarmed man. Not even one who deserved it as much as Seamus. He wasn't that man, never had been, never would be—as much as right now he wished he could be.

Noah clambered to his feet, careful to keep to the shadows and avoid calling attention to himself. Lifting the rifle back up to watch Seamus through the scope, Noah saw him answer a call.

Rage purpled Seamus's face. He threw his phone through the open window of his truck before opening the door and climbing in after it. With a roar, the pickup flared to life, flinging rocks and gravel into the air as the crunch of tires heralded his exit.

Noah's legs crumpled, his bones dissolved, as he collapsed in a heap on the ground, disgusted with himself. Seamus's truck disappeared down the road. A wave of nausea from the pain medication roiled in his stomach. Still Noah sat unmoving, clutching the rifle. All these years. All the torture. All the hate. And he still couldn't pull the trigger.

He stood and flung the rifle away with a guttural roar. It hit the ground and fired off a round. The bullet ricocheted off a rock, screaming upward. Sparks flew. A slight *ping* followed by a massive *boom* knocked Noah on his ass. A spark from the ricochet ignited the combustible gases escaping from the open tank hatch.

Noah's ears rang. Light seared his eyes. Flames danced, illuminating the night. He scrambled to his feet. Grabbing his phone, he checked the GPS coordinates and dialed 9-1-1. He raced toward the rental car.

"Bennett County Sheriff's Office, what is your emergency?"

"Brooke? Noah Morgan here. I'm at coordinates 28.8419 north, 98.7575 west off of county road 1309. There's been…"

The second and third tanks exploded, sending up a giant fireball. The shock wave slammed him to the ground. His phone shattered. Fiery debris rained from the sky. Slapping out flames as they landed on him, he continued crawling to the car. A giant piece of metal clipped his head. The world went black.

****

Get it off! Can't breathe.

Noah swam back to consciousness swinging his arms, swiping at his face. Pressure around his throat strangled him. A band squeezed his arm, growing tighter and tighter. A cool hand brushed the hair from his forehead while another hand applied pressure to his shoulder, holding him prone.

He opened his eyes to find Cat hovering over him. *My angel!* She said something, but he couldn't hear her over the ringing in his ears. She replaced the oxygen mask over his mouth and nose. The pressure on his arm relaxed. The ringing lessened. "One-thirty-two over eighty-two." She jotted the numbers on the back of the latex glove covering her left hand. “Not bad, considering.” She fished in the pocket of her uniform cargo pants and drew out a penlight. She flashed it across his eyes.

The bright light made him flinch. He struggled to sit up. Debilitating pain shot through his body. Warm blood trickled down his side. He collapsed back onto the gurney. His head felt like it was on fire. Trying to lighten the look of worry on Cat’s face, he said, “If you could take my brain off the hibachi, I’d appreciate it.”

“Not funny.” She checked the fit of the cervical collar wrapped around Noah’s neck and tightened the spider straps securing him to the stretcher. “Can you tell me your name? What day it is?” She continued down the scoring system used by first responders to determine the level of consciousness in a person after a potentially traumatic brain injury.

“Cat? Wh-what happened?” he asked, his words muffled by the oxygen mask.

“We don’t really know. Brooke called me. She said you called dispatch and gave your location, but before you could say anything else, she heard a huge explosion, and the call dropped.” Cat kneeled beside the gurney, using the shears to cut away the remains of his shirt. She stopped, dropped her head against his chest. Emotion strangled her voice. “My God! I thought we’d lost you.”

Noah jerked the oxygen mask off. “I love you, Cat.” *Tell me you still love me. Please.*

She jerked away from him as if burned. “Jim, your patient is awake. Vitals are stable. Pupils equal and reactive. A fifteen on the Glasgow scale. Looks like he ripped out his stitches.” She stood, clamped an arm across her slightly pooching tummy. "I have to get out of here." The ambulance rocked as she stepped out.

"Cat!" Frantic, Noah struggled to get off the stretcher and follow her.

Jim restrained him. "Easy, bud, lay still. We're not through assessing you."

"Fuck that. I don't need assessed. I need Cat."

The paramedic pressed him back against the gurney. "And she needs space. I don't know what you did—she won't tell me—and to be honest, I really don't want to know, but you messed up. Bad. Give her a little room. She'll come around." He tugged the scraps of Noah's shirt out of the way. "In the meantime, let's see what we can do to patch you up."

A knock sounded on the ambulance door. The bus sank as Rhyden stepped up on the bumper. "How is he, Jim?"

"*He* can speak for himself. I'm fine. Get me out of here, Rhy."

Rhyden exchanged looks with Jim.

The medic shrugged. "I strongly recommend he go to the hospital. He took a fairly hard hit to the head, has several minor burns on his lower extremities, plus he ripped open the gunshot wound on his side." Jim glared at his patient. "On top of that, someone doubled his ration of asshole know-it-all attitude for the day."

Noah growled. Ripping the blood pressure cuff from his arm and removing the spider straps, he sat up. Tearing the cervical collar from his neck, he said, "I am not going to the hospital."

With a placating motion directed at his partner, Rhyden asked, "Can you just patch him up?"

Jim rubbed the back of his neck as he studied the

bloody bandages littering the floor. He pursed his lips. "I guess so. I can try putting butterflies over the stitches. No guarantees it will work." He glowered from Rhyden to Noah and back to Rhyden with narrowed eyes. "But he needs to get re-stitched…soon. And he'll have to sign a no-transport waiver."

"Just get me the damn waiver and let me the hell out of here."

"Fine," Jim snapped. "No wonder Cat doesn't want to deal with you." He rummaged in the supply cabinet, grabbing a handful of butterfly bandages. He cleaned the wound, a bit rougher than he normally would, and pasted the bandages over it. To Rhyden, he said, "Nothing I can do about the asshole part." Snapping off his latex gloves, he grabbed the rugged laptop designed for field usage from the bench beside the gurney. Tapping rapidly, he opened a waiver form. Shoving it in front of Noah, he said, "Here. Sign this. Use the tip of your finger."

Formalities completed, Rhyden helped Noah from the ambulance. Jim tossed a spare T-shirt at him. "Might be a little big on you but it's better than running around bloody and half-naked."

Noah caught the shirt. "Thank you, Jim."

"Whatever." The paramedic gathered up the used bandages, wrappers, and other detritus and flung them into the trash pail by the side door of the box. He ripped the bloodied sheet off the gurney before turning to face Noah. "I'm not joking. That wound needs tending." His voice dropped to a mumble. "Damn good thing your head is so hard." Raising his voice, he said, "Go on, get out of here. Before I change my mind and strap you back to the stretcher with the real restraints."

Several hours later, the fire finally under control, Noah and Rhyden walked over to the ramshackle farmhouse. They had already investigated the shipping containers and found nothing.

"Feeling okay?" Rhyden asked.

"Oh yeah. Fucking fantastic. I feel like I've been beat up, shot, run over by a dump truck, and these damn drugs making me woozy, but other than that I'm just peachy keen."

"Do you need me to take you to the hospital?"

Noah answered him with a rude gesture and a glare.

"Fine. What were you doing out here in the middle of nowhere loaded for bear?"

"What do you mean?"

Rhyden crossed his arms in front of his chest. He stopped walking and widened his stance. "I mean there is no reason for you to be out here. It's not in our county. It's not even in our region. And what's with the unregistered rifle? Why are you here?"

Noah shook his head and stalked toward the house. He stepped on the front porch. Boards groaned beneath his weight.

"I'm serious, Noah. What's going on with you?"

"I don't know what you are talking about."

He tugged on the rusty doorknob embedded in the wooden door. The sagging door swung open way too easily and way too quietly. Someone had been here recently. He flicked on his LED flashlight, illuminating the interior of the front room. "Son of a bitch! Call forensics, Rhy. Now."

"What?" Rhyden shouldered Noah aside. "What the hell?"

Several racks of skimpy costumes and three vanities covered with a ton of cheap cosmetics lined the walls of the room. The rangers froze in place to avoid contaminating the scene. They swung their lights through the space. Through an open steel door on the other side of the room, stained, wafer-thin mattresses covered the far corner of the floor. A sparkle of green atop one of the mattress pads glinted in the glow of the flashlight. Rhyden darted to the corner.

"Rhy, wait."

A bellow of torment escaped his chest. He slumped to the floor, clutching a blood-soaked, green-sequined tank top. "It's hers. Bree was here."

He stomped back across the room. Dropping the shirt, he grabbed Noah by the throat. Slammed him against the wall. "What. The. Fuck. Is. Going. On? I'm sick of your sketchy behavior. Why do you always lead me to places Bree has been held after she's gone?"

Noah smashed through Rhyden's hands, shoving them from his throat. He pushed away from the wall.

"Are you somehow involved in this? How could you do that to Bree? She loves you. You're her uncle."

Noah bit his lip. The desire to confess was overwhelming, but fear of the consequences held his tongue. "What do you mean 'do this to Bree'? Do you really think I would hurt her? Is that what you really believe?" He shoved Rhyden to the ground and stormed off, leaving his partner staring after him.

****

Driving away from the thwarted assassination attempt, Noah couldn't decide which hurt the most—his body or his heart. He flipped through the radio stations, searching for his favorite alien guy on late night AM radio. The new guy wasn't quite as good as the old one, but unless the dead really could talk, the new guy would just have to do. Noah wasn't sure if he believed in aliens and the paranormal or not, although he had seen some strange things in his day. Tonight—he glanced at the horizon, *this morning?*—he definitely needed a distraction from the crazy thoughts bouncing around inside his skull.

Rhyden was asking too many tough questions. Noah could feel his time running out.

The station faded in and out. "Tell me more about your theory," the host said.

A deep, evangelical voice boomed over the radio. "In the Bible in Revelations chapter nine, John the Revelator states 'And the fifth angel blew his trumpet, and I saw a star falling from heaven to earth, and he was given the key to the shaft of the bottomless pit. He opened the shaft of the bottomless pit, and from the shaft rose smoke like the smoke of a great furnace, and the sun and the air were darkened with the smoke from the shaft. Then from the smoke came locusts on the earth, and they were given power like the power of scorpions of the earth.'

"Then later on, he describes those locusts. He says 'In appearance the locusts were like horses prepared for battle; on their heads were what looked like crowns of gold; their faces were like human faces, their hair like women's hair, and their teeth like lions' teeth; they had breastplates like breastplates of iron, and the noise of their wings was like the noise of many chariots with horses rushing into battle. They have tails and stings like scorpions…'

"Many believers think this refers to a time in the

distant future. It makes them feel better, safer, to think that. But they are wrong, dead wrong. The apocalypse has already begun.

"The smoke? Do you remember the images of the skies over Kuwait during Desert Storm when all the oil wells were burning?"

His thoughts mired in quicksand; Noah snorted. *Really?* He reached up to change the channel, but the next words spoken by the show's guest stayed his hand.

"Those metal locusts aren't mythical beasts from the future either. They are here and now. Helicopters. Think about it… Crowns of gold? Have you looked up into a sunny day as a helicopter swoops overhead? Those rotors reflect the sun, looking like a golden crown. Breastplates of iron? Armor, of course. They painted some of those choppers with ferocious teeth, looking just like a lion as early as 1965."

The radio guest droned on, but Noah had heard enough. He slid the rental car into a rapid J-turn, heading back in the opposite direction toward Redus Crossing, hoping against hope that Trey was home. Noah had questions needing answers only the strange little man could provide.

Fifteen minutes later, Noah drove up in front of another ramshackle residence. The resemblance between the two locations was downright eerie. Trey's house hadn't fallen into quite the same disrepair as the house the captives had been held in, but it was close. An overgrown, abandoned airstrip replaced the helipad. Rusting shipping containers dotted the field beyond the runway.

Thank God. On the rotting veranda wrapped around the farmhouse, a familiar figure rocked. Noah unfolded his lanky frame from the rental car, stretched, and waved at Trey.

"Welcome to my humble abode, Ranger." Trey stood and bowed. "Come in. Come in. Remove an encumbrance from your extremities. Forgive me for saying so, but it appears you were standing directly in front of the fan when the proverbial stuff hit it. What propels you to my doorstep so early on such an auspicious day?"

"Please, sit back down." Noah gestured to the cracked and peeling white wooden rocking chair Trey had vacated before dropping into the matching one beside it. A yawn cracked Noah's jaw. He tried to swallow it, but it was no use. He hadn't slept in over forty-eight hours. A second yawn followed on the heels of the first.

Trey yawned widely, making no attempt to hide it. "Are you testing me, Ranger? Rest assured; I am no psychopath."

"What?" He didn't have time to follow his companion's conversational gambits down the rabbit hole today. "You know what? Never mind." Noah leaned forward on the edge of his seat. "Trey, what do these aliens look like?" He cringed for even thinking the words about to slip past his lips. "Are they gray men with long arms and big heads?"

Trey shot to his feet. His head snapped back. He stretched his neck up and dipped his chin to glare at Noah. "How…dare…you?" he stammered. "After all I have done on your behalf? You insult me like this?"

"Easy, buddy, I didn't mean to offend you."

"Offense meant or not, it was received." Pacing back and forth on the porch, Trey flapped his hands like he was waving Noah's words away. His lips moved, but no sound came out as he searched for words.

Noah placed a calming hand on the other man's shoulder.

Trey turned away, refusing to be placated and refusing to make eye contact.

Noah stepped in front of the old man, forcing him to meet his eyes. "I apologize. I am at my wit's end. You are the only one who can help me. Please. What do these aliens look like?"

Trey huffed out a heavy breath. Dropping back into his rocker, he said, "Fine. Contrary to widely held belief, I am not the village idiot. These aliens are from south of the Texas border, not outer space." He scoffed again. "Gray men with big heads. Pfft! You watch too much television. These men have dark olive skin, brown eyes, and straw cowboy hats covering their shoulder-length dark hair. They wear gaudy pearl snaps shirts left over from the late sixties and embroidered with large roses, blue jeans held up by white leather belts dripping with conchos and rhinestones, and roach-killer boots."

"What the hell is a roach-killer boot?"

Trey rolled his eyes. "Your education is sorely lacking. These boots were all the rage in the 1950s. Roach killers are boots that come to a point at the toe so you can smash the roaches in the room's corner." He shrugged. "Roach killers."

Noah shook his head. *Learn something new every day.* "Where are these aliens now?"

Trey checked the position of the sun. "They should be here any time. Tonight's party night. Then it will be quiet for a few days before they collect more ghosts."

"Where, Trey? Where?"

"No way. I'm not going over there. Nope. No way. No how."

"Just tell me where to go."

"I can't. I have no weapons. My tongue is the sharpest thing I own." Trey sat upright, board-straight in his rocker. He fiddled with the top button of his shirt.

"Trey…" Noah said, warning in his tone.

He rubbed his throat convulsively. "Please…" he begged, his voice rising an octave and cracking. "Please don't make me." His voice dropped to a whisper. "I saved you. Remember? I saved you."

Noah kneeled in front of Trey's rocking chair, a hand resting on each armrest. "Trey, look at me, buddy."

His eyes darted from side to side, avoiding Noah's gaze. His skin flushed. An involuntary whimper escaped. "Trey?"

He squeezed his eyes shut tight and placed his hands over his ears. He shook his head rapidly. "No. No, no, no, no."

Noah reached into his pocket and pulled out his wallet. He opened it to a picture of Bree. It was last year's school picture—he had one of each of the girls—so it was a little dated, but it would have to do. "Trey, buddy, look at her. I have to save her. She needs me." He paused. "She needs you."

Reluctantly, Trey dropped his hands, opened his eyes. He didn't look at the photograph, instead searching Noah's face for something only he would recognize. "If you're fishing for sympathy, the only place you're going to find it is in the dictionary somewhere between 'shit' and 'syphilis.' I read that in a book once." His shoulders drooped. He looked at the picture of Bree. Trey's eyes widened. His breath quickened. He tapped his hands rapidly on the armrests of the rocker. "She's there. I've seen her. Well, come along then, no time to tarry."

"You'll take me to her?"

Trey drew himself up to his full height. "I said I would, didn't I?"

The two men climbed into the car. Noah turned the ignition. The engine coughed once, twice, before catching. He started to slip the vehicle into gear but stopped. "Hang on a minute. What's the address?" Noah slid his hand into his pocket for his phone, coming up empty-handed. "Damn it. I forgot. My phone's gone. Can I borrow yours?"

Trey laughed.

"What's so funny, man?"

"Do I look like I have a phone?" He continued to chuckle. "Come on, my man. Onward we trek."

"Not alone we don't. Time for a detour." Noah spun the peeling vinyl steering wheel, aiming the rental car north toward the Bennett County Sheriff's Office.

****

"Wait here." Noah handed Trey a can of soda and a package of peanut butter crackers from a vending machine. He guided him to an empty seat in the lobby of the law enforcement center. "I'll be back."

After being buzzed through the security door, Noah knocked on the open doorframe of the communications office. "Brooke?"

The perky blonde held up a wait-a-minute finger as she finished reading a teletype across the airwaves. "Ranger Morgan, glad you're alive. You scared us."

She slipped off her headset, gave him a visual head-to-toe appraisal. “You look like shit. What can I do?”

“Is Ranger Trammell around?”

Brooke placed a hand over her heart. “Poor man. He doesn’t look much better than you.” Her features softened. “He’s in the bullpen, harassing the deputies. They’re doing everything they can, but it’s hard when they don’t even know where to start a search.” Her voice dropped an octave. “I can’t even imagine.”

“I think we are about to change that. Can you call in all available officers? Sheriff Preston and his chief deputy?”

Noah hurried down the hallway. He found Rhyden pacing the bullpen, hovering over the deputies as they worked. With a quick whistle and a head jerk, he motioned for his partner to join him.

Rhyden stalked to the door. “What?”

“Come with me.”

Rhyden followed Noah into his office. “What?”

“Have a seat. We need to talk.” Noah tugged his door shut. He could just say Trey stumbled across the kids. No one would doubt him, but he couldn’t live with the weight of his guilt anymore. It was eating him alive. He needed to come clean—now.

Rhyden bounced on the balls of his feet. “Can’t this wait? They’re working a sighting.”

“Rhy, sit down.” Noah blocked his partner’s access to the door. “It’s important.”

“But…”

He pointed. “Sit.”

Rhyden dropped into the chair Noah indicated. His leg bounced. He folded his arms across his chest. Unfolded them. Tapped his leg. “Well?”

Noah perched on the corner of his desk in front of his anxious partner. He bit the inside of his cheek. Avoiding eye contact, he dragged his hand through his hair. His voice barely audible, he said, "I know who has Bree."

"Yeah, we all do. That fucking ghost of a Traveler but knowing who her has hasn't helped us find where she's being held."

Pain hammered the inside of Noah's skull. A heaviness settled in his stomach.

"Rhy…listen. I know these people, okay? I mean I really know these people. I know how they think."

Noah's tongue stuck to the roof of his suddenly dry mouth. He reached back, scooped a bottle of water from the top of his desk, and twisted off the lid. He took a quick sip to moisten his parched throat. His hands dropped to his sides.

"I am these people."

"What do you mean 'you are these people'?" Rhyden jumped from the chair so fast it fell backward, slamming into the wall. He rushed Noah. Grabbing him by the lapels, he hauled him off the desk and smashed him against the wall. "Where the hell is my daughter?"

Brushing Rhyden's hands from his shirt, he shoved back. "Sit down. I'll tell you."

"Fuck you." In a voice that sounded like he could eat iron and spit bullets, Rhyden repeated, "Where. Is. My. Daughter?"

"Rhy, please, sit down. Brooke's gathering the team. We're going to get her. We will get Bree, but first I need to tell you something."

"Fine."

Noah swallowed hard. His hand slipped into his

pocket, his fingers searching out his lucky spark plug. It couldn't save him this time. *This is it—the end. I'm going to lose it all.*

He squeezed his eyes shut, overwhelmed by the thought. Forcing a deep breath in and out, he opened his eyes and faced Rhyden head on. He tightened his grip on the spark plug until the cracked porcelain cut into the palm of his hand. He couldn't hold his partner's gaze.

He dropped his head, stared at the floor. He drew his shoulders up, tucked his elbows tight to his sides. His head hurt, but he forced the words through trembling lips. "When I was young—really, really young—my father murdered my mother. My grandfather and Nana took me in. A few years later, my older cousin moved in with us. Not sure why. We were raised together like brothers…"

"Yeah, yeah, yeah, touching story and all but what does it have to do with Bree?"

"Just shut up and listen to me. I'm getting there. Okay?" Pain from the past and pain from the present rolled over Noah. He tried to understand how everything had gone so wrong; how he had ended up here. He cracked his knuckles. Locking gazes with Rhyden, he rushed on, his words stumbling over one another. "You met my grandda. My name is not Noah Morgan. It's Ferrell Gorman. A Traveler… The guy running the paving company, Seamus, is my family. My cousin. He has Bree."

Slowly, Rhyden stood. Drew himself to his full height. In a deadly whisper, he asked, "How long have you known?"

Noah waited in front of Rhyden, arms dangling at

his sides. “Known? About an hour. Suspected?” He shrugged. “A while.”

Rhyden’s posture tightened. He balled his fists. Through a clenched jaw, he asked, “Were you involved in taking my girl? In taking any of the missing children?”

Noah gasped; his skin blanched. “Seriously?” His hands carved through his hair, tugging in disbelief. He slumped against the wall. A shudder passed through his frame. Unable to speak, he just shook his head.

Rhyden searched his partner’s expression, digging deep. He dropped his fists and placed a hand on Noah’s shoulder. “I believe you, but don’t think this is over. Where are they? Where’s Bree?”

“Trey has the address.”

“Let’s go get my girl. We’ll deal with the rest of this after she is safe.”

Chapter Twenty-Three

Leaning against the wall, Noah tapped his fingers against his thigh. A sense of urgency swamped him. *We know where they are. Why are we still standing around this room flapping our jaws?* Trey said if everything went the way it normally did, they would ship the children out tonight. If they missed this window of opportunity, if the children were moved again, no one in South Texas would ever see them again.

"Okay, are we clear?" Chief Deputy Dannar scanned the room, making eye contact with each deputy, ranger, tactical officer, pilot, and medic. "We will assemble at the abandoned convenience store on Old Kyote road. That leaves us about a quarter mile to cover on foot, most of it through some pretty rough brush. The ambulances will remain in the store parking lot until the scene is contained and we call them in. Understood? No one approaches the building until after Deputy Hendrickson completes the drone fly-over. Once we get the all clear from the deputy, we will approach on foot. People, we don't know what we're going to be dealing with out there. Keep your head on a swivel and watch your six."

Photographs of Bree, Patrick, and Seamus were passed around the room. Chief Deputy Dannar continued, "This young lady is the daughter of Ranger Trammell. She's a good guy."

A strained chuckle circled the room. "The other two are the bad guys. I want to thank all of you for being here and a special thank you to the San Antonio Police Department's Special Response team for helping us out as well. Make sure you activate your IR markers. We don't want to mistake any good guys for bad guys. Radio silence. Got it?"

To the chorus of ayes, yesses, and sirs, the chief deputy gave a sharp nod. "Rangers Trammell and Morgan, am I correct in believing asking you to sit this one out would be a waste of my breath?"

"Sir, my daughter…"

The chief cut Rhyden off with a sharp chopping hand motion. "Like I said, a waste of breath. Okay, load 'em up and head 'em out."

Cat brushed past Noah without looking at him on the way out of the room. He snagged her arm and tugged her into an empty office. He turned her to face him. "Should you be here?"

She yanked her arm from his grasp. "It's my job. What's it to you, anyway?"

"Cat," he pleaded, "I know, okay? I know. I just want to keep you and our baby safe."

Color leached from her face. "You…you know?"

Jim rapped his knuckles on the door and shoved into the room. "Come on, partner, we gotta roll. Get in the box." He scowled at Noah. "You can make kissy faces with this one later…if you have to."

For the second time in an abbreviated period, someone who thought they knew Noah, someone he loved, searched his face for answers. His mouth filled with cotton. Butterflies performed aerial combat in his stomach. He stretched a hand toward her.

Cat recoiled from his touch. She turned and followed Jim to the ambulance.

His heart plummeted. A weight settled on his shoulders, pressing against him. His head throbbed. Eyes stung. He closed his eyes, turned his face to the ceiling. *Breathe, two, three.* He exhaled slowly.

Broken toy, broken toy, broken toy.

Rhyden held the door open. "Noah, you coming?"

He shook himself and shoved the pain deep into a tiny box in his subconscious, banging the lid down and locking it. "Let's go."

Fifteen minutes later, in the parking lot of the abandoned Stop-N-Shop, Noah searched the parking lot for Cat. He caught sight of her in the passenger seat of the ambulance. Their eyes met. She faced away. *Enough. Put it out of your mind. Deal with it later. Focus.*

"Morgan," Chief called, "over here. Now."

Noah joined Chief, Rhyden, and members of the SWAT team where they huddled around a laptop. Video footage from the drone streamed across the monitor. Breach teams were established and gearing up. He tossed a longing glance back at the ambulance, but the medics had been staged where they were now out of sight but could be on-hand within seconds if needed.

"Seems like we've got fifteen or sixteen heat signatures." Deputy Hendrickson pointed at the screen, outlining the figures with the tip of his pen. "One here. One here. And eleven smaller ones huddled here."

He surveyed the officers clustered around him. "I'm betting those are our hostages." They watched the video feed for a few more minutes. "These two appear to be stationary guards while the other two patrol, though they've been standing in the same spot for the past few minutes. Earlier however, they each circled the building in opposite directions."

Chief asked, "Ready to do this?"

Affirmative replies echoed all around. Chief keyed his microphone. "620-Bennett County. Close the channel please."

"10-4 620," the dispatcher responded. "Attention all officers, all units not involved in the special assignment. This channel is now closed. Switch to analog. Repeating, channel is now closed. My time out 20:04."

Chief signaled for the teams to move forward. Adrenaline pumped through Noah's system, erasing all the aches and pains of the past few days. With a nod of acknowledgement to Rhyden, Noah crept forward, moving stealthily through the brush toward the decrepit shack housing the children.

Details of their surroundings faded into the mist that rolled in after the temperatures dropped. Noah and Rhyden communicated using hand signals. A dark shadow popped up in front of them. They drew up short, weapons at the ready, easing forward, one slow step at a time. The shadow gradually gave form to the twisted spine of a mesquite tree. Relief whispered through him.

He inched closer. A shuddering crunch of gravel signaled danger. Noah melted into the shadows. A guard appeared in his peripheral vision. Noah dropped into a shallow, dusty ditch. The guard passed. Noah rose to a crouch in the ditch, preparing to dart forward.

His radio crackled. *Fuck!* He fumbled with the volume button on his radio. "1480-Bennett County.

Traffic stop in front of HEB on 35. John-Robert-Mary six-four-eight."

The guard whipped around, rifle at the ready, searching for the source of the noise.

Dispatch responded to the officer on the radio. "Bennett County-1480. Switch to analog. The channel is closed. Repeat, the channel is closed."

Noah surged up out of the ditch, catching the barrel of the rifle and snatching it from the guard's grasp. Reversing his hold on the gun, he swung it like a club, bashing it against the guard's temple. The man crumpled like a rag doll.

Another guard called out, "*¿Qué fue eso?* Javier? What was that?"

Noah darted behind an ancient mesquite tree. Prickly pear thorns stabbed his thighs as he dropped to his belly. A beam of bright light swept over his previous position.

The guard approached the ranger's hiding spot. "Javier?"

Head down, Noah slithered forward. The light came closer. Jumping up, he slammed the palm of his hand beneath the guard's chin, snapping his head back.

The guard stumbled but didn't go down. He swung the muzzle of his gun toward Noah. He fired just as Noah dove sideways.

Come on, fucker, cooperate. Sweeping his leg out, he caught the guard behind the knees and took him to the ground. Noah clambered on top of him, trying to catch the man in an arm bar.

The guard flipped over, squirmed out of Noah's grasp. He drew his leg up and kicked Noah in the solar plexus. Pain blinded him as the new stitches ripped open—again. Hot blood trickled down his side, soaking his shirt. Diving forward, the guard landed on top of him. He wrapped his massive hands around Noah's neck and cranked them down tight.

Noah clawed at the hands cutting off his air.

The bigger man grinned, his teeth gleaming in the darkness. He squeezed tighter.

Noah's eyes closed. Lightning flashes of red flickered beneath his closed lids. His lungs burned. He batted ineffectively at the guard's hands. Scratched his arms. Arched his back trying to throw him off.

The man leaned forward, pressing his weight into his hands. He squeezed harder still.

The bones in Noah's neck popped. The taste of copper flooded his throat. The lightning flashes became starbursts. A keening wail built in his chest but could not pass the restriction around his throat. His muscles twitched. Cold seeped into his bones. *I'm dying.*

Noah's fingers tingled on the verge of going numb. He dug deep into his reserves. Cupping his hands, he clapped them over the guard's ears with all his remaining strength. The pressure ruptured the man's eardrums.

With a roar of pain, the stranger fell off Noah, releasing his throat. Noah dragged in whooping gasps of air as he lay on the ground, barely conscious.

The guard, caught in the throes of excruciating pain, curled into the fetal position. He moaned.

A second wave of adrenaline flooded Noah's system, blocking out the agony of his injuries, new and old. He knew when this was all over, he would crash, and crash hard, but right now Mother Nature and her fight-or-flight response was serving him well. He rolled on top of the guard, punching. A right to the face, left to the kidneys, right to the face. A satisfying crunch accompanied a spurt of hot blood as the other man's nose shattered beneath his blows. Noah rolled off the man, collapsed in the dirt, and struggled to catch his breath.

"Hey." Rhyden caught up with him. "You okay?"

Still too winded to speak, he rubbed his throat. "Fucking PD," he croaked in a whisper. "Damn near got me killed. What part of channel closed did that motherfucker not understand?"

Rhyden reached a hand down to help Noah to his feet. "Come on, pansy, quit your bellyaching. Bree's waiting for us to save her."

A hoarse chuckle escaped Noah's lips. "Pansy, my ass." He took a moment to drag the now unconscious guard to the base of a mesquite tree, wincing as his bruised ribs cried out in protest. "I hope you get prickly pear stickers in your ass," he muttered as he cuffed the man's hands around its trunk with nylon flex cuffs. "I may never sing again."

"Should I leave him a thank you note?"

"Hardy-har-har," Noah retorted in a voice sounding like sandpaper.

Rapid rifle fire split the air to the east. A frantic voice broke radio silence. "We're pinned down. Taking fire." More gunfire erupted.

"It's hitting the brush around us. Can't see anything."

"Where are you?" asked Rhyden.

"Southeast corner of the building. We're pinned in the brush."

A veteran of many firefights, the chief's calm tones

issued from the radio. "Stay put. Keep your heads down. Backup's on the way. Perimeter is set."

"We can't tell where the shooter is. We're hunkered down in a low spot, surrounded by brush."

Noah and Rhyden raced in the direction of the gunfire. "We're gonna come up behind them," Rhyden radioed.

"Bennett County to all officers. DPS chopper is on the way."

Noah slipped his pistol from the holster. He motioned for Rhyden to follow as he edged forward toward the shack. He pointed toward the back of the structure. "Muzzle flash," he whispered as he corrected course. "We're almost there."

"This is DPS 107, airborne, we're about seven mikes out. I'll circle when we get there. We should be able to spot the shooter for you."

"10-4, we just took three more shots. Seems to be coming from the northeast. Uncertain if we have one or more shooters."

"Roger that. Heading northeast from your location. Five mikes out. Make sure all the good guys have their IR markers activated, please."

Rhyden and Noah met up with a line of officers moving toward the structure. A rustling in the brush caused the officers to pause. As one, they all pointed flashlights and guns at the brush. The brush wriggled again. A member of the San Antonio Police Department's special response team stumbled out. He threw his hands in the air. "Whoa! Hold fire. Hold fire. It's me."

A nervous chuckle swept through the group.

The SAPD officer quipped, "Man, give me the

concrete jungle over this shit any day."

Noah pointed to the northwest. "We're gonna circle around this way."

"This is DPS 107. I see your bad guys. Looks like two armed with ARs. I've got a line of seven good guys in a semi-circle and then two others moving west, northwest. Two more goodies hunkered down about five hundred yards to the east. Okay, your baddies are on the move. Heading back to the structure. Repeat, bad guys are on the move. I've got them pinned in the spotlight."

A volley of rifle fire mixed with small arms fire split the night. The chopper pilot called out. "We're taking fire. We're taking fire." The helicopter returned fire. "They're down. I repeat, bad guys are down."

Noah and Rhyden gave up all pretense of stealth and rushed toward the house.

****

Gunfire shattered the silence. Seamus dropped the child he was examining. *Shit.* He swept his eyes around the building. *Where to hide?*

****

Noah and Rhyden eased up to the fence surrounding the dilapidated house. Noah dropped to one knee and scanned the area with the night vision scope on his rifle. He couldn't see much. Just another ramshackle structure. Trey's home was in better condition but not by much. "Hendrickson, we're getting close. What do you see?"

The drone buzzed overhead. It dropped low, waggling its wings at the rangers, before zooming off to circle the structure and surrounding area. "I've got nothing in the area outside the shack. Thermal imaging shows eleven, no twelve, no eleven… I'm not sure, they keep moving, huddling up, but eleven or twelve heat signatures inside." A pause. "Good guys are joining you."

Noah and Rhyden dropped back to the brush line and waited for the rest of the team. "Okay, who has the rakes?" Noah asked when the group had gathered.

Three men held up metal poles with pointed ends and teeth on them. Noah nodded in acknowledgement. "I need one of you on each team. Bravo team, take the back. Charlie, the left. Delta, the right." Noah pointed where he wanted each team to go as he spoke. "Ranger Trammell and I are marching right in the front door."

He glanced at the illuminated dial on his watch. "Fifteen seconds. Rake the windows. Toss in the flashbangs. We'll make entry after that. Everyone ready?" Affirmative nods circled the group. "One more thing. We have a minimum of eleven children inside—children—possibly including Ranger Trammell's daughter. Let's take it easy. No unnecessary gun fire. Got it? Good. Go."

The men split into three groups and approached their designated areas.

Where is Seamus? Patrick? The thought niggled at the back of Noah's mind. It worried him. "Chief? Ranger Morgan here. Have EMS ready to roll. We go in five…four…three…two…"

Breaking glass and children's screams echoed through the brush. Bright lights and loud explosions lit up the night sky. Rhyden and Noah charged the front door. Rhyden rushed through first, sweeping low. Noah swept high.

"Clear." Rhyden stepped to the left.

Noah stepped past Rhyden, swinging his rifle from left to right. "Clear," he said, pointing the rifle at the ceiling. They continued through the house, the pier-and-beam foundation creaking and groaning at every step.

They entered the last room.

"Daddy!" Bree launched herself at her father, burying her face in his shirt. "You smell like gunpowder and sunshine." Tears streamed down her face. Rhyden wrapped his arms tightly around her, clinging to her.

Noah slid deeper into room. "All clear." He keyed his microphone. "Send in EMS now. We've got them." Emotion colored his voice. "We've got the children."

****

Noah approached the circle of flashing red-and-blue lights—cop cars surrounded ambulances. With the adrenaline fading, he was crashing. Pain rushed through him. Pulling the prescription bottle from his pocket, he dry-swallowed a couple of pain pills.

Relief filled the air. Officers roughly moved suspects—the ones still alive—into the back of marked police units. It still bugged Noah that he hadn't seen hide nor hair of Seamus or his son.

Paramedics tended to the children. Bree still clung to Rhyden. A tiny blonde child clung to Bree. When Noah joined the group, Bree wrapped her arms around his waist, but she never let go of her daddy's hand. "Uncle Noah. I knew you and Daddy would find us. I knew it."

Noah hugged Bree tightly, then released her. "Hey, jump off any cliffs lately?"

A delicate hand tugged on his arm. Bree smiled.

"This is my friend, Sarah."

Noah kneeled so he was on Sarah's eye level. "Hello, Sarah. I'm Noah. How are you?"

Big, green eyes looked at him with an expression of awe. "Are you a Texas Ranger? Bree said you would find us." She looked away, embarrassed. "I didn't really believe her."

"Yes, I am a ranger." He ruffled her hair. Standing, he gestured to the children and asked Rhyden, "How are they?"

His partner gathered his daughter close again. "Physically? None the worse for wear. A little dehydrated, a few bruises. Hungry. Overall, not too bad." He shrugged. "Emotionally? That's a whole other ball of wax."

Noah grasped Rhyden's upper arm. He squeezed and released. "I'm glad she's home, man." His voice cracked. "I am so glad she's home. I'm going to go try to talk to Cat."

****

From his hiding spot, a seething Seamus watched Noah pass. *How many lives does that son of a bitch have?* Heat raced through his body. He gritted his teeth. *What made you so special? Why did Grandda love you and not me?*

With laser focus, he followed Noah with his gaze, searching for a weakness, a chance to attack. *I wish Patrick were here. This would be easier with his help.* He watched Noah approach the pretty paramedic, watched as he pleaded with her. Watched as she gave him the cold shoulder, turned him away.

So that's how it is. Seamus bounced on his toes, felt his cheeks raise in a grin. He narrowed his eyes, trying to figure out how to take advantage of his observations. He slipped out of hiding. Shoulders back, he swaggered toward the ambulances like he belonged there.

"Seamus!" A voice bellowed across the night.

He whirled about. *Damn it!* The pulsing roar in Seamus's ears drowned out the background noise. His breath quickened.

Noah charged his cousin. He rammed a shoulder into Seamus's chest, slamming him backward. Seamus gasped for breath, stumbled, and fell to one knee. Noah lashed out with his foot. Seamus dodged to the side. He grabbed the offending boot and snapped it upward. He swept Noah's other foot out from under him, dropping him face-first onto the ground. Seamus jumped back to his feet. He snapped his leg out, catching Noah in the side.

Noah rolled to safety. Scrambled to his hands and knees. Seamus kicked out again. This time, Noah jerked him to the ground. Wrapped his hands around Seamus's throat and squeezed. Unrelenting pressure cut off his airway. Blackness swirled at the edges of his sight. His head pounded. He struggled to breathe. *When did the broken toy get so strong?* His lungs burned.

Seamus clawed at Noah's hands, his arms. Reached up for his eyes. Noah pressed down harder. Tilted his head back out of Seamus's grasp. Heels kicking on the ground, Seamus dropped his arms. Hands scrabbled against the ground, digging in the dirt, ripping his fingernails. He grabbed a rock. Picked it up. Slammed it against Noah's temple. A heavy weight collapsed on top of him, the pressure on his throat thankfully released. He sucked in whooping gasps of air. Rolled

Noah off him onto the ground. He delivered three brutal punches. Smiled as he felt the crunch and warm spurt of blood from Noah's nose.

"I taught you to fight, maggot. Remember? What made you think you could take me?"

Staggering to his feet, sides heaving as he caught his breath, Seamus rubbed his neck. Stance wide and stable, he glared down at Noah. "Stay down, why don't you?" He kicked Noah in the temple.

****

Noah crawled to his feet. Nausea dropped him to his knees, retching. Blood flowed from the wound on his head, blurring his vision with a curtain of red. The stitches in his side were torn open. Blood soaked through his shirt, sticking it to his skin.

A sharp cry echoed through the night. Noah looked up in time to see Seamus shove Cat into an unattended police unit and peel away.

"No!" A primal roar tore from his throat. With the roar, inhuman adrenaline-fueled strength flooded his system, drowning out the pain. He climbed to his feet and limped to the nearest patrol unit. Falling in, he winced as his chest bounced against the steering wheel. He thrust the seat back to accommodate his height, jerked the door closed, and raced after Seamus and Cat.

"Morgan," Sheriff Preston called over the radio, "where the hell are you going in my county unit?"

"He's got Cat. I'm in pursuit."

"Who's got Cat? Pursuit of what?"

"That bastard, Seamus Gorman. Driving a marked PD unit."

"We're right behind you, son. Hang in there."

Seamus cut into the radio traffic. "Ranger Morgan,

is it? Or should I call you Ferrell—Ferrell Gorman? Come on, cuz. I've got someone you want…again. 'Course she doesn't want a broken toy either, does she?" he taunted in a sing-song fashion. "But hey, catch me if you can."

Noah dropped the mic and pulled in behind the marked unit. The throaty roar of the police package engine snarled into pursuit. The speedometer edged up over eighty, eighty-five, ninety. He pressed harder on the accelerator. Ninety-five, ninety-eight, one hundred. The speed kept climbing. The rear end of the unfamiliar vehicle fish-tailed in the loose gravel. Noah fought for control, fought to keep the old memories at bay.

Seamus reached the main drag, the red-and-blue lights on top of the car clearing a path for him. He wove in and out of traffic. Noah followed, passing cars like they were standing still. The radio chattered in the background. He ignored it. No one existed in his world except for himself, Seamus, and Cat. From the corner of his eye, the telephone poles were passing by so fast they looked like a picket fence.

Faster and faster, they raced on. Noah's heart kept pace, revving with the car's engine. His fingers clenched the steering wheel. All he could see were the red taillights of the PD unit just out of reach. Coming up on a dead man's curve, Noah eased off the accelerator. *Not enough!* He clipped a pickup truck parked on the side of the road just past the turn. The steering wheel jerked in his hands. He fought tooth and nail to keep the car on the road. The rear end started sliding.

Noah steered into the skid. Slowed a little more. Regained control. Straightening out, he mashed the accelerator pedal back to the floor. The taillights grew larger. He was closing in on them.

Seamus took the next curve too fast. He lost control. Brake lights flared. Wheels locked up, squealing and burning rubber on the pavement. Black smoke filled the air. Too little, too late. The PD unit flew off the road. With a screech of crumpling metal, the car tumbled down the hill.

Noah slid to a stop on top of the embankment. He spotted Seamus crawling from the overturned vehicle. He gained his feet and noticed Noah watching him. He took off running. Noah scrambled down the incline to intercept him. Stumbling to the bottom, he raced to Cat trapped in the car.

Hanging upside down from the seatbelt, she struggled with the latch, trying to free herself. Blood dripped from a cut on her cheek and another above her eye. The red-and-blue strobes dug into the ground still fired, reflecting off the fog, adding a surreal feel to the situation.

Noah tugged on the crushed door. He tried to assess her injuries through the unbroken window. Concern for their unborn child filled him. The blood marring her face angered him. *Well, we'll have matching scars.* He tugged harder on the door handle, but the door would not budge.

Cat pressed her palm against the window glass for a brief moment before she waved him off. "Go, get the son of a bitch," she shouted.

Noah paused, uncertain.

"Go! I'm okay. Just go." She returned to trying to unlatch the seatbelt holding her suspended above the caved-in roof.

Noah raced across the river's muddy bank, boots slipping on the damp rocks, chasing Seamus. Fog rolled off the river, obscuring his view.

The edge of a palm knifed at Noah's throat. He glimpsed the calloused hand rushing at him and shifted back. It flashed past in front of him. He roared and charged Seamus, all the hate and anger and frustration of the past days powering his forward momentum. Both men hit the ground hard. Noah pounded a fist into Seamus' side. And did it again. And again.

Gasping for air, Seamus threw Noah off and rolled to his feet. He spat blood on the ground. "That all you got? My boy hits harder than you." He punched Noah, a powerful blow to the jaw.

Noah's head snapped back. Crack! A tooth loosened. The two men circled one another. "Where is your son? Hiding behind his mama's skirts?"

Seamus surged forward, throwing blow after blow. "Far away from here. You'll never find him."

Noah danced backward, dodging the blows. Seeing Seamus tire, the ranger rushed forward, wrapping his arms around Seamus's waist and lifting him from the ground, ignoring the screaming pain from his ribs. Rolling the older man over his hip, Noah slammed his cousin onto the rocky ground. He trapped Seamus in a choke hold and said, "You may have taught me to fight way back then, but I've learned a new trick or two along the way."

Seamus struggled, squirming and kicking, trying to break free. His motions became increasingly feeble.

Noah fought to hang on as his own strength waned. He ignored the warm, wet rush of blood running down his side. His pulse boomed in his ears.

More red-and-blue lights squalled to a stop on the road above the field. Officers swarmed down the embankment.

Noah released the choke hold, dropping the barely conscious man to the ground. A final kick to the side of Seamus' head rendered him unconscious.

The first officers reached Noah. He gestured at his cousin. "Cuff him and stuff him."

He rushed to the crumpled car, brushing first responders aside. "Are you okay? Cat? Are you okay? Is the baby okay?" Noah tugged on the door. Still jammed. Flames flickered beneath the hood. The acrid smell of burned wires filled the air. *No! I will not lose you like this.*

She sawed at the seatbelt with her pocketknife. The webbed fabric stubbornly resisted her attempts to cut through it. Finally, it parted, releasing Cat from its deadly embrace. She shoved against the door from the inside. Nothing. She tried to scramble across the center console and escape out the driver's side door, but the crushed roof and piles of police equipment blocked her path.

The flames danced higher. Smoke filled the interior of the car. Every sight, sound, and scent magnified in Noah's brain. The rescue truck with the Jaws of Life was en route, but as the flames grew, time shrank. The firefighters would not arrive in time. His hands shook. He struck at the car window. Nothing.

"Hurry." She coughed as she struggled to breathe. She fought against the door, trying to open it from the inside.

Think, Noah, think.

He reached into his pocket, pulling out his lucky

spark plug. He slammed it against the glass, shattering the window. He raked it around the edges of the window, scraping out the broken glass. Reaching in, he grabbed Cat with both hands and tugged her free of the car. Together, they collapsed in a heap on the ground. Heat from the growing flames urged them back to their feet. They stumbled away from the vehicle. First responders rushed to them, helping them walk, wrapping them in blankets. Others sprayed the burning vehicle with fire extinguishers.

Noah wrapped her in his embrace, burying his face in her neck. He inhaled her scent—the jasmine sandalwood that always reminded him of her was wrapped in the smoky sulfur-ish tang of burning rubber. He clung to her so tight he couldn't tell her trembling from his own. Without warning, he released her and dropped to his knees.

Alarmed, she dropped to her knees beside him. "Are you okay? Are you hurt?" She ran her hands over his body, assessing him for trauma.

Noah took her hands in his own and gazed deeply into her eyes. "Catalina Maria Ramos," he said, "my name is Noah Ferrell Gorman Morgan. I love you more than life itself. Will you marry me?"

A word about the author…

A sixth-generation Texan with Scottish roots, Glenda Thompson can "bless your heart" with the best of them.

As a former emergency medical technician married to a South Texas lawman, she's used insider information from both their careers as inspiration to build her Broken world of Texas Rangers with hidden pasts and dark secrets.

When she's not busy embarrassing her children or grandchildren by dancing in the middle of a country road during a rainstorm, she can be found huddled in her writing cave with her law enforcement technical adviser/husband working on another story in her Broken universe.

You can keep up with the future crazy cat lady's hijinks at: www.glendathompson.com
Or follow her on: Twitter @PressRattler
Or Facebook @Glenda Thompson, author

Thank you for purchasing
this publication of The Wild Rose Press, Inc.

For questions or more information
contact us at
info@thewildrosepress.com.

The Wild Rose Press, Inc.
www.thewildrosepress.com

CPSIA information can be obtained
at www.ICGtesting.com
Printed in the USA
BVHW091057141220
595676BV00011B/1311